I0788132

BELVIDERE.

VII

X
Sans Nom

Title: **Belvidere.**

Summary: *A mysterious man is sent to a dead-end town; to do what, and to whom, he simply doesn't know. It's all part of a game he neither understands, nor controls. He befriends those he will likely betray; there will certainly be trouble if he does not. A fantastical, mysterious journey; an ephemeral olla podrida of raw erotica, graphic violence, racism, heathenism, bigotry and vulgarity, all buoyed by the providence of friendship, love and kindred souls.*

1.   Fiction-General.   2. Fiction-Fantasy.
17 18 19 20 21   j i h g f e d c b a
First Edition - American

A Special Note To The Reader Who Is A Self-Appointed Observant Orthographer:

To this special group, the spelling and grammar police, please put your pencil down; I will save you the suspense.

This novel may be a grammar and sentence structure nightmare to people who obsess about such things. The pages that follow are vaguely, or not so, reminiscent of Beat literature, which can be described, by some, as a rejection of standard narrative and linguistic values, including, but not necessarily limited to, syntax, punctuation, sentence structure and morphology. The writing style is idiosyncratic; it is how the author thinks, and how the author believes this fictional account should be told. And just as important, it's how real people speak and communicate in the real world, which is rarely textbook or *correct*. It is real, or at least how this author perceives reality, which is all that matters between these end-papers.

In any event, there **will** be mistakes. And all the mistakes in this book were purposeful, and will be defended as such, even if they weren't. After two long years of editing, this writer simply got tired of re-reading and proofing. So what you see is what you get, whether it's *right* or not.

My suggestion is to take the broader view: simply enjoy the characters and enjoy the ride they take you on. Along the way, if you feel the need to get enraged, do so at the abject violence, the graphic sex, the racism, the bigotry, the coarse language, the heathenism....but for God's sake, don't get enraged at punctuation....leave the poor periods alone.

CHAPTER 283 - A LIFELESS FACE, PUSHED LIKE PUTTY AGAINST THE GLASS

He was in the kitchen, without a doubt, he knew it well; it looked the same as he remembered it, but his mother wasn't around, no one was….he was all alone. That was typical.

The humming sound was sonorous, enough to wake the dead, and it was quickly becoming unbearable. Clearly, it was *not* to be ignored.

He opened drawers and cabinet doors, random, frantic, looking for the source of energy, the bad electricity, and he knew it was bad, it had a malevolent feel, as if something wasn't working right. As if something was *terribly* wrong.

He pushed on the kitchen woodwork, like he was looking for a hidden nest, a burrow, a haunt, some sort of breeding ground, which harbored this horrible noise. He knew it was close; to be this loud, it *had* to be close by. As he pushed into the panels, the hum would heighten, like an anger incarnate, like the poke of a hornets nest.

He was scared to death. He needed to fix this right now; to stop the incessant buzz, to knock the static from his head.

He opened the knotty-pine basement door to his left, just beside where he stood, and stared down the worn wooden stairs, painted a drab brown, which disappeared into an abyss. The hair on his arms rose, and then he knew. The source of the badness was somewhere down *there*, wherever those steps ended.

Somehow, without warning, he found himself gliding slowly down the stairs, as if on air, not touching a single tread, slowly descending into the pitch. He couldn't stop, or turn, or anything, just an awful one-way descent into the gloom, the unknown.

And even though he was frightened, he started to scream, some sort of tribal yell, as if he was in attack-mode, to confront whatever lay beyond the envelop of darkness hiding in that horrid basement. His wailing became wild, hysterical, as he neared the bottom, and came face-to-face with the cellar wall, within feet of the last stair tread. He knew that's where it was waiting.

The wall before him was concrete block, but it really wasn't; somehow, it was translucent, with weird white light flashing in, about and through it, like an electrical storm, distorted and bent through opaque glass. He glided closer and closer to the wall, unable to stop himself, until his face was inches from the portal. He raised his arms wide to the sides, horizontal, and shrieked at the top of his lungs, terror-stricken, because he knew, for sure, she was in there, the hag, on the other side of the glass, just beyond the gate, the way in….and he knew in the very next instant, he would see her, waiting for him, her mouth a gaping black hole, with white orbs for eyes and a lifeless face, pushed like putty against the glass.

CHAPTER 284 – DOWN THE DRAIN, OVER AND DONE, DEAD AND GONE

Saturday, October 7, 2006; day one-hundred seventy-one. It should have been the day.

His last scream broke the dream; C never did see her.

Chick woke and bolted in one motion from the end of the bed; she stopped at the bedroom door, quickly looked back, and disappeared into the hall.

He laid in bed, quiet, watching his chest heave from the hyperventilation, his mind processing what just happened. It was a dream, he was asleep, he woke himself up….he's safe. There was no hag in the room.

He raised his eyes to the ceiling and wondered why she didn't show her face, why she let him wake up, why she let him off the hook. He knew she was there, right on the other side of the glass, ready to pull him through. And he somehow knew, that pull would have been a one-way, there was no coming *back* through that wall, ever again, and that she must somehow control these things. That's what he thought. And that was *way* different, and *way scarier*, than the puppet ever was.

And then, inexplicably, his thoughts drifted to pastina.

A bowl of tiny, yellow starchy stars, at the dining room table. There were always two ice cubes sitting on top, his mom always put two in, no more, no less, and the melted water would puddle atop the stars, a miniature lake, till he took his spoon and buried them deep in the yellowness. He liked to imagine they were two people, sinking in quicksand, and it was his job to save them; the saving part always made him smile. He would dig fast and furious to find them, then quickly bury them deep once more with the spoon, only to dig and find them again. He would do it over and over; each time the cubes shrunk, till they were merely thin slivers of frozen water, ready to disappear, melting to nothingness. And then they were gone, the end of the kill. That part always made him sad, the *gone* part, because in the end, he could never save them. Then he would push in two pats of butter, also sitting atop the stars; more quicksand, and more futile saves. Finally, he'd dash salt and pepper on top, and eat in silence, gazing at the jumble of stars in the bowl, thinking of how the ice and butter felt, dying like that, every time.

C wondered where the hell that memory come from? Pastina? He shook his head at the thought, and at how fucked-up his head really was; for some reason, it made him crack a small smile. He swung his legs over the edge of the bed; with the pastina, his breathing had calmed and the darkness from the hag had faded away.

And then it hit him; no visit by Jenny this morning.

And that felt strange, because given his funk over the last several weeks, and given his feelings yesterday, he was convinced today, October 7th, would be the day she would finally show, that the words would come, the box would once again be opened, and the game would be set in motion. One-hundred seventy-one days was long enough.

But instead of Jenny, he got the hag. And even she didn't really show, more of a terrifying tease.

Strange.

He didn't bother to jerk-off or to exercise; not in the mood for fuck-stories, or sit-ups, push-ups, whatever. The day already felt empty, like a throwaway.

Where was Jenny?

He stumbled down the hall, cracking his knuckles along the way. He opened the shower valve, and took a long leak as the water warmed to hot, then to scald. He set it to scald.

As he propped himself against the wall, a trail of urine splashing the bowl, he noticed a small flying ant, trapped inside the shower stall. C assumed it was a she, most ants are, another useless fact buried in his head….taking up space.

She was in there before he turned the valve, and quickly found herself surrounded and overwhelmed by droplets of hot water running down the tile in a space that was, moments before, dry and safe. She got hit by one drop, then another, each bigger than her, which drenched her wings; she struggled to stay stuck to the wall, to stay away from being carried down the drain, to keep away from being dead.

C killed her, or was about to, simply by turning on the valve, to take a shower. And he *couldn't* live with that….he just couldn't.

He would never tell anyone what he did next; no one would ever understand why he did it, and he didn't give a shit what anyone thought anyway. So without hesitation, while still in the midst of a piss, he lunged across the bathroom, into the shower and scooped her off the wall with his finger, leaving a stream of piss on the floor between the toilet and stall. He pulled his finger near his face, to see if she was okay; she was, thank God, struggling to dry her amber wings, which were wet and pasted to her body. He carefully deposited her on the edge of the sink, dry and safe, and stepped into the scald of the shower. He watched her from the shower, slowly dry herself out, a methodical process of antennae cleaning, leg lifting and wing flexing.

As the water cascaded onto his shoulders, and ran down his back, he turned to grab the soap, smiling at the save.

He turned back to the sink, and she was gone.

And he was happy. Much happier than anyone should be for such a foolish thing. But it didn't matter, to him it wasn't foolish, it was necessary; she was saved, and he saved her. His own small shot of redemption. He couldn't help himself, it was just how he felt, it was just how it was.

Maybe today was going to be a good day after all.

And amidst his feelings of worth and redemption, Cord failed to realize he killed her just the same, because he never saw his small friend, dry and safe, fly back into the shower, into the scald of water, which quickly overwhelmed her. She had no chance, none at all, and was quickly swept down the drain, over and done, dead and gone.

CHAPTER 285 – THE BOWL OF BLOOD CORKSCREWED DOWN THE DRAIN

He stood, head down, one arm propped against the wall, engulfed in a stream of recalescent spray, which painted his back crimson.

And as the rush of water passed his ears, it suddenly hit him, and he thought it strange it hadn't dawned earlier, between waking and now, because it was super-important. But maybe because he hadn't seen his friend in awhile, and he was, in more than one sense, already gone, important thoughts sometimes slip.

And this one had, but now it came roaring back.

Today was October 7th.

And although he couldn't say his mood was good, it certainly was better than earlier; as silly as it was, saving the ant had made a real difference. And *better* was important, because today was *the* big day, in planning for months, between Carol and himself. Invitations had been sent, secrets had been kept, itineraries set, and, it seemed safe to say, Earl Liddell had absolutely no idea of the momentous day that lay before him.

How could he have almost forgotten such an important day? No wonder Jenny didn't show; he had no time for Jenny today, although she never made such allowances in the past - Cord's schedule was always beside the point.

He tossed Jenny to the side and focused on Earl.

Now only if C hadn't been such a jerk to everyone, and to Earl, for the last....well, for a while.

But there was no time to dwell on that; suddenly, the urge struck to get this day rolling – he already felt behind, although he wasn't. The hag had roused him early, by about an hour, or so. She did him a favor; he smiled wry at that thought as he jumped from the shower and started toward the bedroom, drying himself on the fly, his mind racing.

Then he stopped dead.

Whenever he got excited, and felt the need to get moving, faster than he was currently moving, it invariably happened. His bowels churned and gurgled, and a new priority would set in. And there was no putting this priority off; morning dumps don't wait. Especially ones that felt *urgent*, like this.

C quickly spun and planted his ass on the bowl. He was pissed; knowing this was adding a good five to ten minutes he didn't want to spend, and fouling a perfectly clean ass to boot, just scrubbed and polished in the shower.

He huffed in indignation.

Chick had resurfaced, sprawled lazily across the bathroom threshold, half in the bath, her other half in the hall. She was busy licking her paws and cleaning her cheeks, first one, then the other, over and over, paying no attention to C, or his squeezes, grunts and goings-on, a mere five feet away.

And as Cord sat and unloaded, he noted nothing particularly special about this bowl-drop, nothing beyond the norm. Until he took the first ass-wipe; he always inspected the wipes, especially the first….it was another ritual.

And there it was, *unmistakable*.

He stared at it, just to be sure, even though it wasn't necessary; it was pretty obvious.

His guest had finally arrived.

He slowly stood and looked into the porcelain hole, and it was clear as day, a titian exclamation. Cord just stood there, bare-ass naked, and smiled. He tossed the soiled tissue into the water and let out a breath, and a long sigh. *Now* it all finally made sense, perfect sense; how could he have not figured it before?

The Jenny-no-show finally made sense; this backwater called Belvidere finally made sense. It had all come together on this day; what were the odds? If it was random, they were astronomical.

But this was anything but random.

C finished wiping his ass, but good; he wasn't in a rush anymore. He hit the handle and flushed the evidence away.

And with it, the bowl of blood corkscrewed down the drain.

CHAPTER 286 – SO BEGAN THE WEAVE OF THE ZOMBIE'S YARN

Earl felt the slightest tickle, right at the tip of his nose, light as a feather, but that's all it took to wrest him from the dream. He barely cracked his right eye, but it was enough to see, through a tangle of lashes.

The puppet's mouth was open wide, cavernous, inches from his face, huge and distorted, with bared teeth and maniacal eyes. And it was just about to get him, to vacuum his eyes from their sockets, like zombies do. On instinct, Earl yanked the blanket over his head and uncaged a wail of words, muffled into the fabric.

"Don't suck my eyeballs out!"

And with a single wave of his tree-trunk arm, he flung the puppet off the bed; it flew into the bedroom wall, landing with a dull thud. And it began to groan.

Wow, that puppet didn't sound so tough Earl thought to himself, still hiding under the blanket.

"Jesus Earl, happy birthday."

The puppet groaned slowly, and it sounded annoyed. And puppets don't usually wish you a *happy birthday*, do they? And that puppet sounded *awful familiar*.

Earl threw the covers off his face, just as Ay struggled onto one knee, moving creaky, like an old man.

"C!!"

Earl jumped out of bed, so happy to finally find his bestest best friend ever, in a lump on the floor. He picked him up like a sock-puppet and bear-hugged him, squeezing the air from the old man's lungs.

"Were you hiding in my room *the whole time*? Were you under the bed? I never looked under the bed; that's a pretty good hiding spot all right! You musta been under there for a week! When did you eat or even blow your nose? You must be pretty sneaky about stuff like that! Hey, are you mad at me? Are ya? Huh? Did I do something wrong? Did I tell a wrong secret? Have you been running? Is that your new secret hiding place, under my bed? When did you ever use the bathroom? Huh? Marty thinks you were hiding in the *Zombie Cave,* but I said NO WAY, that's way too scary a place for C, and he can't run that fast! Zombies would catch him for sure and eat his brains and suck his eyeballs out! And then you'd be a zombie too! Are you a zombie now C? Cause if you are, I'm not letting you suck my eyeballs out, even if we are best friends, because best friends don't suck their best friends eyeballs out, even if they are zombies....just saying. Marty's afraid of zombies, and he even rolled up his windows to protect himself from, you know, the zombies hiding in the tall grass by the road, even though he wouldn't admit it, pretending to pull up his socks....I caught him, but he still wouldn't admit it....he's a real scaredy-cat, when it comes to zombies. Are you *really* a zombie now C? You must be, cause you really aren't fast enough to outrun 'em; sorry to hurt your feelings and all — do zombies even have feelings? But if they do, sorry, but you are way too slow....just saying."

"Thanks Earl, for all *that*. And no, last time I checked, I'm not a zombie. I'm not eating brains and eyeballs just yet, still a vegetarian. Don't think a zombie can be a vegetarian, I think it is kind of against the rules."

C said sarcastic, acknowledging Earl's so-low expectations.

"I'm **so glad** you're not a zombie *[Earl pinched C's face between his two hands, like a grandma does]*, but you do need to start running faster, you know, just in case, for the future. Zombies aren't that fast, but if they were after ya, *I still think you'd be a goner....just saying.*"

Earl whispered that last tidbit, with a tilted head toward Cord, a grandma bent.

C smiled at him, that closed lip, uptick smile that he always used; and Earl smiled back - full of bright, shiny teeth. Really good smiles, both of them, best-friend-smiles.

Then Earl's face contorted, remembering his dream.

"Holy mackerel, I just remembered what I was dreaming!"

And Earl waited impatient, rubbing his hands together and twiddling his thumbs furious, hoping C would ask about the dream, which of course, he did.

"Go 'head."

C said, smirking. And Earl launched, in fast-motion.

"See, I was on the Golden Gate Bridge; I've never been there before, you know, for real, I've never even been out of Belvidere! But I saw it on TV; that's a really big bridge! But it's red, not gold; why do they call it gold, when it isn't....it's red?"

"I don't know, good question; what were you doing on the bridge?"

"Running from zombies!"

"Really?"

"Yeah! I don't know why they were after me, but they were running pretty fast - they got fast ones out there! And I'm pretty fast, and they were still catching up, even to me! You would been eaten for sure, C, for sure;

you'd be a goner....eyeballs sucked right out of your head!"

"Okay Earl, enough already about how slow I am. And zombies do eat your brains, but I don't think they actually suck your eyeballs out."

"*Of course they do*! Don't you know *anything* about zombies!? They're well known to suck the eyeballs right out of your head, like a big vacuum cleaner!"

Earl just stared at Cord, but C didn't have an answer for that one.

"Well anyway, they were getting close, so I jumped right off the side of the bridge, and I just started flying! Just like that! Like Aloysius does! Then I flew down into the water, like he does, and went right under, like I was diving for fish! And the water was cold, but I wasn't scared or anything! And you know what?"

"No, what?"

"I didn't sink! I could swim! I bobbed right up, like Al does, all by myself. And it was really easy! But then I saw one of the zombies swimming toward me; he was pretty far away, yelling at me, but I think he was a good zombie....can you be a good zombie, C? I think he was trying to help me, but I went under water again, like Al does, and I never saw that zombie again. I kinda miss that zombie – I think he was a nice one. Anyway, now the water was warm, and I could see and breathe there too, you know, underwater, like a fish; it was really cool! But I wasn't looking for fish to eat, or anything, I was just kinda hanging. And you know what? I think I was just about to talk to somebody, somebody *really* important, I think, somebody nice. They were floating right behind me, I could feel 'em there, close by, you know? And they were gonna touch me on the shoulder, I think, and talk to me; maybe it was Al, with a fish in his mouth! But I don't think so. Anyway, I didn't want

2160

to share a fish with him, his breath would probably be stinky, like fish, even worse than Lilly's morning breath when she wakes up, before she brushes her teeth, and let me tell ya, *that stink is bad!* So I was about to turn around and tell him so, tell Al that I didn't want his fish, or to smell his stinky fish breath, if it was even Al, and I was just about to, you know, talk to whoever was there, and then you woke me up, when I was still, you know, underwater, just hanging there, waiting. I kinda liked that place; I wish I was back there."

C just smiled at him.

"Sorry Earl, maybe you can close your eyes and go back."

"Nah, I'll go see Al later; then I'll ask him if he was trying to give me a stinky fish, and if he ate it or not. I'd way rather be here with you right now; I'm so happy you came back!"

Earl put his big hand on C's shoulder, gentle, like he was petting Chicken.

"Me too, me too; sorry I've been a bit cranky and out of touch lately....nothing to do with you buddy, just me, being me."

C said, patting Earl lightly on the chest.

"Well is everything okay now; are you still cranky?"

Earl asked, hesitant.

"Nope, all's good."

And Cord smiled sincere at his friend.

"Hey, have you ever been there C? Ever? You know, the big red zombie bridge?"

C nodded a yes.

"*I knew it!* **I knew it!** You've been everywhere! I've been nowhere, except Mr. Gill's farm – he's got lots of cow manure there – I like the smell of cow poop you know. But Mr. Gill's farm doesn't count as being anywhere, does it C? Does it?"

"Sure it does. Mr. Gill's farm is just as good a place as any. But hey, Earl, just so you know, the water's *really* cold out there, under that big red bridge; don't suppose you'd be just sitting underwater, hanging out, not there. But the bridge is pretty cool, so is the city it's in; do you know what city it's in, that big bridge?"

Earl shook his head no.

"San Francisco, in California, all the way on the other side of the country, *way* past the Gill's farm, and the manure, but it's very nice. Maybe we'll go someday, maybe soon, just you and me."

"*Really?* That would be so cool! But are the zombies really there, in California, on the red bridge? Are San Francisco zombies really fast? They ran awful fast when they were after me! And there were tons of them!"

"I don't know about that, maybe. But I can tell you something about San Francisco if you want, not about zombies, but just a little story I remember, if you want."

Earl beamed; he loved C's stories, and C always had a story, and Earl always wanted to hear them, all of them. Every single one.

Ay looked into Earl's eyes and saw a yes.

"Okay, here goes."

But before he could start, Earl squeezed his eyes shut and poked Cord in the chest with an index finger.

"Wait C, I'm gonna pretend you're a zombie when you're telling it to me, okay?"

C smiled and shook his head.

And so began the weave of the zombie's yarn.

CHAPTER 287 – KEPT RUNNING, AND HOPSCOTCHED THE ROT

"It was May, and it was windy, a windy, sunny spring day, I remember that; what May, what year, I don't recall. Not that it matters; it was awhile ago. It always seems awhile ago.

There's a place down by the water, off something called the *Embarcadero;* it's called Pier 14. It's nothing special really, just a long, flat stick of concrete that juts out into San Francisco Bay, with a bulb on the end, like a match.

In the early morning, that's when I went there on a run, to the very end of Pier 14. The fisherman stood all around the bulb, dangling long lines, which disappeared into the choppy blue, far below. Some talked, most didn't, and they paid no attention to people who didn't fish, like me; it was like you didn't exist.

And I remember liking that, being invisible.

And all along the run out to the end of the pier, and on the way back, were these swivel chairs, bolted into the pier, like the kind you find at the counter of an old-fashioned diner. But here, they seemed out-of-place, kind of fancy. I guess they were for the fisherman too, but none used 'em, not a one. Some architect or planner probably thought they were a great idea, but they weren't; in fact, they were a shit idea. They just sat empty, marked with graffiti.

And as I ran Pier 14, on my way from the bulb to the sea wall, back to land, I looked over to the right, south, and I saw a lone cormorant, floating in the bay."

Earl opened his eyes.

"Really? Promise? Did you really see one, or are you making that up C, because you know how much I love

Al....I love him so much. Are you fibbing, just to make a good story?"

"I'm not fibbing, promise, not to you."

Earl was positively aglow. He whispered to C, so low Cord could barely hear him, inches away.

"Do you think it was Al? Do you think he was keeping an eye on ya, so you didn't fall in?"

C shook his head a slow yes. As strange as it seemed, for a second, Cord *really* believed it; maybe it *was* Al that had been following him all these years and he never knew it. He saw cormorants all over the world, and never thought much about it, till he met Al. When Aloysius left Belvidere every year, maybe he just did that, maybe he *did* keep an eye on C, following him around the globe, watching and waiting until Cord finally showed up here, to meet Earl and Lillian. Maybe, just maybe, Al was the one who threw the fourth dart. And that crazy thought maybe wasn't so crazy, especially in this Town, where lots of things just didn't make much sense. A real rabbit hole.

And that made Cord smile.

"I stopped, and watched him, because I knew he was gonna dive, they always do. And he did, just like Al, and stayed under for exactly thirteen seconds; I know, 'cause I counted. And he tossed a little minnow in his mouth, at least it looked like he did."

"He was a good catcher; it must be Al!"

Earl yelped, convinced it was his old friend. He'd have to scold Al the next time he saw him, seeing that he'd been holding out about Pier 14, and hanging with the fisherman, eating California minnows. He wondered if they tasted better than Belvidere minnows....he wondered.

"Oh boy!"

Earl said all of a sudden, for no particular reason, as he rubbed his hands together, fast and furious. Story time always got him excited, and it just caught up with him, and he had to let out an *Oh-boy.* He just had to; sometimes, you just do.

Then Earl took a deep breath, relaxed, and closed his eyes again, playing the zombie, as Cord continued.

"And there was this huge building, kinda slate-blue, called the *Ferry Terminal*, which said:

The Port of San Francisco

That's what it said, in big letters, on its face, just upstream of Pier 14. I remember gulls crying overhead, lots of gulls, and container ships, way off in the distance, beyond the Oakland Bay Bridge, and a big old warehouse building downstream. It said:

Hill's Bros. Coffee

Painted on the side, on the brick.

And there was this big colorful bow and arrow, with bright red quills; it must have been five-stories tall, *huge*, half-buried in the grass, some big public art sculpture, down by the water, between me, and the bridge, and the coffee house. And I remember the water looked pretty calm, for the most part, but in the distance, I remember tiny white caps, so tiny, because they were so far away. And the sky was deep blue, even that early in the morning, with linear clouds, white whispy brushstrokes painted across the blue, east to west *[C ran*

2166

his hand in a lazy line for Earl to see, even though he knew Earl's eyes were closed].

I remember it all, like it was yesterday Earl, every detail, like a painting you just stare and stare at, till it sinks into your brain; I have no clue why that shit sticks with me, but it always does."

C stopped the reminisce, and looked at Earl for answers, who opened his eyes when the story paused, shrugged his shoulders, just once, and closed them again.   C cracked a grin; *that* was the right answer.

So he continued.

"I ran off Pier 14 and headed south, along the water's edge, away from the bustle of the *Ferry Terminal*, the nearby *Farmer's Market* and the tourists, who were out in droves, even that early in the morning.   I wanted to get away from them all, to find the folds in the fabric. That's where I wanted to be.

I ran past Piers 26 and 28, and the crowd quickly thinned to a trickle.   It wasn't even a crowd, really, just a few stragglers.   It's amazing how there are these invisible lines, in cities, where you feel safe on one side, and then you don't on the other.   And it might simply be the width of a city street, safe and unsafe, a mere fifty feet of pavement apart.

Well, I was about to cross into *unsafe*.

Pier 26 and 28 were working piers, you know, fishing and cargo piers, industrial, gritty, dirty.   Further south, I ran past Piers 30 and 32, which weren't even real piers anymore; they were nothing but rotted concrete stubs, decrepit, jutting ugly into the bay, like deformed limbs, which don't work anymore - they just sit there, fetid, dead....ignored.

By now the sidewalk was heaved here and there, broken, full of litter, weeds, and I started to feel better, like I belonged.

The other side of the line.

And the City put up these fancy poles, banner poles, light poles, something like that, all along the *Embarcadero* - the waterfront. They were all stuck in the sidewalk, connecting the *Ferry Terminal* to safer points south; but in doing so, they ran them through this dead zone I was in. It wasn't like they could hop-scotch the cancer, right? So here I was running by all these fancy poles, set in a desolate stretch of broken, weed-filled sidewalk, that no one who dared venture into this dead area even looked at....why would they? But I did, Earl; I did. And each of the poles had fancy writing around the base, you know, quotes and stuff, about times past, cast in bronze, like the writing on a penny.

And I remember, right smack in the middle of all that ugliness, loneliness and fear, what one of them said:

> *Slender spars in the offing,*
> *Mast and yard in the slips –*
> *How they tell on the azure of the sea –*
> *Contending ships!"*

C looked right at Earl's lids as he recalled the verse.

"Isn't it weird, that I remember that saying, every word?"

And Earl, eyes still closed, shook his head no; of course it wasn't weird to Earl, he was an elephant, and forgot nothing.

"What's all that mean C?   *Spar, offing, azure;* why'd they write that stuff? I don't get any of it."

"You know what it means? It means, I think, anyway, that at one time, long ago, that dead ugly area around Pier 32 was anything but; it was alive and hopping like crazy, with hundreds of ships coming and going from port, packed with drunken sailors and goods, with stories to tell and share….times were good."

"What happened C; why'd it stop?"

"Times change, I guess, and the sailor's, the ships and the goods, and all the *good* that came with it, went away, to somewhere else, and the *bad*, and the bums, roll in, with the next tide."

Sadness settled across Earl's face and he opened his eyes, but just a slit.

"Are they *all* bad, you know, the bums?"

C shook his head, sorry he said it.

"No, they're not all bad, not at all."

And C thought about Santa Claus, *his* Santa Claus, in Fort Lauderdale:

Be Good Brother

It was the best Christmas present C ever got….*ever.*

"It's just where they end up is all, unwanted. They don't want to be there, but sometimes that's where the dead-end leads, and you end up there, alone, with no way out. I...."

C didn't finish the thought.

"Is Stinky-Steve a bum?"

Earl asked quiet, then he continued, before C could answer.

"You know, Marty says he was a schoolteacher, or a janitor, or worked in a shop, or something, across the bridge, you know, in Pennsy, a real job. But then he got fired or quit or something, something, and people, and his family, tried to help him and stuff, but he just said no. He lived in a car for a bit - right in Town, I remember that, but then it was gone, the car, it broke, I think, or something, and he didn't live in the car anymore, and then he just started walking around, everywhere....always walking. Where's he go C, walking all the time? You think he would-a got there, you know, by now, wherever he was going, cause he's always walking, and that's a lot of walking; with that much walking, wherever you're going, you should have got there by now. Right?"

C just half-smiled at Earl, and offered no answer.

"Lilly doesn't like him, but he doesn't scare me, even though he smells kinda bad, not just the farts, just overall smelly, the farts just make it worse, you know, when he farts, and he farts a *lot*. I know he farted at you that time. Anyway, he never looks at me, you know, his head is always down, looking at his shoes, or something; I think he's scared a lot too, kinda like me. Hey C, I don't have a real job and I'm scared a lot, maybe *I'm* a bum! Am I a bum too, C? Is someone gonna make me stay out by Pier 32, all alone, by the *slender spars* and all the ugly and the litter and the weeds. Maybe I don't wanna go see the red bridge after all, maybe I'll just stay here; I don't wanna be a bum in San Francisco, C, to be unwanted, in a dead-end, with no way out. And you know what, I'd be real lonely, and I bet Chicken would miss me, for sure – who's shoulders would she sleep on? *Yours?* I don't think so; no offense, but she really would rather sleep on *my* shoulders. And I bet Lilly would miss me too, but maybe she *wouldn't*, maybe she wouldn't like me anymore, maybe she'd even *hate* me, you know, because I was a bum, and she doesn't like bums and maybe I'd start farting all the time too, I mean I fart sometimes, sometimes they just squeak out, you know, by mistake, but maybe I'd start farting more and more, out of control even, and not be able to stop! Nonstop farting! And then I'd be real smelly too! I don't *wanna* be a smelly bum, C!"

C smiled sad at his friend, and put his hand lightly on his chest; he could feel Earl's heart pumping wild, jackrabbit scared.

"You're not a bum, Earl, farthest from it, trust me. And Lilly would *never* hate you for *anything*….promise, except maybe if you really started farting all the time; maybe that."

Earl smiled, scrunched his shoulders and took a big breath; he was *very* relieved he wasn't a bum, but had to remember to concentrate and keep his gas in check, especially around Lilly. Then he whispered to Cord.

"I would help 'em, C, all the bums at Pier 32, if I could, if I met 'em. I'd give 'em a *Vernors* or something, maybe some *Animal Crackers,* even if they still had their heads, even if they were the last *Animal Crackers* I ever had, ever….I'd give 'em all to them, and the *Vernors,* too, because they'd be thirsty, eating all those cookies. I know, 'cause I get real thirsty, eating 'em."

"I know you would, I know."

C gently cupped Earls left cheek with his hand and smiled.

"Why'd you do that?"

Earl asked, but C didn't answer, he just dropped his hand and patted his friend on the chest, as the two sat in silence, just looking at each other, likes best friends sometimes do.

"What happened next?"

Earl finally said; C knew that prompt was coming, and he was waiting for it: *what happened next* always comes from Earl when stories are told, and stories are paused, so that Earl can unpause them, and hear some more. It was just the way stories went, between Cord and Earl.

So Cord carried on.

"By the time I got to Pier 36, I think it was 36, the piers weren't even labeled anymore, not in this part of the City, I was alone, except for a single man....homeless *[C didn't call him a bum]*. He was black, with a scruffy orangy-red beard and glazed eyes, rocking back and forth, sitting on a low crumbled concrete wall, right alongside the sidewalk. I remember he had a baggage cart, you know, from a hotel *[actually Earl didn't know, but he pretended to, so he shook his head yes - he didn't want to interrupt C again]* – he must-a stole it, or found it somewhere, whatever, and all his possessions, *every one*, were piled atop the cart, or hanging from the cart frame, in yellow plastic grocery bags, ripped and torn from constantly flapping in the wind. And I couldn't see what was inside, but I didn't have to; it was just a bunch of junk, other peoples junk, but to him, it was everything....*everything*. And the whole lot, all of it, was covered by a dirty, ratty piece of Visqueen, torn plastic sheeting taken from a job site, you know, a construction site somewhere, probably. And just like the fisherman, back on Pier 14, he didn't see me, and I ran as close to him as I am to you. Frankly, I'm not sure what those eyes saw.

Earl just had to jump in. The whole bum thing was still weighing heavy on his mind, and Earl had no choice but to interrupt; his thoughts spilled as if in mid-sentence.

"....and besides, I could never be a bum, even though I'm kinda black, like the homeless guy, but I don't have orangy-red hair, I don't have any hair at all! And I'm not a rocker, am I C? Do I rock back and forth like the red-haired bum? Do I, huh? Anyway, I wouldn't even know where to find a hotel cart or Visqueen, whatever that is, and I don't have a lotta stuff, important stuff, you know, to cover in plastic anyway, just my Gregson glasses, and my mom's letter opener, and my Santa-Dad letter – my mom would be *really* mad if I forgot that, oh, and my *List Of Ten* - that's really important, and my bumblebee shorts, and my pieces of *Couch Rock*....oh, and my invitation!   You   know,   to   the   *Indian   Summer Bacchanalia - The honor of your presence is requested!* You know the one!   Carol even signed it, in real ink! Can't forget that! And Jonesy....oh my God, I can't leave Jonesy behind – no way! And I don't think he'd like to be under a piece of plastic on a hotel cart – he wouldn't be happy about that, hard to breath, and I can't put him in my pocket, he'd get hurt....and what about Louie the Lobster, I'd never see him again, and what about Chicken *Chimichanga*, can I take her along? But she wouldn't like the zombies, no way, and living under Visqueen, I know that for sure, and besides, you know what I need to take too, huh, *really* important, I need...."

"Earl, Jesus, take a breath! Get off the bum thing for Christ sake, you're *not* a bum!"

"Okay, but I'm just saying."

And then Earl stopped, and they both sat in silence, staring at each other, waiting....waiting. Neither one blinked, not once. Until Earl cracked a mischievous smile and scrunched his shoulders, and said it again.

"So what happened next?"

And C cracked a similar smile, and continued.

"And next to the crumbly wall, just past our friend, was an abandoned building, surrounded by chain-link fence, you know, security fencing. The building jutted out into the Bay, resting on another shitty-broken pier.

Was painted on a broken wooden sign, kinda fake-looking, like someone who puts up a yard-sale sign on a phone pole. It was half-screwed into the masonry wall, above a rusty steel security door, bolted and chained shut ages ago. A plastic sign, duct-taped to the door, flapped in the breeze said, warning:

Unsafe – Do Not Enter

And through it all, I kept running, and hopscotched the rot.

CHAPTER 288 – FOUR WHISPERED WORDS:
CAN I COME TOO?

"Before I knew it, 'cause I was lost in thought, I was in front of the *South Beach Yacht Club,* and I remember thinking, how did I get *here*, from the rot over *there*?

Strange.

I found myself running alongside a yacht basin, with hundreds of crisp white hulls, all covered with bright blue canvas tarps, bobbing in *South Beach Harbor*, all dressed the same….neat, crisp and clean. And I remember all the ropes, hundreds of ropes, slapping against the masts in the breeze, coming off the Bay. And I remember the names painted on the hulls: *Trinity, LuniSea* and *Music*-Man, along with *Goose, Good Omen*, and a hundred more ridiculous attempts at being clever.

It was all so….safe *[C shook his head in disgust].*

And it seemed suddenly, out of nowhere, I was sharing the sidewalk, surrounded by dog-walkers and runners and bikers….all lily-white and *determined*, preoccupied with ear pods and watches and sweat and calories-burned and….whatever.

Simply clueless. Stupidity, all of it.

And I couldn't get out of there fast enough *[to get back to the in-between, the ugly, the forgotten, to sit by the bum, so he could ignore me, and me him – that's where I belong – that's what C thought, but he said none of it aloud].* I turned around and ran back from where I came, back to see my friend on the wall, but he was already gone, Earl, not a trace. And I never saw him again, ever."

C was silent for a bit, and Earl knew the story was over, and that always made him sad.

He slowly opened his eyes - and it was now that C knew the barrage of questions would come; Earl simply didn't know where to start:

- Where'd the homeless man really go?
- Is he okay?
- Will the zombies on the red bridge get him?
- What happened to Al?
- Is he still fishing at Pier 14?
- Did the fisherman hurt the fish, or put them back?
- Why would anyone name a boat *Goose;* isn't that kinda stupid?
- Are you *really* sure I'm not a bum?
- And on, and on and on.

C saw Earl suck in a big gulp of air, and the relentless rat-a-tat was about to begin, so he headed his friend off at the pass.

"Happy Birthday Buddy!"

That one caught Earl off guard.

"Um, thank you, again, I guess, but it's not *really* my birthday yet. My mom said my birthday is exactly 12:31 pm....*exactly*. **Hey Lilly, what time is it?!**"

Earl yelled at the top of his lungs, directing it out his bedroom door, and down the hall. But Lilly was still asleep, at least she was till then.

"Never mind; I gotta clock in here!"

Earl then whispered to C, he was still so excited his best friend wasn't mad at him anymore, he just remembered that again, and that he came to see him, on his birthday! How cool was that!

"It's 8:14; Okay, let's see....nine, ten, eleven, twelve....that's four, and twenty-four, thirty-four, that's twenty....minus three equals seventeen, so it's four hours and seventeen minutes *exactly* to my birthday! Wait, the clock just changed! So now it's *less* than that, now it's....let's see four and....."

C cut this loop off in a hurry, otherwise Earl was going to count down every damn minute for the next four-plus hours.

"What'ya want to do on your birthday?"

And Earl looked at his friend with a raised eyebrow.

"Hey, I know what you're doing! But I still got questions about the zombie San Francisco story; I didn't forget, you know! I know you're trying to change the subject, hoping I'll forget, so you don't have to answer a few questions, but I'm onto you, Mr. C, I know what you're up to; no avoiding the zombie questions!"

As Earl tapped C lightly on the forehead, like he was reminding a little kid.

"I know you didn't, you never do; just ask me on the way."

Earl sat up straight; the zombies could wait.

"On the way....*where?* To San Francisco? We're going to San Francisco for my birthday?! Oh boy, I gotta pack!"

"What?!"

Lilly yelped, standing in a nightshirt, a very short nightshirt, in the doorway. C heard her voice and remembered sitting in the woods, just yesterday afternoon, at *Foul Rift,* and how it ended badly with Lillian; how he was thinking he would never see her, ever again.

But he was wrong; thank goodness he was wrong.

C half-turned and saw her, and immediately turned away. But in that fraction of a glimpse, in that split-second, he saw enough, more than enough. The faint outline of her panties, barely covered by the shirt, and the tiny rounds of her nipples, small and hard, like they usually were, poking into the fabric, wanting out. And in that same fraction, she saw him eye her, up and down, and she knew where his eyes wandered. And despite that, the obvious eye-crawl that C simply couldn't help, there was no annoyed look, no quickly-crossed arms, no rude retort, just a yawn and a lazy morning-scratch of her butt. But the best part of it all, was the shirt - a light-pink shirt, with a little heart on it. It was a girl's shirt….hers, *definitely* hers.

Thank God it was hers.

"C and I are going to San Francisco....***today***! Sorry, Lilly, no-can-talk; gotta go! The plane leaves in a couple hours!"

"What are you talking about? *What?!* **Where?!**"

Earl looked at his wrist, at the watch that wasn't there.

Lilly's voice raised as the sentence spilled.

C whispered to Earl.

"We're not going to San Francisco, Earl; we're going someplace else, someplace *even better*."

"Even better than San Francisco?! How is that *even* possible?"

Earl gasped, as if the mere thought of a better place than San Francisco, at that moment, could even exist was unfathomable, and that no matter where that place was, it would have to be simply beyond the best birthday present ever.

"Yep, even better; you ready for the big four-zero buddy, because this one's for you!"

*"Oh boy, oh boy, **oh boy!**"*

Earl was licking his lips and rubbing his hands and scrunching his shoulder all at once....an *Oh-Boy* frenzy.

C smiled. Right about now, despite what happened in the bathroom bowl not so long ago, life was feeling pretty good. He hoped this feeling would last, just a little while. It always seemed to be fleeting. Maybe this time, it would be different.

Then, from the doorway behind him, out of sight, came four quiet words, leaving the lips of the little girl who owned him, for better or worse, for the past six months, right from that very first day he laid eyes upon her at the market, as he walked to the door, to let her in. Boy did Lillian Liddell own him; totally and without question, from that day, to this. And that little girl uttered four tiny words, that made life for Cord Brin, right about now, feel a whole lot better than good.

Four whispered words: *can I come too?*

CHAPTER 289 – QUICKLY GETTING A LOT BETTER THAN GOOD

Now C was in a bit of a pickle.

Carol and he, well Carol, actually, never included Lillian in *any* of Earl's birthday plans, so Lilly had no idea of the day, and night, her brother was about to have. And remarkably, unbelievably, no one, not a soul, leaked the gig to Lilly; in Belvidere, that was nothing short of a miracle.

C never turned around to face Lillian, but the way she said those four little words, it was clear there was no sarcasm, no set-up, no nothing; it was a heartfelt question that sounded as if the asker would be devastated if the answer was anything but *yes*. It was anything but what you would expect from Lilly.

"You have to ask your brother; it's his birthday present, his day, his decision."

C looked at Earl as he spoke the words, who looked at Lilly, over C's head. And he smiled at his big sister.

"It wouldn't be a *real* birthday if Lilly wasn't with me, ya know; I want her to come, okay C?"

"Of course, your pick, your day! But there's no turning back young lady; once you're in, you're in for the *whole day, one-way ticket; no take-backs!* Sure you want to take the risk? Put your fate in my hands for a *whole* day?"

C asked the question while turning his head half-way toward her, but his eyes stopped, and stared at the wall, never making it to the doorway, never meeting his eyes with hers. He expected silence, a huff, a sigh, a foot-scrape, some evidence of dissension. Instead, he got nothing but this.

"Give me a half-hour and I'll be ready; Earl, let's get egg sandwiches on the way, okay?"

A perfectly compliant answer in the most cheerful tone C had, frankly, ever heard leave her lips. Maybe she was drunk. So he pushed his luck.

"*Uh, uh, uh – not so fast.* My day, my plans; no egg sandwiches unless *I* say so."

C said, as if scolding a child. His words were greeted by silence in the doorway. C turned back to his friend.

"Hey Earl, what'ya say we get some egg sandwiches on the way for you and your sister, my treat, okay? Doesn't that sound good? You okay with that? How about you Lilly?"

Earl smiled wide, and C didn't get a response from Lillian; all he heard was her feet as she half-ran down the hall, more of a deer-leap, toward her room, to get ready.

And Earl whispered a secret to his best friend.

"Hey C, when you said that, she was smiling at you, and it was a *really good* smile."

"Oh yeah?"

C whispered back, sporting his own uptick smile. And he realized this day was quickly getting a lot better than good.

CHAPTER 290– IT WAS FINALLY TIME TO BLOW

The small brown lunch bags, three of them sitting neatly in a row on the kitchen counter, contained a total of six egg sandwiches, one for Lillian, two for C, and three for Earl. Each had salt and pepper and a swirl of ketchup, with extra swirls for Earl. Lilly figured she made egg-sandwiches better than anyone, and for her brother's birthday, they had to be perfect.

The last two lunch bags each had a box of unopened *Animal Crackers*, heads intact, and a bottle of cold *Vernors*. Lilly packed the brown bags neat as a pin, like lunches for three kids on the first day of school. She threw some slices of sheep's cheese in her bag, Manchego, and a half-pack of already-opened, all-grain crackers. Each bag got a fresh napkin...paper, but embossed, kind of fancy. And C got a little surprise that Lillian didn't reveal – a single peanut butter cup - she knew that was Ay's favorite.

Lilly stood at the sink, finishing the dishes and cleaning the kitchen. Cord was at the opposite end of the apartment, in the front room, at the window blinds overlooking Water Street, waiting, alternating his view from between the slats, looking at the curbline comings and goings, and looking down the long hall, to the kitchen, and the back of that lithe little blonde.

The latter view was better; *man,* C thought to himself, *she was an absolute stunner.*

Lilly had on a white cotton short-sleeve top, the fabric just barely thick enough to hide most, but not all, of the details of her tiny breasts, which had no bra to contend with, and a short black skirt, with a pair of flats. Cord couldn't see her tits from his vantage, but he couldn't take his eyes off her tiny firm butt, as she shifted her weight from her left foot to right and back to left, as the water ran in the sink, and the dishes went from dirty to clean.

Carol had made all the arrangements for the car weeks ago; all C had to do was make the call and the convertible would be dropped off within a half-hour, guaranteed.

Exactly twenty-six minutes after the request was made, he peered between the blinds for what must have been the twentieth time, and he saw the baby slowly roll up alongside the curb, just in front of the doorway, fifteen feet west of the *Palace*. It was a sparkling, cherry-red Mustang, and it was already drawing a small crowd on the sidewalk.

"Ride's here! Let's go!"

C yelled, turning and heading down the hall, toward Lillian.

"But I didn't pack yet? What do I need to pack? I'm not ready! Where are we going?"

Lilly yelled nervous; she felt so excited, yet so not-ready for this, whatever *this* was.

"Too late, bus is leaving!"

C exclaimed, as he headed for the exit door.

"We're taking a bus?! Cool! I always wanted to ride on a big bus, like you did C, when you came here!"

Earl yelled from the bathroom.

"But...."

Lilly started to fret.

"Come on, you'll be fine just as you are. Grab the lunch bags and your brother, time's a-wasting and we got shit to do!"

And she just looked at him, and he knew, right then, this was gonna be a special day; at least it had the beginnings of one. Cord simply couldn't keep his eyes off her; she was still smiling, a genuine shine, a result of both being giddy and nervous at the unknown to come. C was sure he didn't know this girl standing before him; an alien must have inhabited Lillian's body overnight.

"Come on guys!"

Was all Earl could say as he sprinted out of the bathroom past them and out the door, bounding down the steps. He couldn't wait to see how big the bus was. He had been pacing the apartment for the past half-hour, rubbing his hands and licking his lips furious, guessing every place, every story, that C had told him over the past six months, sure to guess their destination right. The last of the guesses were yelled from the bathroom.

But Earl never did guess right.

"Is it a long ride C? Should I go the bathroom?"

Earl yelled crazy up the stairwell, waiting for the two of them to come down, not nearly as quick as he'd like. Cord and Lillian finally made it to the lower landing, much too slow for Earl's liking.

"Earl, you just went didn't ya?"

"No, I was just pacing back and forth *in* the bathroom! Sometimes I do that, you know, just pace, when I get excited, and I'm *super-excited!*"

"Really, I couldn't tell."

Cord said, sarcastic. Then he continued matter-of-fact.

"Well, go if you gotta go, go now; there's no stopping in the first hour – none! No exceptions!"

"The first *hour?* How far are we driving? I gotta go too!"

Lilly yelped.

"Well *go* then, then let's go!"

And both brother and sister sprinted back up the steps; Lilly squeezed by and made it to the second floor first, yelled *hah!* to Earl and ducked into their apartment under his arm. Earl yelled *hey, no fair – cheater!* and kept sprinting up to the third floor, to C's apartment. Earl finished first, and he was just passing the second floor when Lilly opened the apartment door. Earl pushed her back in and sprinted to the finish line at the stair bottom, just ahead of her.

"No fair Earl; no pushing!"

She said, and shoved him in the back, out the door, onto the sidewalk.

"Hey, where's the bus?"

Earl said, looking left to right; not a bus to be found on Water Street.

"It's *that* bus, the red convertible one."

C said nonchalant; Linda had come out of *Nonpareil,* and was leaning against the car, talking to the too-cute guy holding the keys.

"A Mustang! We're going in a Mustang convertible?! Cool!"

Lilly said.

"Can I drive?"

She yelped.

"No, you don't even know how to drive."

"I'll learn quick."

She said, with a Lilly-smirk.

"I'm sure you will, *next time*."

C said, deadpan.

"Hey, how are *you* driving? Let's see your license, mister....*Brin*. I'm sure that's what it says, right? Cord Brin?"

Lilly said sarcastic, which C ignored completely.

"Earl, shotgun or back? You get to pick."

C barked.

"Lilly?"

Earl deferred to his sister.

"You take shot-gun next to your girlfriend; I'll spread out in the back."

The second sarcasm of the morning thrown his way; it actually felt good....normalcy returned. And with that, the young man tossed C the keys.

"C this is *yours*!"

Linda whined, knowing she wasn't getting a ride after all.

"For the day; see ya later Chickie! Maybe I'll give you a test-run later."

C said to his little teenage friend, lightly patting her on the butt as he walked by. He had never done that before, and wasn't sure he should've done it then, but Linda gave him a sly between-us smile that said *that little butt-pat was okay.*

Lilly missed that one; probably a good thing. Not sure Buck would have appreciated that either....but, whatever.

"Hey, should we bring Chicken *Teriyaki*?! I could get the Sherpa?"

Earl asked.

"Nah, not this trip; she was sleeping – she'll be fine. We'll see her later, promise."

"Okay, first things first. Let's see if they followed instructions, but I still think we're gonna have a little problem."

And with that, C dropped open the glove compartment, and sitting there were not two, as he pretended there were supposed to be, but three, cheap all-black sunglasses, which were planned the whole time. The third pair, however, originally had someone else's name on them, the third passenger in the original plan. He'd unfortunately have to deal with, and pay for, that issue a bit later, for sure. But later was later, and this was now, so the third set went to the queued-up hot little blonde in the back seat.

"Beautiful, they fucked up, and gave us an extra pair, they must've known cranky-pants in the back was coming."

And C distributed the glasses.

"I'm not wearing these stupid things; that's gay!"

Came the word from behind.

"Wow, what a surprise; you can't just put them on, without comment and drama, always has to be drama. Just put them on, or you're out and Linda's in. Will you wear the shades Linda, and drive around in the convertible with Earl and me?"

"You bet! Give me the glasses!"

She yelled.

C smiled and turned to look at Lilly.

"On or out, make a choice sister!"

With a single huff, on they went. And, of course, they looked great – just about anything on Lilly looked great. Immediately, Lilly was craning forward, leaning between, and pushing the two aside, trying to check her new look in the rear-view.

"For Christ's sake, first you won't put them on, then you can't get in front of the mirror quick enough to check out *the look;* you are pathetic! Sorry Lindy-Lou, next time."

"No prob; have fun guys!"

Linda said, as C turned the key and the engine grumbled sexy in idle; Linda pushed away from the car in envy.

Cord rolled away from the curb, and looked around the car, two pairs of cheap black sunglasses stared back at him. The one to his right was smiling broadly, the one in the back seat stuck its tongue out at him, then looked away, scanning the downtown scene, head back, like a model on the runway.

C smiled, pushed the knob and the radio kicked on, set on a satellite station....1960's. And the first song of what was hoped to be a glorious day, the time of their lives, had just started; it was the *Nashville Teens* and:

Tobacco Road

Earl settled his butt in the front seat; Lilly settled hers in the back; they K-turned in the parking lot across the street and set their black-shaded sights down Water Street, crawling slow through Town, the same crooked way Cord walked into their lives, nearly six months ago.

The *Nashville Teens* sung to them as downtown passed them by:

> *But it's home, the only life I've ever known;*
> *Only you know how I loathe Tobacco Road.*

Earl turned back to look at Lilly, a big smile planted on his face. Lilly returned one in kind, and, it seemed, it was finally time to kiss this Town goodbye.

> *Bring that dynamite and a crane;*
> *Blow it up, start all over again;*
> *Build a town, be proud to show;*
> *Give the name Tobacco Road.*

Earl had waited forty long years, Lilly had waited forty-one; it was finally time to blow.

CHAPTER 291 – *WHAT THE FUCK WAS THAT?*

His April crawl played in reverse.

The bright red Mustang, polished to candy-apple, slowly rolled passed the tired Victorians along Water Street, past the jag in the Pequest River, on by the Municipal Building, the curved entry drive to DSM and the scrub-shrub floodplain that stretched along the river, where he sunk his feet in the river on that first long walk into Town. It felt like a lifetime had passed; this place was nothing but a mystery then, a strange place, with deserted roadside ephemera along the way. But now, it felt like home, a *real* home, the first one in years, since we was a little kid. Who could have *ever* imagined such an outcome? Certainly not him; never would such a play have crossed his mind, especially in a forgotten dead-end like this. Maybe it wasn't a dead-end after all; he smiled at the thought.

Then Cord saw it up ahead, on the right, threading the right-side white sideline, and he smiled wider. How appropriate to see *that* again.

C shook his head at the sight of the balding head, ringed with black and white stringy hair, as much a cartoon as he was that first day. He was hunched over, slight and disheveled, as usual, wearing the one pair of shorts he owned, tan, spotted with ground grease and dirt. Although C didn't know it at the time, back on that first day in April, he knew now; it was Stinky-Steve, heading out of Town, to points unknown....always to points unknown.

And he did it again, like clockwork.

A little less than a half-block away, without hesitation or acknowledgment, he jaywalked and passed to the other side of the street, the left-side, never changing his pace, never once turning his head back to see the oncoming

Mustang. He didn't even acknowledge he knew the car was coming. He somehow had that trick down pat.

"Hold your breath."

C said in a half-snark, mostly to himself, knowing what was surely coming, an ass-kiss.

As Cord approached in the Mustang, still a good twenty yards behind the little man, C pointed and fired a finger-gun at Stinky-Steve's back, chuckling to himself at his little inside joke.

But C's smile erased when he saw Steve stretch out his right arm a mere fraction of a second later and point his own finger-gun directly at C, and he did it *without* looking up, without seeing Cord, without knowing he'd been finger-shot himself, without knowing Cord was even in the car – how could he *possibly* know that car, the Mustang? Steve never turned, he never looked up, his shoulders hunched, his eyes glued to the ground, to his sneakers, as always. But his finger-gun just followed C's head like a laser, as the Mustang rolled by – a direct shot. In the rear view mirror, C could see the little man's shoulders shaking and was sure he was laughing, or farting, at Cord....probably both.

That was fucking creepy strange. C thought to himself.

"Did you see that? Wasn't that weird?"

C asked his passengers.

"See what?"

Earl and Lilly said, in unison. They saw nothing.

"What Stinky-Steve just did – the finger!"

Lillian was looking at her fingers, preoccupied with her nails, too absorbed in her nails to look up. Earl quickly looked about the car – left, right, front and back.

"I don't see anything; there's no Stinky-Steve."

Earl proclaimed, disappointed in not seeing *the finger*, although he wasn't really sure what finger he was looking for.

"Right back there!"

C thumbed behind him, annoyed, scoping the rear view mirror. But there was no Stinky-Steve, walking the white line or anywhere else. It was as if he simply disappeared, into thin air.

The Mustang crested a bend in the road by the old Picnic Grove, and Cord shook his head at the mystery. Earl peered over his cheap shades and gave C the big eye, raising his *have you been drinking?* eyebrows for effect.

C barely whispered to himself, shaking his head slow, in the negative: *what the fuck was that?*

CHAPTER 292 - MAYBE HE DIDN'T WANT THIS DAY TO EVER END

The car clock read 12:15 pm as the Mustang rolled to a stop in the stall, about as far from the front door as you could get. There were no less than thirty spots closer, some *much* closer.

"Are you kidding me? How 'bout just a *bit* closer? There are some spaces, you know, like lots of them, closer!"

Lilly said sarcastically, looking over the top of her shades, annoyed.

"Really?"

C said, with equal sarcasm.

Then Earl chimed in.

"This is it? This is the trip? Not to be a downer or anything C, but, you know, I've already been to the A&P before, *lots* of times! I don't wanna be mean, or anything, you know I like the glasses and everything, but this is kind of a crappy birthday trip C, if I do say so, you know, for a birthday and all….just saying."

"*Really?*"

C said, even more sarcastic.

"And Lilly's kinda right, there are *plenty* of spaces a *lot* closer to the door, just so you know. Just saying."

Earl added, slowly, deliberately, pulling his shades halfway down his nose, a *Gregson-glasses* classic move, and pointing indignant, swinging his finger back and forth across the empty parking lot.

C looked at the both of them, shaking his head and wondering what planet they were from.

"For Christ sake, just stop talking, both of you, take off your glasses and follow me....Earl that is; *you, stick-in-the-mud,* can stay here, in the car, alone, if you like."

C barked at Lilly.

"Oh, *I'm* coming, don't you worry; I don't trust what you're up to. Besides, we already got snacks; what do we need *now*?"

Lilly barked back.

"And I'm *not* taking off my glasses!"

She added, defiant.

"Me neither!"

Earl yelled.

"Jesus; two fucking kids, just come on."

C said shaking his head. So far, the road trip had lasted a total of four minutes, and he was already aggravated by the two of them; this could be the beginning of a *very long,* day.

C made his way down the first aisle on the far right, past the fresh fruit, the nuts and the salad bar; Earl and Lilly in close tow. They were all still wearing their cheap black shades, including C. He turned the corner and started to head past the lobster tank.

"Hey wait C, we gotta say hi to Louie! You almost forgot! That's not very nice; we always say hi to Louie....you know that."

And C did an about face and stopped by the lobster tank.

"How could I forget Louie."

C said, shaking his head.

Just then, an older gentleman that C didn't know came from behind the counter; of course he knew Earl and Lillian. Lilly gave a half-polite half-smile – no doubt some other old man that annoyed her. Earl gave a much bigger smile that was clearly genuine.

"Hi Mr. Sands; how's Louie doing?!"

"Today, he's doing just about as good as a lobster can do in a tank like this."

"Wow! Can I say hi to him? Please?"

"You can do better."

C said, nonchalant.

And with that, the old man reached into the cold, briny water and pulled the large lobster from the tank, the only one with red rubber bands on his claws. He was easily double the size of the other dozen crustaceans crowded around him; he had to be pushing five pounds, maybe more.

As Louie left the tank he flapped his tail and sprayed water over the three of them; most of it covered Lilly, of course. She recoiled in reflex, cursing at Louie, saying she was gonna eat him, then cursed Earl, then C, in that order. Earl paid absolutely no attention to his sister's antics, he just giggled at his fifthest-best-friend. He grabbed him gently and gave him a dry kiss on his wet, speckled orange and brown shell, just below his eyes; Louie's antennae were rotating left to right. Maybe he liked it.

"I love Louie!"

Earl said to C.

"I know you do."

And with that, Earl handed him back to Mr. Sands, who promptly disappeared behind the deli counter.

"Hey, where's he going with Louie?"

Earl protested, as Mr. Sands, out of sight, pulled a white plastic cooler from beneath the counter, the bottom filled with ice and water, with some wet newspapers laid atop. He placed Louie gently in the cooler, reset the lid, and slid the cooler around the counter, at Earl's feet.

"Hey, what's going on?"

Earl protested.

"Lunch, it seems."

Said Lilly, smiling wry behind her shades.

"Hey! That's not funny!"

"Oh, so *now* it's not funny?"

Lilly said, sarcastic, still wet from the spray. C shook his head and snorted a half-laugh at the two of them.

"Louie's coming with us, Earl, on our mystery trip, and then Louie's going home, forever, free....to live with all the other lobsters in the ocean, where he belongs. And maybe, just maybe, he'll find his way to Panama, and we'll see him every time we go down to visit."

Earl's eyes rounded to the size of baseballs, his eyebrows arching above the plastic rims, his mouth was a dead ringer for a codfish.

C's best friend was speechless.

"Really? Really C?"

C just smiled at his friend, shaking his head yes.

"We're going to the ocean?"

Lilly whispered, her own eyes the set of saucers behind the black. A Jersey girl, born and bred, was finally going to see the Shore. C half-turned to Lillian and shook his head once, in a definite yes. He half-smiled, and she returned the look.

"For starters."

C added.

"But I'll miss Louie C; I won't see him up here anymore."

"Louie's lived long enough in that little glass box, just like you've lived long enough in a little green box called Belvidere. Time to expand, my friend, while you're still in your thirties, for what, another fifteen minutes or so. And time to let Louie be free, again; he's waited long enough, don't you think?"

And Earl shook his head a sad and happy yes. And Lilly, out of nowhere, leaned over and kissed C lightly on the cheek.

"Thanks C, that's *really* nice, for Louie….and Earl."

She whispered in his ear; she hesitated, then gave him a kiss on the ear.

"And me."

Cord would never figure Lillian Liddell out….*never*, and he figured that was half the fun. The other half, well, that was another story entirely.

And maybe he wasn't so aggravated after all, just maybe
he didn't want this day to ever end.

2198

CHAPTER 293 – *WHAT A GREAT FUCKING DAY*

Before they left the supermarket, Earl convinced Cord to bring some of Louie's friends, the two that were laying on top of him in the tank - one for each of them, Louie for Earl, and the other two for Lilly and C. Louie wouldn't want to be alone, after all, and his friends looked kinda sad that Louie was on his way out.

It didn't take much an arm-twist; C would have taken the whole tank.

And soon enough, off they went, the six of them, out of the store, and on their way to points, as yet, unknown.

The Mustang pulled out of the parking stall, with Louie and friends safely sequestered in the trunk. Earl was worried, thinking they'd be lonely, and scared, in the dark. C told him Louie would be okay....they'd all be okay.

Lilly smiled to herself and closed her eyes, hidden behind black plastic.

She woke up this morning to Earl's yell down the hall. And, she figured, just another typical Saturday - no place to go, nothing urgent to do, don't have to be anywhere, at any particular time. A too-typical boring, limited, vanilla Lilly day. Maybe a long bubble bath after the first cup of coffee, that would be the day's highlight.

Nice, safe, typical, vanilla….pathetic. Like every other day of her life.

Yeah, it was Earl's birthday, so today *was* a bit different. She would make him a special dinner, flank steak or ravioli, no doubt, and have to go over to Sam's to shop, and she would try to be *extra* nice to him, give him what he wants, when he wants it, with a minimum of fuss, and a big birthday peck on the cheek and a hearty hug, especially because it was his big *four-zero*. But that was about it; Lilly wasn't big on birthdays – frankly she never wanted to see another one of her own; reverse would a better direction.

So this Saturday would have normally shaped up to be another same-old, same-old; Lillian had way too many same-olds. Her whole life was a same-old, penned in a fenced yard called Belvidere.

Laying in bed, she remembered the run-in with C in the woods yesterday, and how that ended badly, and how it made her think about her life, about the things she said, and he said in return. How she told him he was copping out, and that he was just scared, and how he could change, how easy it was to do, it was a choice he made, the wrong choice, but a choice nonetheless....and to just change his choices.

Easy.

And how he scolded her right back; his words replayed in her head. If it's so easy, why doesn't she just talk to her mom, or just leave Belvidere if she hates it so much, or sing Amazing Grace – just once, or extend a hand of friendship to Carol, whom Earl truly loves. How about just one of the above; until she does that, don't be calling me a cop-out, or scared, or tell me it's so easy to change.

Easy.

So when she stood in the doorway minutes earlier, in her nightshirt, seeing the glow on Earl's face, and seeing the man she had roller-coaster feelings about, she decided, right then, *right now*, to change. No more waiting. And four little words reset the board game which had been her life: *can I come too?*

And surprisingly, it wasn't so hard after all.

And now, suddenly, sprawled in the back of a cherry-red Mustang, top down, sporting black shades and a stomach full of butterflies, she had an *olla podrida* of excited and scared and liberated and anxious rolling all around her insides, while she was quickly on her way to destinations unknown.

And today was fast shaping into anything but typical....anything but same-old.

And the faintest hint of a smile, just a shade, really, barely perceptible, cracked her lips; the only one who knew it was there was her. It was a little message sent to herself, and it said one thing:

What a great fucking day.

The Mustang growled as it passed a couple of stray runners and a tight pack of pre-teens on clunkers, tooling about. Cord had traced his way back through Town, heading toward *Nonpareil*, then hung a left at the only traffic light in Town, coursing Greenwich Street, past the Belvidere Elementary School, St. Patrick's Catholic Church and a string of neatly manicured homes.

And as the car left Belvidere's grip, on its way down Route 519, pointed southbound, C watched the familiar landscape slide by: Foul Rift Road - by the sewer plant, Colby Court, the County Jail, and Foul Rift road again – the other end of that infamous loop - with the concrete cooling towers of the power plant looming in the distance, off to the right, across the river, in Pennsylvania.

Cord thought of that day Lilly dusted him, on their run, with Button still very much in the mix. Those were a mix of good and bad memories, but he smiled just the same. Jesus, that seemed a lifetime ago; *everything* seemed a lifetime ago.

They just hit the seven-mile mark, in Harmony Township, when he heard the question he was expecting sooner.

"Hey, where we going C?"

Earl said, looking at C through his shades. It was a half-attempt at best; Earl knew his best friend wasn't gonna spill. C just half-smiled at him and turned back to the road rolling under the wheels; he never uttered a word.

"That's not very nice you know, not answering and stuff."

Earl said, just to set the record, as he poked C in the arm. C just smiled, looking at the road running under his wheels, and continued to ignore his best friend.

Lilly was unnaturally quiet in the back seat.

As the scenery sped by, she had drifted back to the bubble bath she passed up: *this little trip had better be worth it* she thought to herself. Once in the water, nothing short of a fire would get her out before the one hour mark, for sure. The bathtub, one of the most perfect places in the world....her little world, anyway. It was a cure-all, or at least a welcome respite, for the stress and anxiety she carried around most days, like a bag of bricks.

This had better be worth it; the words continued to float around her head.

Cord eyed a wake of black vultures, sunning lazy on the edge of a bleached corn field; there must have been at least a half-dozen. C looked skyward and saw nothing but scattered patches of puffy clouds, balls of cotton set upon a cerulean plate. His eyes returned to the road, and he noticed the clock.

"Holy shit Earl, look at the time!"

The analog had just clicked to 12:31 pm; Cord caught right on the dot – now it was official....forty years of breathing air.

"Should we sing happy birthday or something?"

C asked, excited.

"*NO!*"

Both Lilly and Earl yelped in toto, unplanned, to Cord's suggestion. Then Earl started giggling.

"Sorry C, don't mean to hurt your feelings and all, but you're a *really* bad singer, like an old cat-in-your-mouth-bad....just saying."

"Really bad!"

Came the shout from the back seat.

"Fine, whatever."

C mumbled, in a sulk.

"You can sing it Lilly! Lilly's got the best voice *ever*, even better than my mom's, and my mom was a really good singer, right Lilly? Aren't you a really good singer?"

Lilly didn't answer.

"Well she is, even if she doesn't say so."

Earl said, mainly to himself, as he scrunched his shoulders.

"Happy Birthday little brother."

Lilly said, as she leaned forward and gave Earl a sneaky kiss on the cheek.

"Thank you Bibby; I love you."

"I love you too, and I promise I won't eat Louie, or his friends."

C turned and looked at Lilly, with a sarcastic half-cock of his head.

"Wow, you're the best sister ever, anybody ever tell you that?"

"Watch the road, and stop trying to look up my skirt."

She said, deadpan. C laughed and turned around.

"In your dreams."

He said, under his breath.

"I heard that."

She snarked from the back.

Earl leaned into C and whispered.

"She did you know; Bibby hears *everything* when she wants to."

"Hey, quiet! Stop whispering; that's rude!"

She yelled at the birthday-boy, kicking the back of his seat. That ended the little outburst, and the car was silent once again.

And as they drove along, Lilly found herself staring at the back of the shaved melon in front of her, and she wondered what was going on between those two goofy ears, right, exactly *now*. And how about *now*? And *now*? Was C thinking about her, or the black girl in the VW, or somebody else? She wondered what Cord's real name was, and if she would ever really know. And did she really care?

She did.

One thing she did know, and she would never tell him, never give him the satisfaction, was that Cord impressed her. Partly because he stood up to her, and didn't grovel like most guys; well, he did sometimes, but mostly not. But that wasn't really it, what mattered the most was not how he felt about her, but rather how he felt about Earl. C truly *loved* Earl, and it wasn't fake, or done for some ulterior motive; it was genuine, and she loved C for it. And even though he had been a bit mean and distant recently, she knew that wasn't about Earl, not at all; it was all about C, and whatever demons he had to deal with.

She knew all about demons, having her fair share.

She turned her head slightly, lowered her shades, and looked at her brother's profile. He was so handsome, so happy, with a shaved noggin to mirror Cord, looking straight ahead, the wind washing his face. He had a smile, a shine, that couldn't be wiped, and it was there because of Cord, his best friend in the whole world. Ay truly was his bestest best friend, and Earl loved him, like a brother.

What a great birthday present C was for Earl....the best ever. She was convinced her mom sent C here, for Earl, and maybe her too.

Maybe.

And out of nowhere, without thinking, Lilly found herself leaning forward, into the front seat, and she kissed Cord on the cheek....a sneaky drive-by. No sooner had it happened, before C even knew what hit him, then she was back in the rear seat, a blank slate for a face, ready to deny it ever happened.

C was dumb-founded; he looked at Earl, then they both looked at her in the back seat, but she simply sat stone-faced. Then Earl and C looked at each other and smiled, without a word exchanged, and reset their eyes on the road ahead, watching it lazily roll on by.

The third kiss of the morning, and they were barely out of Belvidere. That had to be some sort of record. And a single thought buzzed between C's ears, as the wry smile never left his lips:

What a great fucking day.

CHAPTER 295 – I DON'T WANNA BE A DIRTY-DOG PANTIE-SNIFFER

"Hey, there it is, slow down! I wanna smell the cow poop!"

Earl sat upright-excited in his seat as the Mustang slowed to a crawl, then rolled to a stop on the grit alongside the edge of the road. C turned off the radio, then killed the engine; suddenly it was quiet; it was easy to forget how much the engine rumbled your brain, till it didn't anymore.

A small gathering of cows, about a dozen, lay less than fifteen feet away, huddled under a lone tree, mostly out of the sun, tails swishing, keeping the flies within reach in a constant circular dance: flies light on the cow, dodge a tail, take off, circle in a chaotic buzz, then light once again - a seemingly endless cycle, en masse, all set to the backbeat of a half-dozen mouths, chewing cud. Just a few of the closest in the herd expended the energy to look at the Mustang, and even that was with indifference; the rest, just chewed, blinked, and chewed some more, as tails forever swished away flies – in futility – as their eyes gazed lazy across the expanse of pasture.

The breeze was light and sweet on the trio's cheeks and the sun warmed their skin. A background of birds unseen, cackling and singing, completed the set. C recognized the call of the crows and bluejays; the rest he couldn't name.

Unknowns.

Earl was smiling wide, looking out over the ruddy green and brown field. He took off his shades and inhaled deep, 'cause you can always smell better without sunglasses on; even Earl knew that.

"This is *the* farm C, Mr. Gill's farm. This is as far as I've ever gone, ever! In my whole life! I haven't been here in years! See that stone row way over there, right by the woods? I used to play in there, playing army, shooting and getting shot and falling over the stones, over and over. Well nobody actually was shooting anybody, in fact, nobody was ever even playing with me....it was just me, all by myself, make-pretend; Lilly would never play with me – she said playing army was stupid! But I didn't think so; I think guys like army better than girls anyway. Ever do that C, ever? Play make-pretend, like army?"

C smirked as he answered.

"Yeah, all the time; I think all little boys do that – kind of goes with the territory."

"Oh boy, oh boy, *oh boy!* If we go any further, even just a *little bit* further, then it's San Francisco and zombies coming right up! Right C?"

"Right, but before we get to San Francisco, we gotta drop off Louie and his buddies, then go to some other places first....okay?"

"Like where?"

Came the line from behind.

"You'll see, soon enough."

C floated in a half-whisper, without turning around.

"Okay, Earl, guess this is the right place to do this."

And with that, C reached into his sport jacket, and pulled out, from the inside pocket, *the* herring gull feather, one of his most prized possessions, a bit worse for wear. Ay slowly ran his fingers along the edge of the feather; it was lightly pinched between his thumb and pointer, like he always did, when he studied the plume, and thought about what it meant, to him.

"I know I've already told you a bunch of times, but I'm gonna tell one last time, just once more, because this occasion deserves it. I was on a morning run, and I came across a dead herring gull; it must've just died, poor thing – I had actually never seen a dead gull – every time you see them, they're always full of life – flying overhead, screeching up a storm, or dodging the surf on a beach, forever looking for the next meal. But this one was dead; that fact alone was sad.

It was on its side, rocking back and forth in the surf, at the top of the tide line, with the water lapping the stony beach, on the edge of some remote bay, down a lonely dead end road, on New Year's day. It was cold, raining, misty - a shitty day - a real shitty day to die.

It was on Martha's Vineyard, that's an island, a pretty big one, pretty ritzy, in Massachusetts; I was running in the outskirts of a little place, a little village, on that island, called Edgartown. It was a tiny place – not a lot of people - bigger than Belvidere for sure, but still pretty small. Anyway, it was just one of those strange places I end up; it was just a place, like all the rest, nothing particularly special about it. Anyway, here it was, the morning of the first day of a new year – I can't even remember which year it was – but still, a new year, a new beginning, full of promise, not fucked-up, yet, and here is this poor gull that had just died. Right at the beginning, it ended.

I don't know how it happened; it didn't look hurt, or mangled – not a feather was out of place….maybe it was just old. But whatever the reason, it was dead when I got there. But the *dead part* must have just happened; it looked so fresh, like it happened seconds before I arrived. It looked like it could just get on its feet and fly away, if it simply just *woke up*.   But there was no waking up; it had dead eyes.

Anyway, as much as I didn't want to disturb it, I felt compelled to pluck a single feather off its side, *this one*, and I've carried it with me ever since, a *memento mori*....a reminder of death.

But just as much as that, for me anyway, it was also a reminder of new beginnings, the ones everyone has right after an ending, when the cycle starts again. And maybe this beginning would be better, I thought; maybe the gull's new beginning would live in me, and it would turn out right....for once. I know that sounds stupid to most people, and in fact, I've never told this story, how I really feel about the feather, to anyone but you, and now Lilly, because if anyone can understand how I truly feel about this feather, it's you, Earl....*it's you*. It's not just a feather, it never has been, and it never will be....not for me.

This feather has been traveling with me for years, waiting for it to bring the goodness, the *better*, I had always hoped for. And you know what I realized this morning; it was *never* meant for *me* - I was just a keeper, of sorts. It never gave me any good beginnings, they always turned sour. I realized that it's been waiting for *you* the whole time, and the goodness it brought to me was in a package called *Earl Liddell*....the best goodness the world has probably ever seen, or ever will. I know that now.

So I want *you* to have it, because with you is where it has always belonged. And once we start rolling again, once the Mustang noses past that stone row over there, by the woods, it's *all* new beginnings for you my friend - the herring gull's in you. It's *your* new beginning, and I got a good feeling about it; it, life that is, is gonna be good for you....*real good.*"

And with that, C turned the feather around and tilted it toward his best friend, his kindred spirit. Earl took it gently, closed his eyes and ran the feather's edge lightly across his own cheek.

"Thanks C, this is the best birthday present *ever*."

Earl whispered, and he meant it.

"Happy birthday buddy."

C said, smiling, looking over the top of his shades. Then, like Earl, he took them off. Earl dug frantically in his front pocket, and pulled out the small, familiar box.

"I gotta show Jonesy!"

"You brought Jonesy along?!   Good deal, he'll enjoy the ride."

C chuckled satisfied.

"Yeah!   I couldn't leave Jonesy home, not today, no way! This is big, *real big*; he'd be mad missing all this sitting in a box, all alone! And now with the feather, it's even bigger than big! Right Jonesy?"

Amid the commotion in the front seat, Lilly was silent, and simply smiling, watching the two of them, acting like excited little kids. She was so happy Cord found his way here, found Earl....found *them*. She was convinced her mom had a hand in it somehow. She didn't remember when she came to that conclusion, but she did. She found herself having more frequent thoughts about her mom, and they were good thoughts, not bitter, or angry, and that, in itself, felt good....*real* good. A burden lifted.

With that, she opened her purse and gazed inside, past the envelope, to a small, neatly folded square of rich, red silk. Her smile widened as she reached in, pulled out the scarf and slowly held it to her nose, breathing in deeply, savoring the smell. She carefully tied in on her head, fixing and fussing with her hair, ensuring it sat just exactly right.

It felt so good to be on, really good.

Earl set Jonesy by his seat, on the console.

"Will he be okay here C?"

"Sure, he's fine."

C said, his eyes looking out at the cows, and the pasture beyond.

"Hey Lilly, do you want to rub my feather? It's really...."

Earl spoke as he spun to face his sister in the rear seat, and as their eyes met, Earl stopped cold, his words frozen. All he could do was stare at his sister.

He saw nothing but the brilliant crimson silk scarf, interlaced with a collage of summer-colors - a bouquet of abstract leaves and blossoms, tied neatly upon Lillian's head. It was all he could see.

It was his mom's *favorite* scarf, the one she wore all the time, the one Lilly and her mom argued over wearing all the time, since it looked so good on both of them. It was the only piece of clothing Lilly saved of her mother's, all the rest was thrown away, every last stitch, even the ones she loved and shared wearing with her mom....all in the trash. Not a piece was given to *Goodwill* - every bit went to the landfill, in black plastic garbage bags. And Lillian had never once worn the scarf, since that April day in 1981, not once. It sat lonely in her bedroom bureau for the past twenty-five years, under some books she never touched, in a drawer she rarely opened.

It never saw the light of day, till now.

"Lilly...."

Was all Earl could say, his mouth open.

2212

Lilly was smiling, and in one graceful sweep, she slipped off her shades.

"What?"

Ay said, as he half-turned and saw Lillian, beaming brilliant.

"Holy, that is really, that looks *beautiful* on you, it really does."

C said, with no hint of anything but awe.

"Thank you."

Was all she answered, politely; nothing more was necessary.

C just shook his head; he couldn't take his eyes off her. And he stared at the scarf, mesmerized; he was sure he had seen that scarf before, but he didn't remember Lilly ever wearing it. Maybe it was in her underwear drawer, amongst the hundred-plus panties he rifled through, hiding the money he gave to Selena. Maybe he thought it was another pair of panties, but somehow, that didn't seem the right answer.

"You look *just* like mommy Bibby! That was your *favorite* scarf in the whole wide world; you loved when mommy wore that!"

"I know."

She whispered; the words came out a bit choked, with emotion. But she was still smiling wide.

Earl turned to C.

"Lilly always said when mom wore that scarf, it was gonna be a good day. Lilly said it meant she was gonna be in a good mood, all day, whenever she wore it, and she would never yell at us, and we never got in trouble or anything! It was good luck, that's what Lilly would say, and Lilly's *always* right about stuff like that. And the two of them would always fight over who got to wear it! Lilly and my mom always traded clothes, all sorts of stuff, but the red scarf, that's the one they fought over the most. Lilly loved that scarf, and my mom would always give in, and let Lilly wear it, because it made Lilly happy. It made her feel all grown-up and pretty, just like my mom.   You look the prettiest ever, Bibby.”

And Earl squeezed her knee and smiled wide at her.

“Do you think mom would be happy Earl, me wearing it? Do ya?”

Earl shook his head an eager yes.

“Why don't you ask her?”

Lilly said, tentatively.

“Why don't you?”

Earl whispered back.

“I did, I tried, but she didn't answer me.”

But Lilly didn't say it with the usual defeat, or anger or angst; her words held none of that. She said it with hope, and that was a first.

“She will, I know she will.”

Earl whispered again, and squeezed her bare knee.

“Have you worn that before? Recently, I mean?”

C asked.

"*No way!* She's never worn it, *ever*, since my mom went away; I didn't even know you kept it Bibby. Where was it?"

"In a special place."

Was all Lillian said.

"Was it in your underwear drawer?"

C asked.

"*No!* Why?"

"I've seen that before, I think."

C said, puzzled.

"Not this one; maybe you were delirious, sniffing all the pantie crotches."

Earl started giggling.

"I didn't sniff the crotches! I counted them, *counted,* not sniffed! I'm not a perv!"

Truth was, C *did* sniff a good half-dozen of them, maybe more, and did at least once whenever he stuffed more money in that drawer. A perv he certainly was, a pantie-sniffing perv.

Lilly looked at him cocked, not believing a word.

"Never once; not a one? *Really?* You counted *one-hundred thirteen* pairs of my underwear, sticking money in my drawer, rooting around in there all the time, running your grubby fingers all over them, even the crotchless ones, and you never took a little whiff, never snuck a tiny sniff of a single pair, ever....*ever?*"

She stared hard at C, and he stared back; neither blinked. Cord felt his eyeballs drying out, and he cracked under the pressure.

"Okay, maybe once, or twice; I don't remember!"

"Hah! I knew it! I *knew* you were an underwear-sniffer! Perv!"

"That's it, time to go, this conversation has nowhere good to go for me."

And with that, C turned the key, and the engine sprung to life in a low, sexy growl; he put the Mustang in gear.

"Did you get your fill of manure yet? Manure-sniffer? Ready to go?"

Earl breathed deep and sucked it in.

"I just can't help it; I *love* the smell of cow poop!"

He yelled as he fell back into his seat, as the Mustang kicked up grit and barreled down the road, punching fast past the stone row, past the horizon of Earl's little world, onward to new beginnings, on its way to San Francisco, and beyond.

They passed a little bridge over a bend in the river, the entrance to the farm, and a faded red barn, slowly being swallowed by vines. And as the Farm, and Earl's world for the first forty years, faded in the rear-view mirror, Earl leaned over to his friend and whispered, his face beet red.

Just once he did it too, he told C; he snuck into the laundry room before Ji-Sue started the laundry, and saw a pair of Carol's black lace panties - *they were so tiny they must not cover up much of anything!* They were sitting atop the wicker basket. He quick-looked around, no Ji in sight, and he got on all fours, like a hunting-dog, *no way* was he touching them, and stuck his nose right up to the fabric in the basket and took in a big swig of air.

It smelled like the best flowers ever, Earl said. And he quickly jumped got up again and no one was the wiser. The whole thing was way too scary for him, no way was he getting caught. He pumped his fist in silence; he got away with it!

Almost.

Big Banana had snuck up behind him and saw the *whole* thing. And now he just sat there, staring up at Earl, who had turned tomato. Busted crotch-sniffing by the cat.

Big B let out a single excited yelp, one big meow, like he always did when Earl just finished cleaning the litter box or just filling the water bowl, and he realized he was first in line.

And with that Big rubbed on Earl's leg.

Earl whispered to B to keep quiet about the whole fiasco, and scratched him under the chin, as a bribe. Banana fell on Earl's shoes, belly up, and got a too-long belly-rub, for extra bribery insurance.

And as Earl finished his story, C smiled at his friend, then posed a question.

"Hey Earl, how do you know you were sniffing Carol's underwear, and not Ji's? She does her own laundry too, you know, mixes it all together, and she's *really* tiny, with tiny panties! Maybe they were Ji's black panties you were sniffing."

Earl gasped; he *never* thought of that. Oh my God! Did he sniff Ji-Sue's crotch by mistake?! If he did, then he could say one thing for sure, Ji-Sue had a very nice smelling crotch – it smelled like the best flowers ever!

"Oh my God."

Was all Earl could say, and he said it a bit too loud.

"Hey, what are you two girls whispering about up there? Cut it out!"

Lilly yelled from the back, kicking C's seat.

"Well, either way, it smelled good didn't it?"

"Sure did....like fresh flowers!"

"You're a dirty-dog pantie-sniffer too; we must be brothers, for sure!"

C said, slapping Earl's leg.

Earl leaned over, and gave one last whisper, so Lilly couldn't hear.

"Just so ya know. I wanna be brothers and all, and we are the bestest best friends, but I don't wanna be a dirty-dog pantie-sniffer."

CHAPTER 296– BLINDING GLINT SPLAYED
AGAINST A BLOODSHOT HOOD

Less than two minutes from the Gill Farm, C hooked a left, ascended a steep ramp, and the Mustang quickly slivered into a mix of early afternoon traffic on a six-lane asphalt ribbon, Route 78, cruising east with the rest of the pack.

The first real highway Earl was ever on. Ever.

He was simply wide-eyed, ogling everything at once - front, back, left and right, a dog sticking his head out of the window, tongue flapping happy in the wind. Then, like a switch, he turned somber, eyeing Cord.

"Are you sure they're okay? I should have kept him on my lap, like I thought."

C sighed.

"No Earl, we're not pulling over *again* to check, they're fine. And he can't stay on your lap; every time we stop, it just delays us. We are on a tight schedule my friend; sit tight and enjoy the view….they're fine."

Earl sighed; he wasn't so sure.

"Keep 'em in the trunk! They're ugly, and they *smell*."

Lilly interjected, from nowhere.

"No they don't Lilly; leave Louie alone!"

"Yes they do; I can't get the lobster-stink out of my nostrils Earl!"

Lilly raised her voice, talking over her brother.

"Blow your nose then!"

Earl yelled at the back seat.

"Give me your sleeve."

Lilly snarked.

"No! Use your own sleeve!"

Earl yelled at the back seat, and then, the switch again, he assumed the role of the dog, happily eyeing the scenery fly by.

"Look at all the cars! The wind is really windy! What direction are we going? Where are we going? Are we almost there? I think I have to go the bathroom!"

With that, C sighed and turned the radio back on, and cranked it loud. This was going to be a long trip.

Lilly grabbed the boys' lunch bags and tossed them in the front seat, like feeding time at the zoo. The egg sandwiches were gone quick. Earl then ate the whole box of *Animal Crackers* and the last half of Cord's box; every one had a head! *That was just about the best birthday present ever*, he thought. He wished he had milk to dip them in, like with Carol, but he didn't, so the lions, tigers and bears were washed down with *Vernors*. After a few sips, C gave his pop to Earl and saved his peanut butter cup for last; he didn't share that. Lilly had a single bite of her hunk of Mangecho cheese and gave Earl the rest, along with all the crackers and her egg sandwich, less the two small bites she took....she was too excited to eat.   Earl vacuumed it all up, and daintily dabbed his lips with his fancy paper-embossed napkin; *if only he had his Gregson glasses on*, Earl thought to himself, as he dabbed some more – then, he figured, he would *really* look smart.

But he was still hungry.

It was now 12:58 pm; the first highway song of their conte began: *Life's Been Good To Me So Far,* by Joe Walsh.

"You like this song C? I like this song!"

Earl was so excited, he just talked to talk.

"It's okay; good song for the road, I guess."

C said.

"Hey Bibby, you know what I'm thinking?"

But before she could answer, he spilled.

"No. 631!"

And Earl turned, all smiles, and Lilly smiled back, not nearly as big. But a good smile, a smile one shares, like a secret.

"No. 631 is the best story ever! Isn't it?"

Lilly nodded a silent yes, and Earl turned back around and was feverishly rubbing his hands together and licking his lips. And that's all that was said.

By this time, Lilly had turned and gazed hollow out the side window, the smile on her face reduced to little more than a line, till it really wasn't a smile at all, as she thought about No. 631. And she didn't want to think about that anymore, not now, not today.

> *If I go crazy then will you still call me Superman;*
> *If I'm alive and well, will you be there a-holding my*
> *hand.*

Kryptonite, by 3 Doors Down, crept onto the radio and filled the car, competing with the buffet of wind cascading the windshield.

C waited patiently, but it was clear there would be no answer without a prod.

"Okay, I give; what's No. 631?"

Before Earl could speak, Lilly blurted.

"Don't you tell him Earl!"

But Earl wasn't gonna spill anyway.

"That's a *super-secret* C, between Bibby and me, a real good one!"

C stared at Earl, his eyes boring holes in his forehead. He knew Earl couldn't last long under the big-eye stare. Earl started to sweat, and quickly turned away.

"Don't you fall for that; keep quiet Earl!"

"Hey, no secrets in the Mustang!"

C yelled above *Superman*.

"Really? Is that another rule you just make up on the fly?"

Lilly snarked.

"Yep, driver sets the rules; driver is king of the castle."

"No secrets? So that's the Mustang rule?"

Lilly said, innocent.

"So says the king; now spill, No. 631."

Cord said, glad at being the king. Lilly leaned forward and whispered in Earl's ear; he scrunched his neck because Lilly's hair, and her warm breath in his ear, was very ticklish.

"No whispering either!"

C yelled.

"You whispered to Earl at the farm, like a little girl."

Lilly said matter-of-fact and gave C a scrunch-face.

"Yes, but the car was not in forward motion, and we were not on a highway; whispering is allowed in those situations, in the front seat, by the driver."

"So says the king."

Lilly parroted sarcastically.

"You're learning."

C said, smiling wry.

"Okay, no secrets; your rules Mr. King. Go ahead Earl, hit him good."

And the one-two barrage, front-seat, then back-seat, hit him like a machine gun.

"Where did you grow up?"

"What's your real name?"

"What are you supposed to tell me?"

"Where'd you really get all that money in the closet?"

"How come you run so slow and sing so bad, like you have an old cat living in your mouth?"

2223

"How often did you pick up the soap in the community shower?"

Lilly raised her eyebrow for the last one.

The questions came rapid-fire, Earl, then Lilly, back to Earl, and Lilly again. C was shelled quick; he stepped right into that one.

All he did was smile. The aggregate age in that car was one-hundred twenty-four years, going on eight.

"I don't care about No. 631 anyway."

Was all Cord said.

"And I *never* picked up the soap in the shower."

He added, staring at Lilly in the rear-view mirror.

"What would you do if you dropped it then? That's kinda dumb; why wouldn't you just pick it up?"

Earl asked confused at the stupid question, and the stupid answer.

"Because Bubba woulda had a big stiff bar waiting for him!"

Lilly said, and laughed at her own joke, slapping her own knee.

C just smiled and shook his head.

"You a regular riot."

"Yes I am!"

She said, sporting a toothy grin.

"So there *was* a shower then; at least we cleared that up."

And C didn't answer; *Freeze Frame* by the J. Geils Band spilled from the radio.

"Hey! Are we going past those mountains way over there C?!"

Earl pointed wildly to the left, to the hills in Clinton; just then a large green marker slipped by on the right:

Newark 36 miles

And it was Lilly's turn to freak.

"We're going to *Newark*?!"

C just turned and, with a quick wink, squeezed her knee. He didn't say a word, he just gave her *that look*. Oh boy, this isn't good, she thought.

"Where *are* we going? It *better not* be Newark!"

She squealed from the back, which C ignored.

"How much longer to Newark C?"

Earl yelled. He didn't give a hoot about Newark; in fact, he didn't even know what or where a Newark was.

"I'm ***not*** going to Newark!"

Lilly yelled.

"We're not going to Newark; but if we were, that's where you'd be going, like it or not – those were the rules when you stepped in the Mustang and donned the cheap shades, remember that. But, I'll at least spill this one fact

- no Newark. So take it easy, and relax; were not in a rush."

"But you said we were! Before! *We're on a tight schedule my friend;* that's what you said!"

Earl corrected him.

"You're right, I did."

With that, C jammed the accelerator, and the Mustang climbed over ninety, snaking the left side, on a serpentine ribbon of black. And that's the way they rolled, for awhile, the three of them, lost in thought on a road journey, soaking in the beginnings of a beautiful Saturday afternoon.

Again, the car was silent, except for the sound of cars they rocketed past, the constant companion of the wind and a new friend *Big Jim Walker,* by Jim Croce:

You don't tug on Superman's cape;
You don't spit into the wind;
You don't pull the mask off that Ol' Lone Ranger;
And you don't mess around with Jim.

The trees whipped by, off the right shoulder, and a big ball of fire hung high overhead, a blinding glint splayed against a bloodshot hood.

Somerville beckoned to the right; the Mustang veered to follow.

"What's in Somerville?"

Lilly sat up straight in the backseat, as Route 78 faded to the rear.

"Not Lobsterville, that's for sure."

Was all C said.

She harrumphed, and sat back in a snit. Earl leaned toward his friend.

"Hey C, what's a Perth Amboy?"

"Just another town we're not stopping at."

"Kind of a funny name, isn't it? What's it mean?"

Earl whispered.

"It means were not stopping."

"Hey! Did ya see that sign Earl!"

"No! What sign? Where is it?"

Earl's head jerked to attention, spinning and spying for the evidence, for the clue he missed that would solve the mystery. Ken and Sandy would have *never* missed such an important clue!"

Lilly leaned forward and spoke into the side of C's face, obnoxious, and smug."

"I believe it said: *Shore Points 10 Miles!*"

"Louie's almost home!"

Earl yelled, arms upright in a touchdown.

"Hey C, do you think....?"

"*YES!* Louie and his friends are fine!"

Cord said, exasperated.

It was Earl's turn to harrumph, arms crossed across this chest. C turned to his best friend, smiled and cracked his knuckles; they all snapped good. Cord liked when that happened. Soon enough, they found themselves rolling along the Garden State Parkway, the *Parkway* in local parlance, heading due south.

"Okay, now pay attention, watch for 117, Exit 117 Earl, that's what we want; make sure we don't miss it."

C stated carefully, slowly to Earl, as if giving instructions upon which his life depended.

Oh boy! Earl thought to himself, now he had a *real* mission, like Ken and Sandy; he wasn't gonna miss *this* clue – no way! He sat up rod straight and squinted, concentration mode was clearly *on*.

"Hey what are those?"

Earl pointed to the right, beyond the guardrail. It was a sea of brownish-green grass waving tall in the wind, bisected by a cobalt blue waterway that snaked into the distance, till it tailed out of sight.

"Salt marshes; were getting close to the ocean."

C's words brought butterflies to Lilly's stomach, her hand clenching the two bucket-seats in front of her. She was excited, and scared, but a good-scared. The trees even looked better here than they did at home, somehow;

they seemed to be a brighter green, if that made sense. It really didn't, and she didn't care one lick. Bottom line, the trees weren't Belvidere trees, and that alone made them better. Earl noticed the trees too, and C was naming the ones he knew. Lilly half-listened, then looked skyward, letting the wind play with the loose ends of her hair, dancing beyond the constraint of her mother's scarf. The sun gently kissed her face, the cotton balls high overhead were floating in a baby blue bath - that's how she would describe it, she said to herself. She tried to make out what they looked like, hoping they looked like something special, but they really didn't look like anything but puffy balls. And that was okay with her; they were still the best clouds she had ever seen.

C looked at the clock; it was 1:25 pm.

"Almost there!"

C announced, and with it, another wave of euphoria washed the car, which Earl displayed prominently, his tongue-wagging feverish. Lilly kept her excitement close to the vest, pretending indifference, but bursting inside.

Welcome To Keyport

The large sign greeted them on the right, with Gordon Lightfoot on the box:

The morning after blues, from my head down to my
shoes;
Carefree highway, let me slip away, slip away on you.

"I love this song; you never hear it anymore."

Lilly waxed, speaking mostly to herself. How cool that song came on just now, like it was meant to, like it was meant just for her – not the blues part, but the carefree part. She sang along silently, the best she could, trying to get the words right, mumbling the ones she didn't know, singing through a smile. C looked back and saw her lost in the song....happy.

And that was just about the best part of the trip so far, for C. *What a gift* Cord thought, and Lilly was none the wiser.

Route 36 rolled under the tires as the trio headed further east, and with it went Keyport. The next town stood ready to receive them:

Welcome To Atlantic Highlands

quickly followed by another:

Welcome To Middletown

"Boy, everybody keeps saying *Welcome;* when are we gonna finally get there C?! You know, Bibby doesn't like surprises."

Earl figured he'd throw that one in. But C didn't answer, he just pointed to the red carpet, off to the left. It was 1:43 pm, and for the first time, the view rolled right to the surf.

"Holy mackerel, holy mackerel, holy mackerel!"

Earl said over and over, as he watched the waves break silently on the distant beach, with thousands of little white caps stretching to the horizon. The ocean, the

Atlantic Ocean....the Jersey shore. The first time it ever met Earl's eyes, and it was beyond beautiful.

Lilly's head, leaned forward from the back seat and shoved between the two of them, watched in silence, as the word *Wow* bounced around her head. The hair on her arms tingled. Then she looked down at C's right forearm, resting on his lap, and she placed her hand gently upon it; a thank you without the words.

"C, Louie's gonna be happy, right? He's gonna be okay?"

She whispered, caring about Louie as much as Earl, although would never admit it. C didn't look at her, he just smiled, facing the road before him, and shook his head in a single nod: *yes.*

"You bet, another mile and we're there, and he's home."

C murmured quietly, and with that, the car went silent. Neither passenger spoke, their eyes glued to the horizon, as the ocean slowly grew before them. Lilly wondered if anyone could ever count all the white-caps off the shore, breaking off the beach. She wondered if anyone had ever even tried. As the nonsense thoughts filled her head, sand dunes emerged and stretched left and right, with beach grass waving lazily in the sea breeze.

The Mustang spanned the causeway bridge, leaned into a tight right loop off the exit ramp and ran the ribbon of pavement along the spine of the sandbar, which jutted for miles into the ocean.

Welcome To Sandy Hook

An unassuming, small brown and white sign announced, planted along the side of the pike.

"*Sandy Hook*? Is this where Ken and Sandy come to the beach? Does Sandy own this hook, C? And what's a hook anyway, and why does Sandy have one? That sounds like a scary, crazy mystery to me, and I have no idea what I 'm even talking about!"

Earl blurted; he was simply beside himself, surrounded by mysteries, waiting to be solved.

"You'll see."

Was the only tease Cord proffered, which made Earl rub his hands faster and lick his lips furious.

"*What's a hook, what's a hook, what's a Sandy hook? And why does Sandy even have one?*"

Earl couldn't stop thinking about it.

From nowhere, a stiff, wicked wind blew in off the ocean, kicking up sand, peppering the side of the car. It was constant.

The National Park was soulless; the ticket booth was empty this time of the year, and the Mustang slid quietly between the pylons, all alone….a silent sentry.

The road stretched flat and straight through the windshield, undulating grassed dunes dipped, rose and dipped again, to either side, with the Bay on the near left, and the Ocean, further off to the right, beyond a wide tan stretch of beach, opaque and hazy from a steady sheet of airborne sand, blowing north. Where the hell did that wind come from?

A half-mile up the ribbon of pavement, they came upon an enormous asphalt lot, empty, with a veneer of silvery sand, shape-shifting across the surface, sculpted by a constant wind.   The bitumen was splintered lacquer, with stunted grass inching from thousands of tiny cracks which spread across the acres of black palette, trying to gain a foothold, till it was beaten down next summer, when this place surrendered to an onslaught of cars and crowds, by the thousands.

But today, nary a soul shared the space.

Just one driver, two passengers and three homesick lobsters.

CHAPTER 298 – QUICKLY SLIPPED BELOW THE WATER, GONE FOREVER

Earl was still thinking hard about this whole Sandy hook mystery; he just couldn't figure the *hook* part. And C wasn't helping one bit, he was too busy struggling to get the lobster cooler safely out of the trunk.

The wind, strangely wicked enough, suddenly become more so, buffeting against the car, enough to give it a mild rock; bits of dune grass and litter skittered across the pavement, quickly on their way somewhere else.

"Ow! Why is it so windy?"

Lilly asked, as if someone had the answer. Grains of sand blasted her legs in a constant pepper; it actually hurt.

"Don't know. Hey Earl, give me a hand, will ya?"

Just as C finished the sentence, the right plastic handle broke free, and the cooler tipped and flipped on its side, crashing onto the pavement. The top flew off, sending a wave of ice-water onto the asphalt.

"Fuck!"

C yelled, as Earl ran over to help.

They righted the cooler and peered inside. Most of the ice had melted, and the newspapers were soaked and frigid. Three cold lobsters were lying on their sides; none were moving.

"Are they okay, C? Are they okay?!"

Earl asked frantic, looking at his friend Louie

"Yeah, they're fine."

C said, dismissive, although he didn't believe it. He carefully picked up one of Louie's friends to be sure, and as he did, his large claw broke off, falling into Cord's hand.

Earl's eyes opened wide and he screamed into the howling wind, closing his eyes to a squint, to fight the grit.

"He's dead! We killed him!"

"He's not dead!"

C responded, annoyed, certainly not sure himself.

Good God, please don't be dead C thought to himself, as he gently shook Louie's friend, praying the other claw stayed put. The cold antennae swirled just a bit, and two of the legs moved....thank God.

"See, he's okay, they lose claws all the time, no problem; check the other two."

Earl got on all fours and stuck his head deep into the cooler, like a mechanic looking under the hood. He eagle-eyed the duo, his nose inches from their shells, and popped back out, with a look of horror.

"I don't see 'em breathing!"

He gasped.

"Jesus Earl, you can't see....never mind."

Cord said, trying to hand the first lobster to Lilly, to hold.

"I'm not touching that slimy thing!"

She yelled, stepping back from the action. C shot her a wicked look, then turned to Earl.

"Christ; Earl, hold him, *gently!*"

Earl held out his hand and gently squeezed the shell between two meaty fingers, bringing the one-clawed lobster close to his nose.

"Hi!"

Earl said, looking squarely in his beady black eyes.

C checked Louie and friend; both were cold, lethargic....and alive.

"They're okay.   Fucking handle, fucking sand....and *where did this fucking wind come from?* **Jesus!**"

C barked aloud, mainly to himself, pissed.

"Earl, where are the scissors?"

C snipped, but Earl simply shrugged.

"Didn't you put them in the trunk?"

Earl shrugged again, holding the lobster like one would hold a dirty diaper, gingerly, and at arm's length. Lilly was right, they did have a bit of a smell.

"They're right there!"

Lilly pointed into the trunk, dismissive; the look she threw Cord was the kind one gives when one thinks the other is some sort of idiot. She followed with a cherry.

"Thanks for bringing me to the beach by the way, *first time ever to the Jersey Shore – any shore!* Boy, this is great! Where's my bathing suit?"

As the wind and sand whipped between Lilly's legs; her scarf buffeting against her head.

"Nice, nice."

Was all C said, shaking his head at her.

C grabbed the scissors and told Earl to take one side of the cooler, after he gently righted Louie and the two others in the cooler, threw in the dismembered claw - rubber band still holding it closed, and shut the top. The two of them hoofed it across the dunes and open seaboard, carrying the cooler between them, the whole time pelted by driving sand, on their way to the surf's edge, which was rough and wild. Lilly was in tow behind, her head turned and tucked from the wind, trying, unsuccessfully, to avoid the sand-blast.

"This is better than the tank at the A&P *how?*"

She said sarcastically.

"The water here is a bit colder than the pot on top of the fucking stove."

C yelled indignant, without looking at her, his shoes filling with more sand each step. They got to the water's edge, and the surf was boiling.

"Jesus, what the fuck? Wasn't it just a beautiful day, like ten minutes ago?"

C yelled out at the ocean, in anger.

They placed the cooler down, just above the tideline, and cracked it open. One-Claw was the first to come out. C's hands were already freezing cold; he grabbed the scissors and tried, carefully, to cut the rubber band, without breaking off the remaining claw. He sliced through the rubber, and the claw, in slow-motion, opened, like a cramped arm straightening out. C felt so bad for the lobster; he wondered how many weeks that fucking band had cinched his claw shut. *Please be okay* was all Cord kept thinking.

C was both anxious and mad; here he was trying to do something good, for once, and it was becoming nothing but a major fuck-up, with sand blasts and broken handles and missing claws and whatever.   Maybe they *were* better off in the supermarket tank, waiting to be boiled alive.

C was pissed, and feeling a bit sorry for himself, which got him *more* pissed.

Without thinking, Cord walked into the frigid surf, shoes and jeans on, up to his knees. The first wave soaked him to his thighs. He never noticed how cold the water was; it had to be in the low 40's....had to be. And the pounding surf was violently rocking him to and fro; it took all his might to avoid being barreled over by the surf, and sucked into the undertow. The surf was vicious.

"Are you *crazy*! What are you doing?!"

Lilly yelled at him, but he ignored her, wading out until the water submerged to just below his knees, chopping wild against his thighs as the waves rolled in.

As best he could, Ay gently submerged One-Claw into the frothy water, down to the sand bottom, about two feet deep at that point. He rocked back and forth on the bottom, with the churn of water. He seemed okay.

Maybe it *would* work out; maybe the lobster rescue was going be okay after all.

He gave another glance; One-Claw was holding his own. C smiled and went back to get the next.

"What am I supposed to do?"

C asked, a delayed answer to Lilly's prior crazy-yell.

"I don't know; didn't you think about this first?"

Lilly yelled into the wind.

"This is my first lobster drop; kinda winging it."

C said, sarcastic, happy one was down, with only two more drops to go. He went over to the cooler and got friend number two, and started to cut the bands. His hands were ice-cold – he couldn't feel his fingers, which made it next to impossible to work the scissors.

"He's back!"

Earl yelled.

And sure enough, One-Claw had washed up on the beach, rolled over on his side in the chop-surf and looking the worse for wear. Out of nowhere, three seagulls had already landed nearby, like little white vultures, squawking loud, announcing to all an easy meal rolling along the tideline….lobster tartar.

*"Are you fucking kidding me? **ARE YOU FUCKING KIDDING ME?!**"*

C screamed flush into the wind, which, somehow, was getting stronger, blowing the words back into his face, mocking him.

C quickly cut the two bands for the second lobster, and both claws slowly opened, like an automatic door. And they stayed attached. He placed the second lobster on the sand, kicked off his tassel-loafers and stripped his pants and sports coat, throwing them down; they got caught in the wind like a kite and landed a good ten feet down the beach, in a tangled mess.

"What the hell are you doing!?"

Lilly yelled, chasing after his clothes.

"Are they gonna be okay C?"

Earl asked, looking like he was ready to cry.

"Yes Earl, I promise; I just gotta get them out farther, so the surf doesn't wash 'em back in. They aren't strong enough to walk along the bottom and fight the surf, fucking waves....*fucking wind!*"

C grabbed lobster number two and ran to the surf's edge, scooping up One-Claw; the gulls took off and relit about twenty yards away....they had all day to wait for lunch.

C charged into the surf - bare feet, bare chest, bare everything, except his boxer briefs, and suddenly the cold saltwater seized him – and it took his breath away. *Fuck* was all he could say, as his nutsack shriveled and tucked inside his body.

But he was so mad, he didn't give a fuck, not one lick; he rushed out till the water was waist-deep.

He plunged both hands and arms into the freezing water, turning and laying his head on the surface. He couldn't reach the bottom without submerging his head, so he gently dropped the lobsters. The water swirled around him, and a wave came in and submerged him to his shoulders. The broil of sand and water made it hard to see...but it looked like the two had landed soft on the sand, and were holding their own, since this water was a bit deeper. He gave them a second, then waded as quick as he could back to the shore. As his body left the water, the wind whipped him hard, and he was shivering uncontrollably.

Earl was talking to Louie, whispering into his shell where his ears should be. His antennae swirled in a circle, one clockwise, the other counter. Earl had already cut off the bands; Lilly was sucked next to him, not to say goodbye to Louie, but to use Earl as a windbreak. Her head was buried in his armpit.

"Here C, he's ready to go home! He's happy; he told me so!"

"Good, give him to me, quick, before I fucking pass out!"

Earl handed Louie to C; Cord looked at the large lobster, and wished him luck. With that, he went a bit down beach and dashed into the broil of the surf, right up to his waist. C's skin was splotchy-crimson and half-numb; he didn't feel the water this time....that must not be a good thing, he thought – well on his way to hypothermia.

He needed to get Louie as far away from the shore as possible, to raise the chance that he would stabilize and be able to find his way to deeper, calmer water. But if Cord waded out any further, he would quickly be in water too deep to stand. So, standing there, Ay slowly half-turned, and, as gently as he could, with frozen fingers, launched Louie through the air in a graceful lobster-toss, like a discus. *Please don't lose your claws* was all C could think as Louie sailed through the salty air, on his way back to freedom.

"Bye Louie! See you in Panama!"

C heard Earl's muffled yell from the beach fifteen yards behind him.

Louie hit the surf sideways about twenty feet further from the beach, and quickly slipped below the water, gone forever.

CHAPTER 299 – SHE CALMLY BENT OVER AND JINGLED OFF THE SILICA

Lilly gathered C's clothes, rumpled and covered in a skin of sand; she tried to shake them clean, but it was pointless, flapping like flags in the grit-choked wind, they were catching as much sand as she was trying to release. She gave up and rolled them in a boy's laundry ball, tucked under her arm.

Earl had packed the cooler, including the amputee claw, all that remained of the Belvidere lobsters, and hoisted it upon his right shoulder; the sand-storm, as if it was even possible, had gotten worse. Lilly was already half-way through the gauntlet, on the way back to the lot. There was no getting dressed on the beach, C ran, wearing nothing but bone-chilled wet underwear, barefoot across the sand, heading for the warmth of the car, his teeth clicking uncontrollably in his head, which brought thoughts of the puppet. The grains stung as they pelted him; a cake of moist sand formed slippers, sticking to his wet feet.

Earl and C got to the car just behind Lilly, popped the trunk and threw in the cooler. The three dove into the safety of the cab. There was no towel, so C had nothing to dry with, except his shirt, and the top half of his jeans, which were freezing cold. He fumbled in his jean pockets, looking for the keys to start the car, and turn the heat to high.

No luck, no keys.

"Earl give me the keys."

C said, still shivering herky-jerk behind the wheel. Earl just stared at him.

"The keys, *the keys*; I'm fucking freezing!"

C yelled.

"I don't have the keys."

Earl said timid, his shoulders raising to his ears as he spoke. C looked over his shoulder at Lilly, and before he could utter a sound, she shot him down.

"Why would *I* have the fucking keys?! *You drove!* Where did you put 'em?"

"*Christ!*"

Was C's answer, as he frantically shoved his hands along the seat seams, along and under the floor mat, beside the center console....everywhere they might have fallen, and then everywhere else in the cab he knew they couldn't possibly be, because maybe they somehow were.

Nothing.

At first Lilly and Earl just stared at him, like some freak show.

"*Excuse me?!*"

He barked, not needing to finish the sentence that said: *how about some fucking help!* With that, the two started the same fruitless hand-sweeps, digs and drags in all cracks and crevices in the car.

No keys.

"*Are you fucking....!*"

C didn't finish the screamed sentence, still shivering.

Without warning, C pulled down his wet underwear in one shot, right to his ankles, and kicked them off on the floor, somewhere by the gas pedal. He had to get those God-damn clammy wet things off....***now!***

Earl quickly swung his head away from the action.

"Don't look up here Lilly! Nothing going on up here! Nothing to see up here!"

Earl jumped between the seats and waved his arms frantically, like trying to block an extra point.

"Cut it out Earl, cut it out!"

Lilly yelled, trying to juke and sneak a peek. Earl snagged her and cupped his hand over her eyes like a blindfold.

"Earl, cut it out, *I can't breathe!*"

Yet Earl knew he was nowhere near her nose, or her yappy mouth; he didn't fall for her shenanigans one bit. She wasn't tricking him.

C paid no attention to the ruckus, cursing and fussing, trying to pull on half-wet jeans. He wriggled into them and carefully buttoned and zipped the fly, pushing his prick well out of the way; catching cock-skin in a cold, wet zipper would be the *perfect* ending to this beach trip, for sure.

Sensing the scene was safe, Earl removed his hand from Lilly's face; she lunged forward to bite him, but he was too smart and quick for her, and she snapped the air futile, like an angry piranha.

He grabbed his dry shirt and whipped it on, buttoning as fast as he could, realizing he buttoned wrong, and redoing it all over again, through a fresh stream of expletives.

"This is fun!"

Earl said, and he really meant it.

C swung open the door and fought the wet fabric of his jeans, twisting and cursing the whole time. He ran his hands over and between his toes, trying to get off the half-wet sand; he got most, but not all. He threw on his shoes and ran around to the trunk, popped it, and frantically tried to find the keys; they were nowhere to be found.

"Are you fucking kidding me? Where are the God-damn keys!"

He said to himself, coming to the sinking realization the keys might well be on the bottom of the ocean, sleeping with the lobsters. But no, they can't be; they didn't float out of his pocket, he was only in the water to his knees before he tossed his trousers. They couldn't have fallen out in the drink, could they?

As he debated himself, he saw Lilly and Earl, without words, head back to the beach. He slammed the trunk and ran to catch up, his wet jeans fighting the whole way. How he didn't split the seams, he had no idea.

As as he ran to catch them, he came to the realization that they were fucked, he simply knew it. How the hell were they going to get out of there? They would have to be towed, and then what? Get a taxi home? The whole fucking day shot?   That simply couldn't happen, couldn't, not today; today was too big, too planned, and Carol would *kill* him, for sure! What the hell was he gonna do?

His mind raced, watching Lilly and Earl walk through a blinding sandstorm, back to the beach, in a futile attempt to find keys that were long, long gone.

Another ten minutes, at most and the driving wind, and the sand it carried, would have surely buried them below the beach, out of sight forever. Walking a mere ten feet to the right or left, and Lilly would have surely missed them on her blind amble.

But twenty yards off the edge of the parking lot, in an endless sea of rippled sand, that all looked the same, in a raging windstorm, futile, Lilly spied the half-buried keys.

She calmly bent over and jingled off the silica.

CHAPTER 300 – RUNNING TO SAVE A SCARED AND LONELY LOBSTER

C stood dumbfounded as Lilly walked back at him, her mother's crimson head-scarf buffeting in the wind, with the biggest shit-eating grin on her face that she could muster.

"Lilly found the keys!"

Earl yelled the obvious.

"You're the best Lilly! You're so smart!"

Earl planted a big one on her cheek, just as she came face to face with C. He wasn't cold anymore, he was steaming.

"You must have dropped them when you were *struggling* with the cooler."

She said, dropping them into his palm, and walking by, with a long, straight stick up her butt.

"You're welcome."

She yelled, as she walked away.

And as Earl and Lilly strode triumphant back to the car, C stood staring at the ocean, at the surf in the distance, which was a good fifty yards away, and looked more like a hundred, obscured by the wash of sand blowing by his face.

But even through the haze, he thought he saw it. He squinted a bit, then didn't squint anymore. A flock of seagulls had congregated at the break of the surf; he could hear, if he tilted his head just right, their constant squawks....some sort of cheer. And amongst them, on the beach, he thought he saw something low, and black, hugging the sand, but he wasn't sure, and he didn't want to know. It didn't look like many, it looked like one, maybe just one.

He lowered his gaze, turned, and shuffled, in no particular hurry, back to the car, in silence, wondering why he wasn't running to the surf, why he wasn't running to save a scared and lonely lobster.

CHAPTER 301 – MAY I HUMBLY PRESENT: SKELETON ISLAND

"What's the matter C; aren't you happy Lilly found the keys?"

C was staring blankly through the windshield, melancholy, looking out toward the wicked ocean, at where the gulls were, squawking with delight, beside whatever washed up on the beach, one, two, or all three helpless creatures – nothing was for sure, because none of it could really be seen from where they were parked, in the car, doors closed. And Ay shook his head slow, in the negative, almost imperceptive, left to right, knowing, once again, although he tried, something likely died, badly, because of him. A one-way he could never seem to exit. Yet another fucking mess.

The car was idling and the heat was pumping; it was warm, safe and dry. Lilly didn't say a word; the smug smile on her face said everything it needed to say. C didn't answer his friend, he simply put the Mustang in reverse, looked at Earl, who was all smiles, and cracked a small forced one himself. There would be no more rescues, no run from the car to check the surf one last time for stranded lobsters, being pecked apart, eaten alive. It is what it is, C thought, they either made it or they didn't – the outcome was set, like it always was in the end....with him. Nothing he could do would change it – it never did.

Cord slowly looped the cavernous, empty parking lot and swung around the entrance, took a right and headed further up the peninsula, toward the end, which pointed north. He drove several hundred yards, to the next parking lot, which was even bigger than the first – acres upon acres of pavement. It too, was sand-swept and empty. He pulled in, looped around and faced the nose of the Mustang back out toward the road. He put it in park; the car rumbled low, at idle.

"Wow, now *this* is an *amazing* parking lot! Way better than the first one!"

Lilly exclaimed sarcastic, but C didn't take the bait. She immediately became pissed, and prattled even louder from the back seat.

"Come on, come on! Are we staying here all day! Enough of the beach-from-hell already, and stupid parking lots!"

Lilly whined from the back.

But Earl was studying C intently, ignoring his sister; he could sense C stopped for a reason, for something important. It had the feel of a juicy mystery; it just did. Earl leaned in and whispered to his best friend.

"What is it C? Is it some kind of mystery? A puzzle to solve, perhaps?"

Earl was doing his best to sound smart, like Ken and Sandy.

C slowly turned his head and looked at Earl, then pointed out the windshield, across the asphalt ribbon road; it was called Hartshorne Drive, but they didn't know that, and they didn't care, because the name of the road didn't matter, not one bit. What *really* mattered, lay just beyond.

C got out of the car, without a word. Earl followed him in silence.

"I'm not getting out! *Have fun!"*

Lilly yelled from the back seat, finally warm and still content, reveling in her *car-keys-win.* But the boys both ignored her, and she followed them with her eyes as they crossed the road. She folded her arms across her chest in a huff, and after another second or so of hesitation, she kicked open the door, indignant at the diss.

"Hope nobody steals the car! I'm letting it run; hope the doors don't lock! You're fault if they do!"

She yelled at them, but the duo never broke stride.

"This is **stupid!**"

She yelled, as she kicked the door shut and half-ran to catch up with them, mumbling mad and cursing to herself the entire way.

"What's the big deal? More water, sand and grass? *Wow*, you're right, this is *way* better than the parking lot!"

She said as she bellied up beside Earl, purposely bumping into him, trying to knock him off his feet. Fat chance; she bounced right off him, which enraged her more. C ignored her and the intrusion; he climbed to the top of a little dune fronting the road, placed his hands on his hips, and silently gazed at whatever lay beyond. When it was clear he had found what he was looking for, whatever that may be, Earl followed suit, and then Lilly, sulking and kicking the sand along the way, just to be sure they both knew she was *really* annoyed.

Atop the knoll afforded a view across a calm bay, off the west side of Sandy Hook. The water barely rippled in the wind, which, strangely, had died considerably on this side of the sand spit, no more than several hundred yards from the lobster-drop. Here, there was no sandstorm, just a steady, cool breeze. As Earl followed the sight of C's eyes, out past this protected cove, about a quarter-mile away lay a low sandy isle, crescent-shaped, like a waxing moon.

"Bet you can't guess what that is."

C finally said, in just above a whisper, to Earl.

"Boring."

Lilly answered, deadpan.

"*No way.*"

Was all Earl said, in awe, ignoring his sister's sarcasm.

"No way *what*? What do you see? I don't see anything but more stupid sand! Get out of the way! Let me see the nothing you're seeing!"

Lilly was shoving C to the side, trying to muscle in between the two, to eye the prize. But no luck, Cord wouldn't yield, instead, Ay leaned into Earl, sporting a crooked smile.

"Mystery solved, in the flesh. May I humbly present: Skeleton Island."

CHAPTER 302 – *WILD THINGS* DANCING CRAZY ABOUT HIS HEAD

"You're lying!"

Lilly yelled, setting up to punch C in the arm. She wanted to hit him so hard, she round-housed, telegraphing the punch, giving Cord enough time to juke just a bit, which made her blow land askew on his shoulder, knocking her off balance in the loose, shifty sand. She half-spun and tumbled, backwards, down the little dune, landing on her rump. The indignity made her all the more livid.

She sprung to her feet and charged C hard, her face beet red. He held up his hands in a defensive posture, never letting her get off a second round. She wrestled with him as he tied up her arms, spewing venom the whole time, back and forth between Ay and her brother.

"There's no such thing as Skeleton Island! That's a stupid made-up place for kids; It's a kid's book....*kids* Earl, not forty-year olds! Don't lie to him like that!"

She screamed at Cord. To which C answered calmly, which enraged her even more.

"I'm not lying; that's Skeleton Island, at Sandy Hook. Actually, it's officially called *Skeleton Hill Island*, but that's just semantics; it's the real deal Earl. *The Secret of Skeleton Island*, solved, right in front of your nose."

Earl couldn't drink in the scene enough; it was simply too big to comprehend. He had so many questions, he didn't know where to start. But before Earl could utter a word, C grabbed him by the shoulders and quarter-spun him to the right. There, miles away, across an expanse of open ocean, seeming small and hazy on the horizon, as if it were merely a mirage, Earl saw the faintest outline of skyscrapers. *Lots* of skyscrapers, all jumbled in a long row, one after another, like people standing in line.

"Is that *really*?"

"Yep, it really is. New York City, Manhattan. Look close, to the left a little more, see the tallest one? It's hard to make out, but that's it *[Earl tried to follow C's finger]*, the *Empire State Building*. Not too far from Skeleton Island is it? Just like the book says."

"*Oh boy!*"

Earl said, licking his lips frantic and rubbing his hands together.

"Stop lying to him!"

Lilly punched C flush in the solar plexus; she got that one in, because C was distracted. And it was a pretty good sock; hard enough to knock his wind, and piss Ay off.

"Hey shit-for-brains, stop punching! And I'm not lying to him; just because *you* don't believe in something, doesn't mean it isn't true!"

C yelled at her, between gulps of air, trying to catch his breath. And they both realized that statement could have meant a lot of things, and applied to a lot of topics, between the two of them.

"Where's the resort, C? There's supposed to be a big building on Skeleton Island, you know, where the bad guys are hiding; I don't see it."

Earl asked, and that first question was a direct hit. Lilly stared hard at C, waiting for his wiggle-lie on *that* one, lining up for punch number three.

"Well, this island doesn't have a resort, not now anyway. But Sandy and Ken were here a *long* time ago, and maybe it was here then, or maybe *that* part of the story was made up."

Lilly guffawed at C's answer, the cackle of a crow.

"Are you kidding me?! *That's* your answer?! That stupid sand pile isn't big enough for a garage, let alone a resort! Earl, don't believe a single word he says, not another word! Some birthday present! And why didn't you put the lobsters in the water over *here*, by the way; the water is nice and calm, and there isn't a God-damn sandstorm....*good job,* Mr. lobster-saver."

C was getting mad.

Lillian was spot-on, of course, about the lobster-drop; he didn't have a good answer, any answer, for why he didn't think to put them on the bay side, because there wasn't one – he simply fucked-up and picked the ocean instead of the bay. He didn't think it out; he had some sort of brain fart on that one, and such a silly oversight, that could have been easily rectified, by going left, instead of right, likely killed Louie and his friends. And that made Cord even more pissed. And the sandbar stretching before him *was* pretty God-damn narrow, and shrunk with the incoming tide; it was much smaller than he expected it would be. And although Lilly exaggerated about the garage-thing, she was right – this shifting sand spit wasn't nearly big enough for a resort of any size; maybe in the 1940's it was different, bigger, but at least now, circa-2006, it was picayune at best.

So Ay shot off.

"Okay, big-mouth, I'll prove it to you, okay? But if I'm right, I'm so tired of all your shit, I get a chit, a *real* chit – a no holds barred chit! *Deal*?"

"And what do I get?"

Lilly shot back, just as nasty.

"Same fucking thing!"

C yelled at her.

"And what do I want *that* for?"

She said, sarcastic.

"Because it has no rules, no limits, and unlimited chit for *anything* you want from me, *anything*. But same goes for you! Come on, smart-ass, put up, or shut-the-fuck up! Are you in or not?"

Lilly mind was racing; Cord was angry, and yelling in a tone that wasn't playful, or fun. He was mad, really mad, and she knew it. But he was also a skilled bullshit artist, almost as good as her, but not quite, and his tone had the feel, the tinge, of a con. She rolled the options around her head, her mind calculating quick; there had to be some catch. She looked to Earl for help, but he just looked at his shoes; no way he was getting in the middle of *this* one.

"Come on! Come on! Put up or shut up....bitch!"

C yelled at her, and extended his hand, shaking it within inches of her face.

She was enraged; C wasn't allowed to talk her like that, he doesn't boss her around!

"OKAY! BITCH!"

She screamed back, and slapped his hand away.

"And you better pay up pal, no take-backs Cord, you little cheater; right Earl?"

"Right."

Earl said calmly, not exactly sure to what, or to whom, he was saying *right* to.

He was preoccupied, rubbing his hands together and gazing in awe at Skeleton Island, adventures with Ken, Sandy and the *Wild Things* dancing crazy about his head.

CHAPTER 303 - A PEGGY-SUE, AND IT'S GONNA FEEL GOOD

They spanned the causeway, with the Hook to their backs, in silence.

C couldn't stop obsessing about the fate of the lobsters; *why* didn't he just go to the bay side? How didn't he think of that? *Why* didn't he think of that? The lobsters all washed up on the beach, picked apart, eaten alive, by seagulls, all because of his stupidity. He hoped at least one made it; he hoped at least Louie made it; maybe he threw him far enough, deep enough, that the undertow didn't drag him back to the beach. He thought he only saw one on the beach, maybe just one. He couldn't shake the image, the guilt; it raced his brain in a never-ending loop. He shook his head, sullen.

"So?"

Lilly finally said, snapping C back.

"So what?"

He said, curt.

"Where's the proof, and where's my chit? Skeleton Island is fading fast."

Lilly pointed over her shoulder from the back seat.

"Keep your pants on sister."

Was all C said.

"Yeah, you wish."

She whispered under her breath, as Earl's fumbled in his pocket, looking for his phone. He hit *Speed Dial No. 3.*

A single, nondescript beep chirped in the dimly lit bedroom; that was all it did, and just once. He didn't go for any of those queer ringtones everyone uses....never did, never would.

After a brief hesitation, Mac reached over to the nightstand, spied the display, and flipped open the phone.

"Hey Earl, kinda busy dude!"

"MAC, guess what?! I'm at the Shore with Lilly and C! And C just showed me Skeleton Island! For real! You know, where I told you Ken and Sandy solve the mystery, and the *Wild Things* live! Although I didn't see them, you know, the *Wild Things*, they must have been hiding under the water, because they are *really* big! Anyway, I'm way past the Gill Farm, *way past*! This is the farthest I've ever been, anywhere, ever! I can even see New York and the *Empire State Building*, kind of, and everything. And Lilly's gonna owe C a big chit too, she's gonna, I just know it!"

"Am not!"

She yelled from behind, kicking the back of Earl's seat.

"You're outa Belvidere, huh? For real? That's great man, congrats! But hey, I gotta call you back in a quick bit, okay? Sorry about that, but I got a beer in one hand, and I'm driving, you know?"

"You're not supposed to drink and drive; *that's not safe*!"

Earl yelled frantic into the phone.

"Not that kind a drive, brother; I'm going for a Peggy-Sue - *that* kind of ride....remember?"

"Oh, sorry. **Sorry Lucy!**"

Earl yelled the last part into the phone.

Lucien smiled wide at hearing Earl's voice and lunged her full figure forward - one swift motion, and just like that, Mac was left hanging in the bedroom breeze - the Peggy-Sue came to an abrupt halt. She swung around like a rhino and grabbed the phone. She was a plus-size girl; big, but not sloppy, with an almost empty canvas in contrast to him....no piercing, no ink, sans a small rose, riding camel-jockey atop her right butt-cheek. She was sheathed in a beautiful Caribbean-brown spread of skin, stretched just right over heavy curves, top to bottom. She had an infectious smile, which lit a beautiful Dominican face. That was her true cherry.

And Lucien loved Mac, and he her. And they both loved Earl. She spoke gently into the phone.

"That's okay Hon, *Papi* was taking way too long, know what I mean *[Lucien poked Mac, her Papi, in his big beer belly, and smiled at him – he smiled back. Mac never got mad at Earl, never, even for breaking up a bang]*? Hey! Happy Birthday, big guy! I gotta get in the shower, I'm running late; got lots to do before the big night tonight, right?!"

Mac, horror-stricken, smacked the phone from her hand, and Lucien realized she almost blew it. She mouthed *Sorry*, smiled at Mac, and made her way to the bathroom; he half-watched the small rose and double-Ds bounce in the mirror as he found the phone amongst the crumpled sheets.

"What'd she say?"

Earl asked innocent, and a bit confused.

"Nothing, you know girls."

Mac answered, trying to be dismissive.

"Not really."

Earl said, to which Mac laughed his response.

"Count yourself lucky."

"Hey Mac, why'd you pick up the phone during, you know, a Peggy-Sue?"

"Why? Because it was you! And I pick up whenever you call, you know that, no matter what."

"But why? You don't hafta, you know."

Earl asked.

"Yeah I do. And why? Because you're my friend, one of the, no, *the* truest friend I have, ever had, I've told you that, and I'd do *anything* for you, buddy, told you that too. And if you're calling me, it must be important, so I pick up the phone, even during a Sue. So, you outta Town *for real*?! And you finally found Skeleton Island, huh? That's pretty cool, man, very cool....I'm happy for ya. You're gonna have to tell me all about it, and the Shore, and anything else you do today....big day for you! Hey, isn't it somebody's birthday?"

"Yeah, it's mine! I'm forty! I turned forty at exactly 12:31 pm! That's *exactly* when I was born; my mom told me that, so I know it's gotta be true. And that was hours ago! I'm really old now!"

"Join the club brother."

Mac said, deadpan.

"We'll, I'll try and come see you sometime soon, one of these days, and give you that ride I keep promising, okay?"

"Okay, thanks Mac; say bye to Lucy!

"Will do, take it easy brother."

Mac smiled, flipped the phone shut, and shuffled naked into the bathroom.

"Sorry about that Papi; can't believe I almost blew it! Did he figure it out?"

"Nah, no clue; he was too excited about other stuff."

Mac stared blankly at his reflection in the mirror, an old worn face, grizzled, pocked and tired, stared back. But it was still content, something it hadn't been for most of his life. Lucien stepped out of the quickie-shower and was drying off; she noticed the reflection, the blank stare that meant he was somewhere else, far away.

"Where are you? What are you thinking Papi?"

Mac slowly turned to Lucy.

"Just thinking, about how good he is, so forgiving, and how, and he'll never really know or appreciate this, how, in the short period of time I've known him, how he's made me a better person, a person I don't hate....and that's not so easy.

Lucien dropped her towel and came up behind him, in a gentle, naked bear hug. She kissed him on the back, and for a bit, she didn't say anything. They just hugged, sharing their warmth, feeling each other breathe.

Then Lucien whispered softly into his back.

"We're together, and we're good, because of Earl, you know that, right? I've known you a long time, Papi, and I've loved you just as long, but we couldn't be together, no one could really *be* with you....you weren't in a good place. But you've changed for the better, sweetie, you did good. I'm so proud of you, and I know Earl loves you just as much as you love him, and you do....Si, Papi?"

He shook his head slowly, in the affirmative.

She kissed him on the back a second time, and gave him a little squeeze. She reached around and affectionately rubbed his Buddha-belly, covered in gray and black hair. Mac whispered to Lucien, his head down, shaking his head as he spoke.

"You know, he calls me *every* week, sometimes two or three times a week, and, you know, he's never angry or anything....he's always *up*. C said he never used to talk to strangers, still doesn't, gets scared, you know; but some people, a few, for some reason, he just talks to, and he's not afraid....and *I'm* one of them. Of all people, *me*. Don't know what I did to deserve that, but whatever I did, I'm glad I did it. And Jesus, can that boy talk! He's always telling me about Cord, or Carol or Lilly, or Marty, or you, or Chicken-Little or all those other cats - Big Banana - and most of all, he talks about his mom. He *loves* his mom, he talks to her almost every day, and she's been dead, for, like, twenty years. And you know what, I *believe* him; he really talks to her, and she talks to him; I believe him."

"Me too, me too."

Lucy whispered.

"Did you decide about his birthday, tonight? Are you giving it to him?"

"Yeah."

Mac raised his head and smiled, while he shook his head slow....a good slow.

"Are you sure?"

"It's the most valuable thing I own, I've *ever* owned. I've been offered thirty-five grand for it, and would never sell it....*never*.   I love that bike, and I'm giving it to him....and I've never been so sure of anything in my life."

Mac turned to face Lucien.

"Earl said his mom used to ride on some guy's *Knucklehead,* just like mine, it was her favorite – she loved it. I think he thinks she rode mine, somehow; he never said it outright, but that's why he was looking at it that day in the Park, you know, in Belvidere, Rolling *Thunder,* when he knocked it over....it's crazy important to him. And Lilly and Cord were asking me all those questions about where I got it, and how I somehow remembered that guy's name, Jones, that rich, white dude who sold it to me, when I can't remember anything; how did that happen? Just by a fluke? Strange. I'm so happy he knocked over my bike that day; he changed my life, our life, forever. So yeah, I've known for awhile, just didn't tell ya. I'm giving the bike to Earl because it feels like it's really been his all along; I'm just kinda like a placeholder, sweetie. So yeah, I'm giving him the *Knucklehead,* and it's gonna feel good."

She smiled at him, took him by the hand, and headed back into the bedroom.

"I'm proud of you Papi. And know what, I'm gonna give you the second half of the Peggy-Sue, and it's gonna feel good."

CHAPTER 304 – A SEASONED SHIT-SHOVELER CAN SNIFF ONE A MILE AWAY

The Mustang climbed ever higher, weaving through a series of switch-backs, in a residential neighborhood, venturing further from the highway and the beach, far below. The nose of the car was sniffing for clues, marked by small, scattered signs along the side of the road, that made the same promise, over and over:

Mt. Mitchell Scenic Overlook

Always somewhere further up the road, around the next bend, beyond the next rise, higher and higher they climbed.

"Hey C, that water we saw, it didn't look oily; I thought it was supposed to be all black and oily, at least by the *Westside Piers*. And what are *westside piers* anyway? And where are the smugglers if there's no resort on the island to hide in? Were they hiding behind the grass, where we couldn't see 'em? And do you think Ken and Sandy are in the City, hiding in the underbelly of the ferry? And I guess the *Wild Things* really don't live on Skeleton Island after all, do they, because they're way-big, and we would've seen 'em, right? Unless they were hiding under the water or were buried in the sand, or something, then we might not have seen 'em, and they could still be there, right C?"

Cord smiled at him, and didn't say a word. Lilly harrumphed from behind.

"Jesus, enough already!"

But no one paid attention.

"I told you the water wasn't oily; you could have stuck your toe in."

"No way! I saw you come out of that water like an ice-pop! You weren't very happy Mr. C."

Earl yelped.

"Enough!"

Lilly yelled, louder.

"Hey it's my birthday Bibby and you get to do and say what *you* want on your birthday! Actually you get to do and say what you want *every* day! And besides, C **did** see the monster in the clouds, with the curly lips, just like I said it was there, at the beginning of the book, you know, Ken and Sandy, the pictures at the beginning of the book, so there! I was right; you saw it, didn't you C?"

"Sure did!"

C chimed chipper, even though he never really could see that monster either.

"Big surprise, your girlfriend saw it too."

Lilly yawned from the back.

"No, Carol didn't see it, I did."

C said deadpan.

Which earned him a swift kick to the back of his car seat. C just laughed; it was worth a kick to the backside.

Then it hit Earl, and he sat up, accusation scrawled across his face.

"Hey! You still didn't get me the next two books you keep promising: *The Riddle of the Stone Elephant* and the *Black Thumb Mystery;* you lost the bet mister!"

"And you cheated, with you-know-who!"

C shot back.

"I didn't cheat! I never cheat! You don't keep your promises, and that's not nice! I keep *my* promises."

Earl whined. And Lilly, who was having real bad feelings about this whole chit thing, saw an opportunity to exit.

"You're a welcher, *I knew it*! Bet's off! Chit's off!"

She announced, absolving herself of all liability.

"The bet is **not** off! No way! And I'm not a welcher!"

C yelled back at her.

"And as for *you*, maybe those two books are already bought, wrapped and ready; maybe they're the best surprise birthday present ever, that you just ruined, ever think of that?"

C looked stern at Earl, like he just blew the biggest birthday surprise ever. Earl put his head down, a scolded pup.

"Really C?"

"Maybe, just maybe."

Was all C said, contrite.

"Oh brother."

Was all Lilly could come up with, knowing C was as full of shit as she was most of the time; a seasoned shit-shoveler can sniff one a mile away.

CHAPTER 305 – ANOTHER SWIFT KICK IN THE BACKSIDE, AND HE LIKED IT

"So, where are we, on the numbers."

C had hopped to a new subject, as the Mustang continued to scale Mt. Mitchell.

Earl knew exactly what C meant, but he had to speak in code; the *Top-Ten To-Do List* was a not-so-secret secret amongst the boys, no girls allowed, and Earl rattled them off, sneaking thoughts about each and every one.

No. 1 – Done!

[Go on a date with Carol, to Couch Rock! Oh boy, that was fun, and he didn't even know it was a real date till C told him it was, and it was easy! He could do that lots of times, no problem! In fact, he already had! He ignored the sex part C threw into No. 1, of course, but he wanted to think about it, but it way too scary, and he'd probably mess it up, even though he read the Kama Sutra book, like a hundred times, but Carol would laugh at him, but maybe not, but maybe - too much thinking - he quickly moved on to No. 2]

No. 2 – We'll do it later, but not much later, right C?

[Go to Panama with C, swinging slow on the hammock in the sun, with his butt scraping the dock; he really wanted to do that! He never did a real butt-scrape before – not a real one, on a hammock! And to meet Earl, the little blue fish who swam circles around the coral, and to say hi to the lobsters hiding in the mangroves, and maybe even see Louie! Maybe he'd get there by then, even though C said he liked cold water, he knew Louie pretty well, he was pretty sure he'd like warm water too, but not too warm, like on the stove!]

No. 3 – Done!

[Solve a mystery – he just did it! He figured out it was Skeleton Island, before C even told him! But he still didn't figure out the whole Sandy Hook thing, and what Sandy's hook had to do with anything, and why he even had a hook. He had to think about that some more, and he still don't know where those smugglers were hiding, or where the Wild Things were – how could they hold their breath under water for so long? He would have to deal with these major mysteries later! Oh boy!]

No. 4 – Done!

[Go to Skeleton Island – just did it! Although it wasn't very impressive, if he did say so himself, but he would never tell C that; he didn't want to hurt his feelings or anything. And sorry, but no way the Wild Things were hiding in the sand, or under the water, no way....or were they? If so, they were really sneaky!]

No. 5 – Done!

*[Get real mail! He looked at that invitation and read in over and over, every night, counting off the days; **only 7 days to go!** And then it was the big sleepover party at Carol's – next Saturday! Oh boy! And he still didn't know what a bacchanalia was, but its gotta be good, cause Carol was doing it, and he'd get to sleep over again, and then he started thinking about the 's' word, got scared, and moved onto to No. 6]*

No. 6 – Done!   Wow, we got lots done C, haven't we?!

[Cord to be his brother, which was the bestest-best, but he wanted C to be his real brother, even more real than he already was; that would be even better than the bestest-best, and that's about the best that it could ever

*get.   Earl squeezed his eyes shut, hoping C and Lilly
would get married; that would be the best ever! He
squeezed them harder, figuring maybe that would help it
come true]*

No. 7 – Later, but Mac promised **soon**, right C?

*[Ride a Knucklehead, **the** Knucklehead, the same one
his mom rode on. He was so sure, even super sure, even
though his mom would never answer him when he asked
about it; she always ignored that question! He was a
little cranky at her about that, but not really too cranky;
she'd tell him eventually, right? And maybe he'd even
get to ride on the levee road that C always talked about,
beating the dust. He knew he could do it; his mom told
him he'd beat the dust, and she was never wrong – ever!
But he didn't even know where the levee was! But that
was okay, 'cause C would show him]*

No. 8….

No. 8 had crept up on him without warning, and he
didn't have time to prepare. And he didn't finish the
sentence; he just thought it, as his head slowly fell
forward.

*[Hope Little-Earl doesn't die, but he did, he died….he
already did.   But C said No. 8 was to make him happy
until he does, and Earl tried his very best to make him
happy; he hoped he made Little-Earl at least a little
happy when he was sick, his mom said he did, and she
knows about those things the best, and she would never
lie. But he was still sad; he wished he could have spent
his birthday with him - he missed Little-Earl so much.
He didn't deserve to be sick; he never did anything to
hurt anybody]*

Earl kept his head down, the excitement of the *To-Do
List* drained out of him. C realized what had happened,

frowned and leaned over, whispered to him, but loud enough for Lilly to hear.

"Sorry Earl, I forgot the first part of No. 8. But Little-Earl *was* happy because of you; he loved you very much - don't you ever forget that, because it matters, it's all that *really* matters, in the end."

Lilly hadn't said a sarcastic word, although there was plenty of opportunity to do so, as Earl trolled from Nos. 1 to 7, and now, she was happy she hadn't. She sat up and kissed Earl on the cheek whispering gently in his ear.

"I loved Little-Earl too sweetie. And C's right, he loved you, very much; he was a good boy."

Earl just shook his head in a sad yes, and gave her a thank-you smile. C looked at Lilly; he heard everything she said.

"You're amazing, how can you be such a bitch, and then so incredibly nice, so sweet, two seconds later?"

"Shut up asshole."

"And then such a bitch...."

C said, without missing a beat. And that earned him another swift kick in the backside, and he liked it.

CHAPTER 306 – WITH A HAND MUFFLING HER MOUTH: *OH MY GOD!*

"Hey Earl, what about No. 1? I don't think that's really done, is it? Or you do have something to spill?"

"We're here!"

Earl cut him off; saved as the Mustang crested the hilltop and was greeted by an oversized sign:

Mt. Mitchell Scenic Overlook

No way he was talking about *that* stuff, especially in front of Lilly. *Thank you Mr. Sign!* he said to himself.

The Mustang weaved through the parking lot; this one had a scatter of cars and some people milling about under a small pavilion and plaza, at the top of a grassy knoll.

"That doesn't make No. 1 go away mister."

C whispered, as he shoved the gear into park; Earl couldn't get out of the car quick enough.

"Okay, enough girl talk; spill Earl, what is No. 1?"

Lilly said, sarcastic.

"*NO!*"

Earl yelled, a little too loud.

"I don't wanna talk about No. 1! What about Nos. 9 and 10 C? We still need a nine and ten you know. A top ten needs a nine and ten, or it's not a *Top 10* you know; you need all of them....all ten, ten is ten, not eight, just saying."

"I know, know, and we'll let No. 1 drop for now, since it's your birthday and all."

"Hey! *Rude!* I'm right here! Stop talking secrets like little girls!"

They both ignored her, which steamed Lilly even more, which was the point.

"Now what? What are we here for anyway?"

The Lilly-whining started yet again.

The wind was gone, or at least most; it was more of a sweet kiss, on the left cheek. The windstorm, like the beach, fell far behind. C climbed the knoll, with Earl, and Lilly – reluctantly, in tow. Before them was a slanted Park Service board, mapping Sandy Hook and its environs far below them, the exact stretch of shore they just left, twenty minutes prior.

"Hey, we were just there C; that's where the lobsters went free!"

Earl pointed to the horizon, and then to the board, and back to the horizon.

"You got it."

C said.

"Look over there *[C pointed to the far left]* - see it? You can really see it from up here; say hello to Manhattan - New York City!"

"Wow."

Was all Earl could say.

"I wish we could go there someday!"

Earl said.

"We'll go someday, Earl, promise....someday."

C assured him.

"Really? 'Cause that would be the coolest ever!"

"Really, I promise."

C said sincere. And Earl hugged his best friend.

"Oh my God! *Oh my God!"*

Lilly said it twice, then a third time, with a hand muffling her mouth:

Oh My God!

CHAPTER 307 – SMILES….THE KIND THAT SCARE LITTLE GIRLS

There it lay, plain as day, in perfect black-block letters. The exact crescent of sand that all three could see from their vantage, the same nondescript spit first eyed in the sandstorm. Three little words laid quiet on the slanted Park Service board, and C creased the biggest shit-grin he could muster:

Skeleton Hill Island

It was 3:15 pm, and, for C, all was right in the world. It took Earl a second to register, then he victory-hugged his best friend.

"You won! You won!"

And as quick as he hugged Cord, he let go and put on a face of utter condolence.

"Sorry Lilly."

She didn't buy it for a second, and proceeded to punch Earl in the gut, which was like punching a rock. He smiled the roundhouse away, and hugged her hard, even as she tried to wriggle free, playing the sore loser. Earl held her like a wriggling fish and planted a big wet kiss on her forehead. And just as quick, he let her go. C cracked his knuckles in anticipation of the chit; so many possibilities, *so many*.

"Don't get any sex ideas, mister, that's off the …."

He cut her off, with a dismissive wave of the hand.

"You don't get to say shit. I won, no exceptions, with nothing out-of-bounds, and no time limit. Jesus, this chit is literally good for….*years!*"

C and Earl high-fived, throwing caution to the wind, and sported devilish, teenage-boy smiles….the kind that scare little girls.

CHAPTER 308 – INTO THE QUICKIE WORLD
OF *CLERKS*

Lilly's shoulders deflated in defeat, letting out a long drawn sigh. Then, like the turn of a page, she recovered.

"Okay, whatever, no big deal, whatever you want, you got it. You won, fair and square."

She tossed her head to the side in typical Lilly move-on fashion, and the indignity of the chit was filed under *forgotten*. C and Earl looked at her, then each other, and just laughed. They both said it, simultaneous, as if rehearsed.

"Yeah, right."

And into the car they piled. The Mustang nosed north, destination unknown. The clock turned to 3:30 pm; it was a mere fifteen minutes into one big chit, the biggest ever, and not a single word was spoken. But that baby was doing multiple rolls in both Lilly's and C's melons. He had a goofy smile plastered to his face. She didn't.

C pulled off the highway into a little town called:

Leonardo

Somehow, that rang a bell. He crawled two blocks along a nondescript street, where absolutely nothing was anything but same-old, blue-collar Jersey suburban ordinary. Gray and dull.

Then he saw it, just ahead, on the right.

"Holy shit Earl; do you know what that is?"

Earl sat up and studied the scene; clearly this was another mystery to solve. But all he saw was a little storefront, sporting three words:

Quickie Stop Grocery

Some dumpy hole-in-the-wall. This was a tough one, for sure; C had him stumped, but good. Ten seconds passed, Earl's finger tapping his lips, with his sister sighing in the back seat. Then it hit him, and Earl busted.

"Holy mackerel! *Clerks!* That's the store! The real store! Isn't it C? For real? This is the best ever!"

C couldn't stop smiling.

"I didn't plan this part Earl, I promise, it's just a weird fluke. I didn't know it was here, or even where it was; I'm not sure if I even knew it was in Jersey."

Lilly sat up, with a look of utter disgust on her face.

"I don't get it. You two are so gay, it's scary; when are you going to grow up?"

"Hey, chit-girl, guys get old, but they *never* grow up, it's a fact *[Earl shook his head in eager agreement]*. Haven't you figured that out yet? By the way, I've got some ideas for...."

Lilly closed her eyes and put her hands over her ears, humming loud to drown out whatever depraved idea Cord had in mind. C smiled and turned to Earl.

"You know, the first *Clerks* was pretty good, not great - it was no *Neighbors*, for sure, but still, okay. But the second one, *Jesus,* that blew dog."

"Yeah, blew dog."

Earl parroted.

"Really sucked-ass."

"Sucked-ass."

Earl whispered, as he shook his head in agreement, because it *really did* suck ass.

"Hey Earl, let's go in and get some junk food for the ride, just so we can say we went in; whaddaya say?"

"Are you serious? This is *so gay!*"

Lilly protested, knowing it was in vain.

"Hey! Get off the gay thing, it's old."

"Stop acting gay and I will; you're both ***embarrassing!***"

"Then stay in the car, chit-girl."

"Then you get off the chit-girl thing!"

"Never, not until you pay up, and that could be a long, *long* time."

Was all C said, through a cheeser, as the two boys barrelled out of the car and into the quickie world of *Clerks*.

CHAPTER 309 - SHE KEPT SWALLOWING, ONE AFTER ANOTHER

They came out mere minutes later, with Earl's favorite, a jumbo bag of *Pizza Supreme* nachos.

"Well, that was a disappointment."

C said, flat.

"Yeah, and it didn't even look like it was supposed to, and the floor was all sticky!"

Earl said, clutching his prized nachos.

"But at least they had the best, the *Pizza Supreme* tortilla chips, right C?"

"Right, and we voted, unanimous; Lilly gets none, right?"

C snapped at her, playing the victorious dick. But before Cord could even laugh, in the lightning strike of a snake, Lilly leaped from the back seat and snatched the *Pizza Supremes* from Earl's grasp....a deadly viper. In a flash, she ripped open the bag, chips flying everywhere and shoved a wad in, chewing with her mouth wide open, like a cow's cud in the field.

"*HAH!*"

Was all she could muster, being her mouth was full of wet, mashed orange cornmeal.

"*HEY!*"

Earl screamed, his prize in pieces, being mangled in the back seat, like the heads of *Animal Crackers*. He knew a complete slaughter was on its way.

"Nice, nice."

Was all C could say, as he turned away, with a look of disgust.

"Nice food-mouth, Buck."

Cord added, as Lilllian chewed with her mouth wide open, the contents in full view of anyone who dared look her way. It was disgusting.

"Want some, *chit-boy*?"

Lilly said, sticking her tongue out, covered in a thick wad of saliva and half-chewed orange goo.

"That's unsanitary!"

Earl yelled, backing away in abject horror.

"Yum!"

Was all Lilly said, as she kept swallowing, one after another.

CHAPTER 310 – I DIDN'T WANT A STUPID CHIP ANYWAY

The boys never got a chip, not a one.

Lilly ate as many as she physically could, till she felt ill, then proceeded to lick every last remaining *Pizza Supreme*, both sides, and threw them back in the bag; sad, soggy triangles.

C ignored her, but Earl was devastated, just like beheaded *Animal Crackers*. He kept saying, over and over, right before she licked clean the next kidnapped chip.

"Can I please have one?"

And she ignored him every time, her fingers dyed orange, and covered in saliva, cause she kept licking them clean, like you do when you eat chips, lots of chips.

"Earl give it up, don't beg; that's what she wants you to do."

"I know, but I *really* want one! It's my birthday you know, Lilly, it's *my* birthday! You should be nice and not lick your fingers in front of me; that's **rude!**"

She licked another one.

"The whole car smells like your pizza breath! **Stop breathing all over me Lilly!**"

"Oh for Christ's sake Earl, just grab the stupid bag, you can take her; go for it!"

C said, exasperated.

For a second Earl lost his senses; the aroma of *Pizza Supreme* tortilla chips had clouded his thinking, and he turned to make an assault on the back seat.

Lilly simply smiled evil at Earl, with wild cat eyes.

"Sure Earl, take the bag; come on, *take it*!"

She taunted him, and Earl quickly recoiled in fear. They both knew that bag was staying right where it was; an assault on the backseat was simply too dangerous to risk. Earl accepted defeat with grace, his arms crossed in front of his chest.

"I didn't want a stupid chip anyway."

CHAPTER 311 – HE'S IN....DEEP

The spicy chips were gone, eaten or licked into submission. It was a wholesale slaughter.

The sun kissed the Mustang hood and the radio blared as the very first sign for the *Lincoln Tunnel* approached overhead, without warning, and quietly passed by, both Lilly and Earl, lost in their own thoughts, missed it.

C didn't.

"Wonder what's next? Bet you wish you knew!"

Earl smiled and rubbed his hands together furious; he knew whatever it was, it was going to be good.   He was *so* past those stupid chips; who wants a tasty tortilla chip anyway – they aren't really *that* good....too spicy.

Lilly leaned forward, breathing hot, spicy chip-breath in her brother's ear.

"Open your hand."

"Don't do it Earl; it's a trap!"

C warned his best friend.

Earl looked at his big sister, and obliged, like he always did.

"Both hands."

Earl did as he was told.

Out of nowhere, from thin air it seemed, Lilly proceeded to dump a huge pile of fresh *Pizza Supreme* tortilla chips, all virgin, unlicked, into her brother's outstretched hands.

"*Oh boy!* Thank you Lilly; you're the best sister ever!"

She kissed him on the cheek; *now* her hot spicy breath smelled pretty darn good.

"Hey, how 'bout some for Cord?"

Earl yelled. Lilly turned to C, with mischief in her eyes, and spoke with her best, most innocent, school-girl charm.

"I saved you some too, Mr. Brin; believe me? Close your eyes and open up daddy, and I'll slide one right in."

She taunted him.

He stared at her, and she at him, smiling angelic. It was scary, and gave him a chill. He stared at her some more, as Earl chomped away next door. This was surely a deal with the devil.

"Licked?"

He said, but she didn't answer; the creepy plastic smile never left her lips. He stared hard, studying her poker-face, and simply couldn't shake the bad vibe. He was always right about such things.

"No thanks, I'm not getting a soggy licked one shoved in my mouth, that's gross; no way, not taking the chance."

He finally said, refusing the dare. But he *really* did want a chip; the whole cab smelled like yummy pizza.

Lilly smiled and produced a handful of beautiful, perfect, virgin tortilla chips; she sexily slipped them into her mouth, eating them in slow-motion, for added effect.

"*Fuck.*"

C whispered, as she crunched away.

Just then, *Katrina and the Waves* queued on the radio:

and it *was* sunny, that rarely happened to C. More often than not, whenever that song hit the car radio, it was night, or raining, or snowing, or something....anything but sunny, which made today's song that much better. And it suddenly put him in a good mood, even without the pizza tortilla. He was about to start singing, looked right and got the evil-eye from Earl.

"I was gonna sing low."

C said, almost apologetic. But Earl shook his head no, a parent's no, which is a *real* no. C singing on Earl's birthday was simply not allowed.

Out of the blue, Lilly leaned forward and kissed Cord's cheek warm, not a peck, but something much more, then whispered low in C's ear.

"Hey, thanks for the beach, I mean it, and thanks for saving the lobsters, not just for Earl, but for me too. I think they're gonna make it after all; I mean, they survived the tank, the ride, and they'll look out for each other, *right*? Because that's what friends do."

C smiled at the unexpected gift, but she didn't see it, because her face was buried in his neck. She whispered to him, as she gently kissed his nape, radiating warmth.

"Hey, look on your seat."

C's eyes dropped, and there, beside him, was the most perfect tortilla chip....unbroken, untouched, probably the best chip in the entire bag. He raised his eyes, pulled his head away and greeted her beautiful gaze. Then he simply shook his head.

"How do you do that? How do you *always* do that? When am I *ever* gonna get you?"

"Hopefully never; what fun is that?   Oh, and I decided
what your chit is: it's not the chip by the way. I'll give it
you later, *in private*. I think you'll like it; I hope so."

C could do nothing but stare like a little kid at her
beautiful face, framed in red silk. He was mesmerized,
like the day he first saw her through the plate glass at
Sam's; the way one stares when he knows he's in….deep.

CHAPTER 312 – MOUTH STRETCHED WIDE, READY TO GREET A THREESOME

At 4:15 pm, even though they were still a good fifteen miles away, the Midtown skyline, crystal clear, fit neatly inside the windshield frame. But not for long; it was growing.

Lilly hadn't noticed the unfolding scene, silent in the back seat, playing with her hair, fussing over her mother's scarf, smiling to herself, thinking about Cord. About how goofy he sometimes was, and how sensitive, and how smart and….how much he loved her brother. C loved Earl just the way he was, like a little kid, shoulder-to-shoulder, with no qualifications, no exceptions, no *except-for-thats*. It must be nice to have someone love you that much.

And then Lilly wondered: does C love *me* that much? Why is he here, *really*? Who sent him, *really*? And does it really even matter anymore?

Lilly closed her eyes. *If I died right now, I'd be okay, I really would. I'd die happy, because I am, me and my mom's scarf. And I know Earl would be alright; C would take care of him....he would never leave him.*

And as Lilly rewound, the smile never left her face. The radio brought her out:

> *Won't let nobody hurt you;*
> *And I'll never desert you;*
> *I'll stand by you;*
> *I'll stand by you.*

I'll Stand By You, by *The Pretenders*. How do things like that happen? How do songs come on at just the right time, that make sense, played just for you....talking *just* to you.

Earl had been fidgeting with his fingernails, head down, never seeing the screen in front of his face, till now, when he lazily raised his eyes to the stage, as they rumbled down Route 3.

"Hey C; *what's that?*"

Earl pointed to the distant row of super-tall buildings, about a dozen miles away, on the far horizon.

"That, my friend, is New York."

"It's straight ahead Lilly, **look!** It looks *fake!* Hey C, what's the big building, the biggest one?"

Earl shook his finger at the right side of the windshield.

"The *Empire State Building.*"

Came the answer from the back.

"Remember mom used to talk about bringing us all the way to the top, like she did when she was a little kid? She said you had to hold onto your hat, it was so windy up there!"

Earl shook his head a happy yes.

"C, are we going there? For real? Now?"

Lilly half-asked. Cord grinned Cheshire, and didn't answer.

"But you said we'd go to New York someday....*maybe* someday."

Earl chimed.

"That's right, I did. But nobody said *maybe* someday couldn't be today; what do you say Earl?"

C whispered to his friend.

"Welcome to the end of the road, I guess."

Earl said, through a wry smile. Then the two of them erupted, simultaneous, like the little kids that they were.

"Neighbors!"

Another classic quote from their favorite goofy movie. C turned and saw worry settle across Lilly's face. He spoke gently to her, looking into the rear-view mirror.

"What? Nervous?   I'll tell you what *I* think; *I* think Manhattan, after forty-one long years, waiting with bated breath, is finally ready to meet *the* Miss Lillian Liddell."

Lilly proffered a weak smile.

Lilly had heard it all before, too many times to count over the years; Carol running her mouth about Lilly thinking she's something special, but she swims in a small, no-name pond in the middle of nowhere, called Belvidere. In New York City, in the *real* world, she would be less than a footnote. No one would even notice her, no one would even care; there were a thousand prettier girls, ten-thousand sexier girls, a hundred-thousand whatever.

Truth was, Lilly believed it, *every* single word.

Her mouth got pasty, her heart was in her throat, and she was scared to death, as the miles ticked away, and they got ever closer to the *Emerald City*.

A sign for:

Lyndhurst

2290

passed, and the *Empire State Building* loomed ever larger through the windshield, growing by leaps and bounds. Lilly felt she could put her arm out the window and grab it, an icicle off the roof.

"How much further?"

Lilly asked, feigning calm.

"About fifteen minutes and we'll be Midtown, if we don't hit traffic at the tunnel."

Both Earl and Lilly were glued to the screen; *Hoboken* and *Ferry* signs passed on the right, traffic was light, and the Mustang found itself descending in a clockwise loop, corkscrewing through the helix, toward the mouth of the *Lincoln Tunnel*, passing jumbo billboards, watching the sunlight glint off the Hudson River and canyons of steel and glass on the far shore, which all looked anything but real.

As they approached the mouth of the tunnel, it was almost too much to drink in, with Earl craning over C's head, and Lilly, her nose pressed light against the left window. Both had Christmas-morning mouths, slightly agape, with eyes saucer-wide.

The City was busting at the seams, building upon building, each bigger than the next, pushed hard against the west bank of the island, a ribbon of shimmering blue water laid before it. And they saw sailboats, *real sailboats*, plying the waters of the Hudson River, dodging a ferry heading toward New York, just like them.

"It's beyond….it's *beautiful*."

Lilly whispered.

"It's way big, Bibby, *way big*! King Kong was way up there, you know! I saw it! Right there!"

"Yeah, he was."

Lilly agreed, without a hint of sarcasm.

"But he fell off – I feel bad that he did *[Earl hung his head, then quickly jerked it up]*. Hope we don't fall and get smooshed too!

Earl yelped.

"Yeah."

Lilly whispered to herself, desperate, afraid she was about to do her own King Kong and fall flat on her face in Carol's home town, on *Carol's* home turf.

Earl was holding up Jonesy, to give him a birds-eye of the view; he was so excited that Jonesy got to come along.

The clock tripped 4:25 pm and the Mustang slipped quietly into the middle tube of the *Tunnel*.

"Hold your breath under the river!"

C yelled.

Earl didn't even question, he parroted C and took a big gulp, miming frantic to Lilly to suck in some air. Earl cupped his hand over Jonesy, just in case.

Lilly ignored them, and sat quiet in the back, surprised that she felt a bit claustrophobic and a bit panicked, a sardine in that long narrow tube, watching dingy white wall tiles whiz by under the fluorescent.

Earl stared at C, and C glanced over every two seconds or so, seeing who would drown first. As if there was any question, after thirty seconds or so, C was beet red and done; he exhaled hard. Earl was still smiling, his cheeks the size of a chipmunk, full of nuts.

"I win! Jonesy wins!"

"No shit."

C said, and Lilly breathed relief, as the stifling tube finally yawned to daylight on the far side; its mouth stretched wide, ready to greet a threesome.

CHAPTER 313 – NONE OF THEM WERE ANY THE WISER

A quick bank to the left and they found themselves knee-deep in bumper-to-bumper traffic, stuck at the first red-light, by the *Port Authority Bus Terminal*. Earl was craning his neck, trying to see the tops of the buildings; Lilly did the same from the back, typical tourist pose.

"This is like Belvidere on *major* steroids."

Lilly whispered to herself, knowing that wasn't even close to true. This was a whole different world, a different planet.

"Who owns all these buildings, C? Must be rich people!"

Earl said, his face vertical as he spoke.

"Yeah, there are lots of them, for sure, but lots of others too, lots of renters. There are about eight million or so, I think, but that's *all* the boroughs, not just Manhattan."

"*Eight Million?!* **People?!** All in one place?! *No way* I could ever count that high! Do they all know each other? Are they friends? We only have, like, two thousand in all of Belvidere! I know that 'cause Marty told me once. Are there any cows? Do cows live here too? Is there a lot of cow poop?"

Earl was chirping like a little girl.

"Earl, there are two thousand people in some of these buildings *alone*, easy. You could fit the whole of Belvidere in a lot of these buildings, just one building, with plenty of room to spare. And no, don't think there are any cows, unless they are hiding somewhere. But lots of horses, horse poop, but they just pull tourists around; they can't be very happy living here."

C said, cracking his knuckles, waiting for the light to turn. Earl hung his head a bit; he felt bad that eight million people couldn't smell cow poop; they didn't know what they were missing. And he felt bad for the horses, because C felt bad for them; and if C did, he did too.

"I always wanted to own that big white house on the Park, the one on an angle; you know which one I'm talking about C?"

Lilly said, still spinning her head left, right, up and down, trying to drink the scene. Everything she looked at was big, or bigger.

"Yeah, I ran by that thing enough times; why that one?"

C said, as he jockeyed from lane to lane, as lights turned and the pack of cars surged and dodged one another and jaywalkers sprouting from all directions.

"Rumor is that house used to sit straight, then the old lady who owned it a hundred years ago wanted to look at the Park - she loved looking at the Park - so she had the house spun, literally picked it right up and spun it, so it looked right down the gravel path, to the middle, to where my mom and Earl's bench is; do you believe that?"

Lilly asked, genuine.

"Sure, why not?"

C said.

"I've always wanted to believe that, that somebody really spun that house because they loved the Park so much; that they were rich enough to afford it, and crazy enough to do it, just because they loved it. My mom loved that Park, sitting in the middle with me."

Lilly said, waxing nostalgic. It was a good memory, and she savored it.

"*And me!*"

Earl yelled.

"And Earl. Actually it was mostly Earl and her who sat on that bench, but it was me too, sometimes. My mom liked that big house too; she was the one who told me that story, about it getting spun around; she'd rub my leg when she told me, and I'd get goosebumps and she'd rub them away. I don't know why I got goosebumps, excited I guess. Anyway, I always wanted to live there, to own it, to sit on that big porch and just look at the Park. My mom said she'd buy it for me one day, when I was old enough, and I asked her if we could put a big sign in the yard that said: *Lilly's House – Keep Out and Get Off the Lawn!* I threw in the *lawn* part, because old man Beaumont, the veterinarian that owned Crowhead's house on the Park always yelled at me when I was a kid and cut the corner, and rode my bike across his crappy lawn. My mom would always laugh about my sign idea – she said why don't we just call it: *Lilly Liddell*, or maybe just *The Lillian* – it was classier, more dignified, with an *air of mystery*, she said. I still liked my idea better, but she was right, of course. I still would like to own that house, I think that would be nice....someday, maybe."

Lilly's voice trailed off, thinking good thoughts about her mom.

"You got it; I'll buy it for you."

C said, and he sounded sincere.

Lilly just smiled, appreciating the gesture, knowing Cord couldn't buy it anymore than she could; it would take a lot more than a couple of foil packs hidden on the upper closet shelf, that's for sure. Lilly wondered what her mother thought of Cord; did she really like him, like Earl said? And what would she think about today, about *right now*, with her and Earl smack in the middle of New York City of all places, with her red scarf on. She hoped she'd be proud of her, for finally leaving Belvidere, even though it was just for a day, *part* of a day. It was a start. Thinking of her mom in that way made Lillian smile wider.

"What about you; what one would you like to own?"

Lilly asked Ay.

"I don't know, it'd be fun to own that little brick one on the Park, with the eagle statue set atop the chimney, overlooking the Green. I don't know why, just kind of like it. My dad always liked eagles – had lots of statues and sculptures of them around. But it doesn't have a front porch, and having a front porch is nice, to drink and smoke and nap on, maybe do some people-watching. Maybe I'll put a big sign in the yard that says: *Cord Brin*, or maybe just *C. Brin*, or *The Cord*."

Lilly guffawed.

"How gay, *The Cord*; how about calling it *The Dork*? And **no way** are you buying the house next to Crowhead and people-watch, while you smoke, drink and nap with the neighbors, so just forget it *[never mind the fact that he would have to buy it from Carol, since she owned that building too, which everyone in the Mustang knew, but neither boy dared say aloud]*!"

"Hey Bibby, don't call her Crowhead! That's *not* her real name!"

Earl defended his play-pretend girlfriend.

"Sorry Earl, you're right, it's not Crowhead, it's Shithead; my mistake."

Lilly said, matter-of-fact.

"Hey! That's not nice, you know! She doesn't call you that!"

Earl yelped.

"How could she? I'm not."

Lilly said, as if the fact was obvious.

But as quick as Earl protested, defending Carol, he stopped, dropping the conversation cold – he was getting too distracted looking for horses, *any* horses, and getting shell-shocked by the ever-changing cityscape unfolding before him, along with the hundreds of people of every shape and size, at every intersection, and on every sidewalk, walking in every different direction before him, most in a hurry, and nobody was smiling! How could you not smile being in New York City?! That made absolutely no sense to Earl; it was yet another mystery he had to work on. Earl figured they *all* must be going somewhere *very* important, to be in such a hurry; maybe they were going to the dentist, or something scary like that, since they all seemed kind of cranky. Must be *lots* of dentists in New York, and they must be very rich, fixing all those cranky teeth; maybe it was the rich dentists that owned all the big buildings! Maybe. Now it was all starting to make sense.

C continued.

"Or maybe I'd buy the old *Goodwill Firehouse*, down on Water Street - that's kinda cool – and call it *Esprit,* 'cause I like the word. I'd make it into a private cigar club, you know with individual humidors and private liquor lockers, big leather chairs, dim lights, dark walls, jazz on Friday nights, blues on Saturday, *Casablanca* forever playing on a big screen; how cool would that be? But no girls allowed, just *real* men, right Earl?"

"Right."

Earl parroted blindly, not knowing what he was even agreeing to. His mind was preoccupied with a mystery: *man, the horses must be hiding really good*; he hadn't seen a single one yet.

"Just *real* men? Then how are you going to get in?"

Lilly said, deadpan to Cord, and grinned at her own joke. C smiled, knowing he had served her a grapefruit with that one.

"Or maybe buy the old Georgia-Pacific building down on the water, and do all sorts of cool stuff down there – big outdoor movie screen, like the old days, and bike trails, and zip lines, luxury camping, maybe some kayak rentals, and whatever else; that would be fun; right Earl?"

"Right."

Earl said again, still not paying a lick of attention.

"But it would be good to live on the Park, you know, in that little brick building next to that Lion House; not sure who lives in that big white lion house; heard it was some rich hottie."

Lilly kicked the back of his seat.

"Forget it mister – I suggest you get the brick house and the trampy neighbor out of your head, or that little chit you stole goes out the window, no matter what your stupid *rules* say. And I don't think you want *that* to happen, do you, especially since I have some interesting ideas for how you can cash in that chit?"

C didn't answer her, he just smiled and eyed her through the rear-view mirror. She saw his grin, and knew that chit meant more to him than ten houses on the Park, surrounding the crowhead. She smiled at the easy win.

"In the end, maybe I'll just buy the big white house on the Park, you know, the one the old lady spun around, and give it to a friend of mine *[Lilly smiled]*. Maybe this friend of mine will let me live in the basement, or maybe the attic, if I'm lucky, and let me out now and then, you know, to see the sun, feel the grass."

C said, through a smirk.

"I don't know about that; I've heard that friend of yours is a bit unpredictable."

Lilly said wry.

"Yeah, that's kind of understatement, so I hear. Anyway, so, what about you Earl? What building do you want?"

C said, and was startled at the quick bark of a response from his co-pilot. Earl had apparently started listening.

"I want the King Kong building, that's what I want! But that would mean I would have to be a dentist, I guess, and that's probably pretty hard to do, but that's okay, I'll get smart, and then look at cranky people's teeth all day, and smell their bad breath. I know they don't mean to have bad breath, but they don't floss and gargle! You have to floss and gargle every day not to have to stinky breath! It's a known fact! Just saying. But I'll become a dentist if I have to, and smell stinky breath, like Lilly's in the morning, before she brushes her teeth....yuck *[that prompted a 'hey', along with another swift seat kick from the back of the Mustang]* because ***I want that building***; the *whole thing*, just for me and Jonesy!   And my good-luck herring gull feather too! Thanks C, for the feather; so far it's bringing *really* good luck, just like you said! We saved Louie and his friends, and they're on their way to Panama; we found Skeleton

Island; Lilly lost the big bet – sorry Lilly, but you did lose, fair and square, and C gets a big chit, and I wonder what that will be? And the *Wild Things* were hiding in the water; and we saw the *Clerks'* building, even though the floor was sticky; Lilly shared her *Pizza Supremes* with me – and they were *really* good – 'cause I had a hankering for some spicy pizza chips – she's the best sister *ever*, right Bibby? And I got to talk to Mac, and he even picked up the phone during a Peggy-Sue, and that's because he's my friend – not just *anybody* gets to interrupt a Peggy-Sue you know, just saying, and now we're in New York, like Ken and Sandy, solving mysteries about the sneaky hiding horses, and the water isn't even oily! So far, everything has been pretty lucky, right C?"

"Right!"

C exclaimed, astonished, yet again, that Earl could rattle that monster off without taking a single breath between. And what *dentists and hiding horses* had to do with absolutely anything he would never know, but this was Earl speaking, and that explanation was good enough.

They were on 10th Avenue, stopped at yet another light. The blink turned green and the mass of gridlocked cars surrounding the Mustang surged north, carrying them along. Throngs of people were still everywhere they drove, but the queue was getting thicker as they worked their way up the Avenue, heading north, walking the sidewalks, crossing and dodging traffic, all in a hurry somewhere else.

"Oh my God, there are more and more people every block we go! Jesus; I never saw so many people in one place in my life!"

Lilly said, trying to scope out the women, seeing how pretty they really were. She never saw so many people, so many ears! For some reason, she couldn't stop looking at people's ears. But none of the women were lookers yet, none so far – what a crock this *they're all gorgeous thing* really was! Oh, wait, there's one, and another, but her legs aren't so great, but that's only two, one and a half really, nothing special….no biggie. Wait, holy shit, she's fucking *gorgeous*; her legs go on forever, and they're the size of my arms! How does she do that?! Lilly stopped looking, dropping her eyes, information overload. She started to hyper-ventilate.

"This is *Hell's Kitchen*, just for your information; lot of good restaurants. But we're not stopping, just passing through."

C said, playing the tour guide.

"Lilly, look at that funny-looking guy; hey look at that building – holy mackerel, its got statues on it and everything! You gotta be *really, really* rich if they put a statue of you on a building, right C? That must be some good dentist. Whoa, watch out for that car C! Wow, that guy is really tall like me; hey Lilly you watching? You're missing *everything*!"

"Uh huh, great."

She said, keeping her head down. It took less than ten minutes to get up to 78th; soon, they were circling the complex, looking for a place to park, with no luck.

"Holy cow! Is this a museum or something?"

Earl gasped. The building looked half the size of Belvidere.

"Well, it's not *something;* Jesus, where the fuck you supposed to park?"

C said, cursing under his breath; every street was jammed with cars, some double-parked, without a parking garage in sight.

"Hey, this place closes in about an hour, so we gotta hustle. I'm gonna drop you two off in front, go in and get tickets, or just wait for me outside. No, forget that, you gotta go in and get the tickets, now, in case there is a long line. Go inside, get 'em and wait for me in there, in the lobby; got it? We're running out of time; *shit*!"

C stuck his hand in his pocket and pulled out a clip of greenbacks; he peeled off a Franklin and threw it at Lilly.

"A hundred? Jesus, how much does it cost to get in?"

"I don't know, but that should cover it; it better. Get us three tickets for a fucking hour, okay? I'll meet you in the lobby....say hi to Central Park, by the way; now ***get out** [C waved his hand in a hurry at the long expanse of wooded green across the street, just thirty feet away]!"*

C was idling double-parked, with jammed-up cars blaring horns, flipping fingers and cursing all around him. Lilly and Earl scooched onto the sidewalk, and in a flash, the Mustang melted into a sea of traffic, disappearing, leaving them alone amongst thousands, all ducking, weaving and jostling all about on the wide sidewalk fronting the immense structure towering above them.

Already, there were looks at Earl from all directions. Even in New York, a six foot eight almost four-hundred pound man, built like a mountain, gets attention. Not that either Lilly or Earl even noticed; the two of them looked around with that lost tourist gaze, a deer in headlights, a dead giveaway.

"Look at the woods Lilly! I didn't think they had *real* woods here – there's trees and everything! I bet that's where the horses are hiding, and maybe C is wrong, maybe they got cows in there too! It looks really big; see how far it goes; it goes forever!"

Earl pointed up the broad avenue, choked with jockeying cars; the woods disappeared in the distance; he couldn't see the end. Lilly tugged on his arm, pointing to the immense structure before them.

"Earl, this is the *American Museum Of Natural History;* don't you remember learning all about it in school?"

"Nope."

Earl said, deadpan.

"Me neither."

Lilly said, honest.

"Hey, I know you, *you're big*! He thinks you're a bison, but we're not scared of you! Sign this please!"

Two little beanpole boys saddled alongside Earl, one hugging his leg like a tree trunk, the other shoving a piece of paper and a pen up at him; they both must have been no more than six years old. The pen-holder had a mop of brown hair and oversized doe eyes. Earl was positively terrified, and couldn't say a word, looking down at one set of big brown eyes staring up at him and another with arms latched in a death-grip to his right leg.

"Sure he will; what's your name?"

Lilly said, as she smiled at the little mophead.

"*Colin, Colin James*; that's not me, that's him, my brother; do the signing to him; he saw the bison first!"

Colin James didn't say a word, he just hugged Earl's leg, petting it and delicately drawing figures on Earl's pants with a long thin finger, as he stared down at the sidewalk.

"Okay, *Colin James*, you got it."

Lilly said to the silent beanpole, and with that, she took the pen and paper, and handed it up to Earl.

"We're twins! But not exact-exact, just kinda-like exact. Some people can't tell us apart; even my mom sometimes!"

"I can see that, and what's *your* name?"

Lilly had bent over by this time, to get closer to the fast-talker's face.

"I'm *Quin*, with one *n*, which is much more sophisticated. Are you the bison's girlfriend?"

He batted his big lashes at Lilly, a six-year-old player.

"Kinda."

Was all Lilly said, through a half-smile.

"You're *really* pretty, just like my mom! I like your scarf, it brings out your features. My name's Quin!"

"You told me that already, I didn't forget! And thank you for the compliment, compliments actually....*Quin*."

And Lilly smiled wider at the six-year-old pick-up artist. *I guess at least someone thinks I'm pretty; shit-in-your-hat Carol Crowe,* she thought to herself.

"And you're right, your mom is *very* pretty."

Lilly looked over and met eyes with a petite, thin woman who looked about Lilly's age, maybe a bit older, but not much. She had a short blonde bob, straight and stylish, professional, with warm slate blue eyes and a tiny upturned nose. She smiled at Lillian, white picket-straight teeth, a bit large for her face, but not too much so, enough to notice. The kind of smile that says: *thank you for being nice to my children, for playing along with the charade.* Lillian could tell, in just one look, that she was a good person, a good mother, she could just tell. And she seemed happy, but who can really tell? The woman was holding a large souvenir bag from the museum gift shop, chock full of dew-dads the boys had just bought, after romping through the Natural History museum for the past two hours, past all the crazy animals, including the stuffed bison.

Earl wrote slow and hesitant on the paper, a nervous-cursive, his tongue sticking out in concentration-mode. This was hard work, and since it was his first autograph, he wanted it to be perfect. What exactly he was supposed to be writing, and signing, was a mystery he had no clue how to solve. So he wung it.

Done, he handed it to Lilly:

I'm Earl
I'm not a bison
Thank you for stopping by

He finished it with a block-letter *Earl Liddell,* with a little curl on the last ell. It was the first and last time Earl ever did that; an original. Lillian read it, smiled, folded it thrice and bent over to Colin-James, who still had a tight grip on Earl's leg.

"Now don't open this till later; this is his *very first* autograph of the day, and it's *very* special.

"Okay! Thanks!"

Quin yelled, as he grabbed it; Colin never opened his mouth, or made eye contact, from beginning to end. And before Lilly could respond, Quin planted a hard

2306

smooch on Lilly's left hip, right on her skirt; it was kind of a drive-by head butt, with a loud lip smack to boot.

Lilly's first New York kiss.

Before she could respond, Quin dashed off, Colin James poked along behind, unimpressed by the whole bison affair. They both ended up on each side of their mother's legs, girdling her, standing not twenty feet away. She smiled again at Lilly, mouthing *thank you* for the *entertainment.* Lilly returned the expression with a silent smile, and the three turned and headed up Central Park West, away from the museum, and quickly disappeared, swallowed in a swell of strangers.

And so it happened. It was *that* close; thirty-two long years, and C came *that* close. Ten minutes, no more than ten minutes, made the difference. If there had just been a parking stall, or a lot, nearer by, if he hadn't dropped the keys at the beach, or stopped for *Pizza Supremes* at the *Quickie Mart,* if the lobsters had just stayed put, if a dozen other events had broken the other way, and he had gotten back just a bit sooner, the story may have taken a marked turn, a node on the branch would have veered his course a bit to the left, or the right, and maybe things would have turned out better. Maybe C would have seen her, maybe even recognized her, on the sidewalk with her children; maybe he would have seen the same eyes, the same smile, that the little knobby-kneed girl from the school bus still had, all those years later. And maybe then, all would have been right with the world.

Maybe.

But things didn't work out that way. They seldom do.

And the life that could have been, wasn't. There was no finding to be made, no one was saved, the regret remained, and none of them were any the wiser.

The whole autograph incident caused a bit of a commotion afront the museum; those two little skinny kids must have recognized Earl as a professional player of some sort: football, basketball, professional wrestler; somebody heard the kid say he played for the Bisons, and a second wave of onlookers moved a little closer, looked a little closer at Earl, squinting, knowing they saw him on television, and just trying to remember his name, trying to figure out which celebrity athlete was standing next to the little blonde model in the red scarf.

And at some point, collectively, like water that forms from nothing into a great wave, it was decided amongst the rabble: *yeah, it's him, it was definitely him,* they recognized him for sure, whomever *him* actually was.

Earl noticed the hunt, the tightening circle, and was whispering frantic to his sister.

"Lilly, I think they're onto us, that we're *alive*! I think they're all zombies, and they're gonna suck our eyeballs out! We gotta go! *We gotta go right now!*"

Before Lilly could answer, he took her arm and whisked her away; he would have carried her under his arm if he had to, and they quickly bounded the steps, into the cavernous museum lobby, buried in a crush of bodies queued at bag check, brushing past a stream of tourist maps and the bulbous bellies and fanny packs of the proletariat.

The two of them threaded through the gauntlet, finding themselves along one of the Memorial Hall walls, beyond the large double-doors, scanning the surging crowd, waiting for C to show; it seemed like forever.

"We lost 'em! We ditched the zombies! This is *way* too many people for me Lilly; I'm kinda scared."

Lilly grabbed his hand, and he squeezed hers tight.

"Don't worry, no one's gonna bother you."

"Then why were those zombies looking at us like lunch? Do they live in that park, and come out to feed! I'm not going in there, *ever*! No wonder I couldn't find the horses, the zombies must have ate 'em all!"

"This isn't Belvidere sweetie, for sure, but even in this place, you are a pretty big guy, tall, big, muscular, and people think you're somebody famous....maybe an athlete, or something."

And the light bulb suddenly lit; Earl solved the mystery. It hit him, like a ton of bricks; he was getting pretty smart about stuff like this – another mystery solved!

Somehow, they must have found out about his eight-hundred-thirty pound world record squat in Margie's gym; that's it! Billy must have tattled in New York, maybe he was even walking in the zombie park outside, and talking too loud - that must be it! C would have never told, never! *It was Billy for sure!* Oh boy, Billy was going to get yelled at by Earl, 'cause he's a tattler! But no time for that now! Word travels fast in Belvidere, and there are only two thousand people; word must *really* go quick around here, 'cause there are eight million of them! Oh boy, now Earl was in even *bigger* trouble, because these weren't eye-sucking zombies, they were much, much worse - *they were panty-throwing groupies*! And they were after him, just like C said they would be, after squatting all that weight!

Earl started to sweat, talking to Lilly a mile-a-minute.

"I knew I should've done a do-over and dropped it! Are the girls gonna start throwing their panties at me? I don't want the groupies, and I don't want their panties....none of them!"

Earl was looking mighty desperate; Lilly eyed him like he was a nut.

"What are you talking about? Dropped what do-over? What panties? Groupies? *What?!* Who've you been talking to?"

Earl's eyes darted around the room, as he slid into a nook in the wall, as much as a guy his size could slide into a nook.

"They're not taking me away from *Chicken Teriyaki*! *No Sir!*"

He whispered defiant, eyes darting about the crowd.

"Oh they will, trust me, they will!"

Lilly said, rolling her eyes at her nutty brother. Just then C caught sight of them, and jogged over, out of breath from the no-stop parking garage run he just did; eight God-damn blocks!

"Jesus, I'm parked a fucking mile away! You got the tix? We only got, must be, less than an hour, way off schedule! Lobsters and *Clerks* and parking is fucking us up; did you get a map *[Lilly waved it in his face]*? Good girl."

Lilly handed him the exhibition map and cocked her head to the one hiding in the shadows.

"What's up with *him*?"

C said, watching Earl cower in the shadows, eyes darting around the room.

"I don't know, something about *do-overs* and *girls throwing panties* and *groupies taking him away;* don't suppose you know anything about that?"

C sighed.

"Yeah, I figured as much. Good job."

Lilly said with a snark. After a short huddle in the corner with Earl, the twosome came out for the second round.

"He's cool, no problems."

Earl smiled and leaned over to Lilly, tickling her ear with two words purred:

Baba Ghanoush

CHAPTER 315 – NOW SHE'S ONE OF *THEM*, A PANTY-THROWER!

The three of them half-jogged to the staircase, and made their ascent, past the second floor birds, mammals and butterflies, past the third level reptiles and amphibians, up to the fourth floor landing....the top floor.

"Okay Earl, this one's for you. You've been dreaming about this guy since you were a kid, chasing you around, so I figured you might want to really meet him, face-to-face, real-deal....ready?"

"Ready."

Earl parroted; for what, he didn't know. But just as soon as they crossed the wide hall, before they even got into the massive room, Earl saw him. His eyes bugged; his heart raced.

"Holy mackerel! He's way *way* bigger than me! Way! Holy cow! Hope he's not hungry!"

And Earl ran, dodging and weaving amongst the dozens of little kids that always circle the exhibit, always, trying to get closer, leaning over the glass.

"That's pretty cool C; do you know how many times I've heard about that dinosaur coming up over the *Big Hill*, with the eyeballs stuck between his teeth, snorting snot and drool whatever other gross descriptions run around his nutty head. Pretty cool to finally meet him, thanks."

And she kissed him on the cheek; Cord was losing track of the number of kisses she gave him today; he would have to plan forty-year old birthday trips every weekend, maybe every day.

The T-Rex looked like a runner in the blocks; ready to sprint out of the hall, crouched over, his back parallel to the floor, his long tail sticking out straight behind him.

He was walking on what looked to be a white rock, like sandstone, behind a tiny glass fence; his six-inch teeth looked dark-chocolate, his bones, a half-lighter shade of same.   He was everything in Earl's dream, and more. Lilly circled him slowly, looking at his barrel rib cage, his tiny arms, his enormous three-clawed feet. She was so tiny, she was so beautiful....that was all C could think, as he watched the two of them, brother and sister, circle the big lizard in awe.

"Now don't be jealous, you're still my favorite, but look how *big* he is!"

Earl had snuck Jonesy from his pocket, and let him eye the T-Rex, then shut him safely back in his box, and slipped him in his pocket. He didn't want to take any chances with the T-Rex getting jealous and eating Jonesy!

Earl was so mesmerized, he forgot how scared he was; not of the dinosaur, but of the swarms of little people around him, and the parents trying to corral the herd. Every now and then, when the scary thoughts crept in, he did what C told him too, he said that funny eggplant word that Cord taught him, and that helped, it helped a lot: *baba ghanoush.* They might even eat some later, some real baba ghanoush C said, which made it even better.

Baba Ghanoush.

Parents and kids standing a bit too close heard Earl talking to himself, repeating it aloud, over and over, in all different accents, all different voices, from baritone to soprano: *baba ghanoush, baba ganoush, baba ghanouj.* Not a one stayed very close beyond the third iteration; they discretely backed away from the eggplant man; *it worked!*

Earl rushed from one dinosaur to the next, with Lilly and C in tow. The three of them wound their way through the rest of the fourth floor, seeing the brontosaurus (now they called it an apatosaurus - news to Earl – and a name he simply refused to use – it was a brontosaurus, always was, and always would be), the barosaurus (the biggest dinosaur there; Earl thought for sure it was really a diplodocus - they must have labeled it wrong) the triceratops, the stegosaurus, the dimetrodon....all the ones all the little boys, and Earl, had long committed to memory.

In the end, he was exhausted.

"That was the coolest ever!"

"Yeah it was. Sorry we don't have more time, but this is what I really wanted you to see anyway, the T-Rex; glad?"

"Best birthday ever! *Baba Ghanoush!*"

"Stop saying that Earl; it's annoying."

Lilly said.

Earl leaned into her and whispered, ever-so-low.

"*Baba Ghanoush.*"

She mumbled and cursed under her breath, as she walked away in a huff.

"It works!"

Earl yelled again, his arms up touchdown style.

"Good. Okay, let's go; lots more to do and running out of time to do it."

C announced.

"*More?*"

Earl asked, as if there could possibly being anything cooler and better than what he had seen so far.

"*Way more!* No time to rest."

Ay said, which Earl responded to by rubbing his hands together furious, whilst his tongue quickly ran over and under his lips double-time....vintage Earl.

Down and out and off they went, waving the museum goodbye. As they walked the eight long blocks to the parking garage behind the museum, C stopped to kick yet more Sandy Hook out of his shoes; it seemed like an endless supply of sand. As Cord rapped his shoe against a lamp post, Earl noticed the store before them; it was closed, but the front plate glass was dimly-lit nonetheless, and basking in the amber light were draped, dangled and displayed a menagerie of lingerie.....*vintage* lingerie.

"What the heck?"

Lilly's voice trailed off, as she peered into the window, eyeing antique mannequins and a large French commode, the drawers half-open, neatly displaying a panoply of panties, bras, corsets, slips and nightgowns....intricate weaves of silk, velvet and lace, in muted colors of the night. They were *beautiful*, more beautiful than anything Lillian had ever seen, or worn.

"They *sell* you other people's *used* underwear?"

Earl said, with a boys-scrunched face, then added.

"That's kinda yucky."

"Lilly, clean out that pantie drawer; you'll be rich!"

C said through a smirk.

But Lillian paid the boys no heed; she was mesmerized by the couture laid before her. Her underwear were *nothing* like this, not even close. If the shop was open, she'd be inside and a customer, for sure, for life. How cool was New York? Somebody actually thought about, and opened, a used lingerie store....*used!* And they are *in* business; people are buying their stuff! And why wouldn't they? The pieces were simply breathtaking, like art you could wear. *Could you imagine such a store in Belvidere?* She thought to herself; it would be the talk of the decade, and not a single person would *ever* buy a single thing. All they would do is complain and snicker and laugh and berate, and never once step a toe inside. But here, in New York, such a store is tucked-in on a simple street, just like all the rest, thousands upon thousands of stores on thousands of streets everywhere. And people were looking, and enjoying, and, apparently, buying.

Used underwear.

This was, indeed, the coolest store she had ever seen, ever. She turned to C and purred like a kitten, sliding her hand gently along C's cheek.

"You *wish* I cleaned it out, so you could see me in some of *this*, and some of *that*! Isn't that right, chit-boy?"

She grabbed C's chin, and turned it, like a mannequin, to the left, and to the right, eyeing the goods like candy. And of course, she was right; spot on.

The underwear shop unfortunately stayed behind; Lilly committed the name to memory, soon to be a customer online. She couldn't wait; that stumble-upon was, by far, the trip highlight for her, and the fact it was just happenstance made it all the more special.

Serendipity.

Only in New York she thought to herself, picturing that lovely couture hugging her body. She was already in love with this City, madly in love.

Soon enough, the trio were in the car, top-down, and headed back to *Mid-Town*, half-around *Columbus Circle* and down Broadway, heading south. It was 6:19 pm and the sun was hanging low, about to fade, when they came upon the constant flash, blink and blitz of *Times Square*.

It was sensory overload.

A non-stop staccato of lights, color, words and figures on too-tall pixel boards affixed to every flat surface, stretching for city-blocks. Forever glass towers rising like pikes in the sky, covered in blinking neon – pinks, blues and ruby-reds, reflecting kaleidoscope off each other. Billboards swathed in green superheroes and women and men in tight underwear with so much skin, shaved and smooth and stubbled and rough....bronzed bodies and bathing suits and beach scenes....too-tight jeans and cowboy hats and Levis and white teeth and smiles....everyone with smiles. Pepsi and Coke and beer and pop and Virgin and Disney shouting at the Mustang from all sides. Hordes of people hustling across intersections, side-stepping scaffolding and traffic cones....dodging taxis and buses, trucks and pedicabs, cruisers and bikes. Flashing *Walk* and *Don't-Walk* and *Don't-Block-The-Box* and *One Way* and *No-Left, No Stopping, No Standing* yelling from all directions. Earl and Lillian looked left and right and up and down and back again, taking in snippets and splashes of coffee and cameras and Hershey and watches and boobs and maps and flags....flags *everywhere.*

The sidewalks oozed crowds, mass migrations of tourists moving east and west, with equal numbers moving north and south, up and down, here and there....armies of ants....madness. The Mustang crawled along, wading slowly through the jetsam.

Earl and Lilly drank it all in, drunk on the electronic *Kool-Aid*.

Starting blocks before, and through the heart of the *Square*, Lilly tried to commit the theaters, the signs, to memory: the *Ambassador*, the *Walter Kerr*, followed by the *Barrymore*, the *Brooks-Atkinson* and the *Richard Rodgers*....the *Lunt Fontanne*, the *Minskoff*, *Winter Garden*, *Helen Hayes*, the *Shubert*, the *Broadhurst*, the *Lyceum*. In the end, cramming her brain, going by way too quick, too fast, she'd end up forgetting them all, except the *Minskoff*, because it sounded like a fancy coat....one you take off, wearing nothing underneath.

"Hey Earl, remember staying up with mom and eating popcorn and watching the ball drop on New Year's; this is where it always was!"

"Always is; still is."

C corrected, as Earl nodded yes with a smile to the memories.

"Can we come in this year, C, you think, and see the ball?"

Earl asked.

"Sure, why not; you're seasoned New Yorkers now, don't see why not."

"Cool, maybe Car...."

And Earl stopped his sentence cold; Lilly finished the thought for her brother.

"She can come too Earl."

"Really Lilly?"

Earl perked, spinning and smiling at his sister in the back seat.

"Sure, she just has to stay in the trunk."

"*Hey!* That's...."

And Earl saw that Lilly was smiling devilish, with her black shades back in place, sunglasses at dusk. So Earl smiled too, and put his on. C saw the drill, and completed the trio, slipping on his cheap sunglasses.

Cruising Manhattan in a Mustang, top down, shades on, with the night sky creeping up on them. Life was pretty damn good.

Lilly was feeling better about herself; she didn't see any knockouts in the museum (not that the hotties would necessarily be hanging out with the dinosaurs, but hey), or on the ride since. It got her confidence up. And as she watched the Broadway show houses pass on the side streets, she remembered always wanting to see a play, a real Broadway play. Maybe she would come in on her own and do just that. Yeah, maybe she just would - *alone*. And that's when the feeling rushed over her; it started with the lingerie, but it blossomed in *Times Square,* the feeling that this place, New York, was pretty damn cool, and she could see herself here, visiting here, living here, staying here....*forever.* It felt that good, that right, that fast. And all of a sudden, Belvidere felt so backward, so remote, insignificant, so non-vintage lingerie....so *not* her.

Maybe she was meant to be a New York girl after all; maybe Carol knew that too, deep down, and had discouraged her because of it. All of a sudden she was feeling good, confident, sassy, like she could *own* this City.

And it felt better than good.

"**Serve it up bitch!** *What's next!*"

She yelled from the back seat, all cocky.

"This is the best birthday ever, for as long as I live!"

Earl announced, from nowhere, as the Mustang jumped a wobbly manhole cover on 40th Street, where they had turned a few moments earlier, out of the *Times Square* thicket.

"Good, and it's gonna get even better!"

C slapped him in the chest as he said it.

"And you, *Serve-It-Up* girl, just chill and keep your panties on back there."

C yelled.

"Maybe I will, maybe I won't."

C looked at Earl, and him back.

"Wow girl, we haven't even *started drinking* yet! That sexy little store got a hold of ya, huh? Maybe we should go back."

And they both heard her rustling around behind them, slipping and sliding on the leather seat.

"What the hell you doing?"

C yelled, trying to catch a glimpse of something dirty in the rear mirror. And from nowhere, a pair of the tiniest, frilliest black panties landed square on C's bald head, followed by a hysterical cackle from the back.

Earl eyes bugged, eyebrows topping his shades.

"Did you hear that laugh! We're in trouble for sure! She's one of 'em, C! The groupies must have got her in the dinosaur place, like the body snatchers! Now she's one of *them*, a panty-thrower!"

CHAPTER 316 – STOP QUICK; SHE WAS THAT CLOSE. *THAT CLOSE*

"I'm *keeping* these you know; you're not getting them back."

C stuffed them in his jacket pocket.

"So keep 'em, sniff 'em, wear 'em if you want! I'm buying all new ones, or maybe I don't need any at all! I kind of like the breeze."

Another hysterical cackle from behind. Oh, how C wanted to be that breeze.

"Did you bring booze or something?"

Cord said, convinced she was already half in the bag.

"No, just *feeling good;* is that okay with you?"

"Yeah, absolutely. If you want to throw any other clothes up here, that's fine too!"

"**No it's not!** No more clothes-throwing Lilly! I'm your brother and it's *my* birthday; no more breezes and no more nakedness allowed in the car, keep your clothes *ON!*"

"Hey, close your eyes then!"

C yelled, hand-slapping Earl in the chest.

"Ow!"

"Sorry Earl. Okay, I'll be a good girl, give me back my little black panties C, and stop sniffing them."

"I'm not sniffing them, they are in my jacket pocket! But *no way* are you getting them back; that was a one-way toss. They're off for the duration; no good-girls are allowed in this car, and keep quiet Earl!"

C said.

"I think I saw you sneak a sniff, C; I think I did. You didn't sneak very well, just saying."

Earl said, with an air of disapproval, his nose scrunched.

"I didn't sniff the underwear; Christ!"

"I think you did; Jonesy thinks you did too....you're a sneaky sniffer."

Earl looked matter-of-fact, he had Jonesy's box open, and the lizard was giving C the evil eye.

Lilly smirked at the show; it was a play and she was center stage! C could keep her underwear, and sniff away, she didn't care one bit! She knew he would never give them back, and she didn't want them back. Just having them off, the freedom, the air circulating under her skirt, between her legs, the feel of being a little dirty-girl, got her so juiced, so fast, she could have finished herself with the two of them right in the car in less than ten seconds....she was all-of-a-sudden wired. And she liked it. She rubbed her legs together, clit-friction, but had to stop quick; she was that close.

That close.

CHAPTER 317 – NEITHER WAS THE WISER....YET

On came the night sky; reluctantly, off came the shades.

The Mustang slid through the end of dusk down 40th; in two blocks they passed a small green gem - *Bryant Park*, now cloaked in the charcoal of early evening. The car saddled alongside a massive, three story edifice, polished white blocks of *Beaux Arts* stone, eleven palladium windows topped with eleven lions, heads and manes glaring down at the trio from the second story facade....icy stares, with ears perked, nostrils flared and teeth bared.

They let the Mustang pass without a word.

The light was green, and they crossed 5th Avenue, never seeing the two regal marble recumbant lions - *Patience* and *Fortitude* - in front of the massive Library entrance; either one could eat Carol's front porch lions in one snap....chicken-feed. But the two massive lions also let the Mustang pass in silence, as the ink of night swallowed them whole in the rear-view.

Lilly and Earl missed it all; they had eyes peeled down the long narrow canyon, sliced between skyscrapers whose tops they couldn't see; the scene through the windshield was a medley of cars, people, bikes and lights cutting the night; a migration heading east, to points unknown.

Including them.

Cord caught a second green and hooked a left on Park Avenue, heading north and idled at a red. He depressed the button on the dash, and the roof responded, folding back into place. The lid quietly clicked shut, and the open-air ride came to an end.

Rising before them, two blocks away, reaching high into
the night sky lay Earl and Lillian's next destination, but
neither was the wiser....yet.

2325

CHAPTER 318 – THE KNOCK-OUT PUNCH:
BABA GHANOUSH

"Pop the trunk."

No *please*, no nothing, just a flashlight-in-the-face from the tree-thick, butt-ugly security guard, who appeared at the driver's side door, after a slow shuffle; neither foot left contact with the floor. It apparently took too much effort.

The Mustang idled mild about two car-lengths into the parking garage ramp off the sidewalk. Cord eyed the gnome, with her neatly sewn, over-sized flag-patch affixed to her uniform, stretched tight over ample folds of fat.

It read, in bold blue stitching, affixed to an unfurled American flag:

Viper Two Strike Force
Security Management Consultants For Freedom

He should have laughed at the troll; instead, he was annoyed.

"Pop the trunk? We're just trying to park."

She eyeballed Cord hard, processing his response in her tiny brain. From nowhere, she yipped like a toy dog into a shoulder-mounted mike, which made Earl jump.

"Ricky! Viper's got a problem here!"

She laid a beefy mitten, with squat chubby fingers, on the edge of the door, like she was holding it in place.

A sloppy, half-tall Latino with a scraggly goatee, baggy black pants and untied designer high-tops ambled over, seeming taller when saddled up beside the four-foot round viper. He was one of those guys in a perpetual state of half-sleep, annoyed at being distracted from doing nothing in his plexiglass parking garage *command* booth.

He didn't say a word, he just stared at Cord, curled his nose and gave a half-nod to the butch-dyke, all the while working hard a wad of stale gum.

"Whatever; I'll find another garage."

C said, more than mildly annoyed.

"Do you realize this is a sensitive building sir, priority parking?"

"Obviously not; step aside and I'll back up, find another garage."

And to drive home the point, C glared at the hobgoblin as he depressed the gas heavy, revving the engine. The Mustang responded, growling loud, like it meant business, while standing in park.

She tightened her grip on the car door, like a don't-let-go candy bar, and pushed here fat face closer to C's, staring at him with her best *security-guard-stare*. Her chubby cheeks were inches from Cord; and he, for some reason, focused on a smear of half-dried barbecue wing sauce tucked in the corner of her distorted mouth, residue from an early-shift, fast-food chicken snack.

"Oh no you won't sir; no you won't."

She warned, a hint of hot sauce mixing with the words, enveloping Cord in a toxic waft. He pulled back in disgust at her warm exhale, a mix of moist, tangy barbecue and bad breath.

"Listen, I have an appointment I'm going to be late for; either let me in, or let me out! Pick a door!"

C snapped annoyed, trying his best to avoid her breath.

"What's *that* supposed to mean sir? What kind of *doors* might you be referring to? Evil-doer doors? *Ricky, some help here! Viper One to Viper Two!*"

The Latino, on cue, leaned lazily into the window, pushing his scrawny face next to her round one, looking for those supposed suspicious *doors.*

"Oh for Christ's sake C, just pop the fucking trunk for the lard-ass!"

Lilly yelled from the back, which promptly got her a flashlight high-beam in the face.

As one could imagine, that wasn't such a smart move by *Viper One*, nor was Lilly's immediate response.

"Hey! *Ass-Munch!* I'm gonna take that flashlight and shove it up your fat...."

"It's my Birthday!"

Earl shouted over Lilly, which got him the swing of the flashlight beam, which wasn't nearly big enough to take all of him in.

Both vipers instinctively recoiled; they never saw something so massive wedged in a car seat, made all the more ominous by the shadows of the night. In fact, it wasn't entirely clear where the shadows ended and the mammoth began; but whatever was planted in that co-pilot seat, it was fucking *huge.*

Earl took in a mighty gulp of air, and began to spew rapid-fire.

"....and I'm already forty! And I've never, *ever* been forty before, but it didn't feel any different at 12:31 than it did right before that! I don't what the big deal is, I can still run fast, *way faster* than C, sorry C, just saying, and this is my first time ever, *ever* past the Gill farm, I've never even been past the stone row! I used to play there all by myself and I fell off once and hurt myself, but I was okay after my mom rubbed my elbow and kissed it, it felt way better then, and I fell another time in the chicken manure coop, but I didn't *really* fall that time, my sister pushed me, she always says she didn't, but she did, I *know* she did, and *she* knows I know she did, don't you Bibby, and *don't fib*! And I didn't smell good; chickens don't smell good, but I like the cows, they smell good, they're my favorite! And they keep me company; I like the smell of cow manure, not chicken poop, but *definitely* cow poop, I really do! It makes me happy, and I don't even know why! And then we were in the car and we talked about Squirrel No. 631, but I can't tell you about that, 'cause it's a big secret and I'm not talking about that anymore, 'cause I sometimes tell secrets I'm not supposed to and then I get sad, and then we saw signs for Newark, but we didn't go there, no way, but we did go to Sandy Hook and let the lobsters go free, but we still have a claw, 'cause it fell off of Louie's friend, and that's all that's in the trunk, a lonely lobster claw in the cooler, and I feel bad about that, but they are on their way to Panama, all three of them, Louie and his lobster brothers....*right now!* So I feel good about that, and I'll see Louie when I'm swinging in the hammock, my butt scraping the dock just like C said, right C? And we'll see the little blue fish swimming around the coral who's name is the same as mine! And I still don't know why Sandy has a hook, that's still a big mystery, but we did find Skeleton Island, we solved that one, didn't we C *[Earl poked Cord in the side, and he nodded yes, smiling the whole time]*?! But Ken and Sandy weren't there, and the water wasn't oily at all, and there were no *Wild Things* either, unless they were hiding in the sand or in the water, but I don't think so, 'cause they're too big. **Let the Wild Rumpus Start!** And that's my favorite line: **Let** *the Wild Rumpus Start!* I love saying that! And I saw dinosaurs on the fourth floor and they were even bigger than me! But I still don't know how they got up the steps, I forgot to ask about that one, and even though some of the names were wrong I still liked them. And there were zombies in the park, but I don't think they were zombies at all, I think they were really groupies pretending to be zombies, but they didn't throw their underwear at me, like groupies are supposed to, but Lilly did, even though she's not supposed to do that, especially in the car, but it was okay, because Lilly is wearing mommy's favorite red scarf and she looks so pretty in it and that made me happy and I know it makes my mom happy; she didn't tell me yet, but I just know, and I gave my autograph by the dinosaur place to two little brothers who looked *exactly* alike, and one was hugging my leg and the other was kissing Lilly's hip and even though they thought I was a bison, I'm not, I'm Earl, not a bison, I'm Earl, and it's **my birthday today**! And *this is the best day of my whole life, so far; the best day ever! And it's not even over yet, right C? Not by a long shot!"*

And Earl smiled wide, showing off that goofy, toothy grin, at the ugly troll, leaning into the Mustang driver's side window. Earl never took a *single* breath, not a one, through the entire recount.

Till now, now he took in a big one, heaving his huge chest.

Viper Two Strike Force stood silent, mouths agape, and simply stared at the monstrous smiling man in the front seat, speechless. They seemed to be teetering on the edge, not quite sure what to do, or what to make of the man in the co-pilot seat.

Then Ricky slowly started chewing his stale gum again. He shook his head and cracked the slightest half-smile, a convert. The little round troll, however, with the bad, barbecue breath, hadn't been turned, not yet; she was still on the edge.

So Earl leaned toward the driver-side window, half into C's lap, smiled wider and delivered to her, in the sweetest whisper, the knockout punch:

Baba Ghanoush

CHAPTER 319 – CRANED HIS NECK NORTH, AND HIS MOTHER SMILED

"Wasn't that the best ever C! We got *priority* parking, for free! We're VIPs! And Juanita, wasn't she nice? Okay, her breath was a little stinky, I'll give you that, but nowhere near as bad as Lilly's in the morning!"

"Hey fuck-nuts, enough with the breath shit!"

Lilly snapped, shoving her brother in the arm. Earl ignored the shove and the snark, continuing to prattle on.

"And she even wished me happy birthday and asked me if I wanted one of her chicken-wings! She doesn't look like she gives them up too easy, just saying, so that was pretty nice of her, wasn't it C! And Ricky even shook my hand, but he gave me a limp fish, those are the worst shakes ever, but he was nice anyway, for a limp fish. *Baba Ghanoush* really works!"

"Yes it does, it certainly does."

C said, as he pushed opened the second door, and they spilled into the massive space, the *Main Concourse*.

And what a space it was.

Lilly stopped dead in her tracks. She kinda knew where she was, then she saw the ceiling, and the hundreds of points of light, and smiled broad, murmuring *Oh my God* to herself.

She *definitely* knew where she was. She whispered to Earl, pulling on his arm.

"Sweetie, do you know what this is? Where we are?"

She placed her left open hand on his back, and rubbed it in a light circle, just like her mom did.

"No Bibby….no."

"It's *Grand Central Station*! Remember mom was always gonna take us here and show us all the animals and people and stars up on the big ceiling? *Remember?* Well, we're here, we're *really* here, and so are they, just waiting for us all these years, like she said they would. Look up, look up!"

She whispered to her little brother.

So he did; Earl craned his neck north, and his mother smiled.

CHAPTER 320 – IT NEVER HAPPENED; SHE WENT AWAY, AND IT NEVER HAPPENED

Before them lay eighty-thousand square feet of Mediterranean sky, illuminated with countless scores of sparkling stars, pulsating white-light, high overhead, spanning the ceiling of the grand hall that engulfed them.

And stretched in a graceful arc across an otherworldly cerulean night, woven amongst the thousands of gold leaf points, was a parade of men in togas - brandishing swords, followed by jumping fish, a raging bull, a giant crab, and off by itself....a unicorn.

A *beautiful* unicorn, wings spread, emerging from the clouds, as if to greet the trio.

Lilly, mouth agape, couldn't believe it; she couldn't peel her eyes from it. Since she was eight years old, she had waited to meet the unicorn, a promise made long ago, never forgotten, finally fulfilled. She smiled to herself.

"It's backwards, you know."

Lilly said aloud, to whomever was listening. And they both were.

"What's backwards?"

C said.

Lilly pointed and swept her hand gracefully, left to right across that magnificent ceiling, following the trajectory.

"The zodiac, the astronomy figures up there, across the sky, it's backwards."

C just shook his head, waiting for more. Earl listened intently; he knew this must be important stuff - Lilly had her important-looking face on, and whenever she did, it always made Earl pay extra-special attention.

"It's because it's not *us* looking up at it, it's heaven looking down *at* it, looking at us; it's *their* perspective, heaven's that is, not ours. That's the story anyway; not everybody believes that, they think the artist just made a big mistake, but my mom believed it was really from heaven, and so do I….*so do I*."

Lilly's voice trailed off with the second one, as if she was talking to directly to her mom.

"And so do I; if Lilly and mom believe it, then so do I."

Earl whispered, poking C in the side, to be sure he was listening.

"Me too."

Said C, matter-of-fact.

Lilly turned to Cord, with serious search in her eyes.

"How did you know? How did you *know* to come here?"

Lilly questioned, and following the first two was the implicit third question, the unasked one, the most important query; did her mom tell him to bring them here? She must have, to have Lillian finally meet her unicorn, she *must have*! This was simply too important to be just dumb-luck; there was no other explanation. Lilly was convinced.

"I didn't."

C said, flat. Lilly pressed, brushing aside Ay's answer.

"Then *why* are we here? Come on, you just picked *here* by chance? One of the most important places in the whole world to me that I've never been, and never told you about? My mom always promised to bring me here, to this place, to meet *that* unicorn, *my* unicorn; I was eight years old when she first promised, and I've dreamed of this day ever since. And this, coming here, was just a fluke? Really?"

"Lilly I swear. We have an appointment here, but I didn't *pick* here, where we are going, for the appointment, was already here – you had to come here to do it. Actually, you could do it, this appointment, either here or downtown, at the *Trade Center*, well, what used to be the *Trade Center* anyway. That was my first choice, downtown, but when I tried to set it up, they told me it was completely booked, for weeks out. *That* was my first choice, downtown, not here. So we *had* to come here; this was the only other choice."

Lilly wasn't convinced.

"What appointment? What was booked? What are we *doing here*?"

Lillian pressed.

"*That* is a surprise, young lady; and at exactly 7:45 pm you'll find out, which is in, can you see the clock? What time is it?"

C pointed down the grand sweep of regal marble stairs before them, which led like a carpet to the *Information Booth*, smack in the center of the *Concourse*.

The *Information Booth;* it still was, and had always been, *the* meeting place, the perennial spot for anyone and everyone who chose to meet in *Grand Central* since the *Station* was born, almost a hundred years ago. And the majestic, four-faced clock set atop the booth – that regal timepiece **was** *Grand Central* incarnate, more so even than the famous zodiac ceiling. There was even talk of a *secret* door in the floor, beneath the clock, that concealed a spiral staircase leading to points unknown below the station; it was another fantastical morsel her mother dished to a wide-eyed eight-year old Lilly about this special place, when she would tell her daughter bedtime stories, sitting ginger on the edge of Lillian's bed. It was some of her favorite quiet times with her mom, those bedtime stories, shared just with her. Lilly didn't share that tidbit mom-memory with the boys, she kept that one to herself, to just between her and her mother, as it always had been.

Lillian didn't answer C's question; rather, she simply began to ramble, to reminiscence, providing an explanation to a question that wasn't asked.

"We were always going to go, together, to that clock, in the middle, my mom and me. She said it was a *really* special place. And then we'd look up at the ceiling, together, and find my unicorn; she always said he was jumping out of the clouds, because he was so happy he was gonna get to finally meet me, to see me. He'd been waiting a long, long time, she would say, and soon, we would finally meet. Then she said we'd walk, arm in arm, to the ticket booths and I could just: *pick a train, any train, going anywhere [Lilly waved her hand effortlessly across the broad stretch of digital board, listing the comings and goings of scores of locomotives, of passenger cars carrying pilgrims to points unknown, far and wide] and we'll go, just you and me, best friends forever, on our own little adventure.* Anyway, that's what my mom said. But it never happened; she went away, and it never happened."

CHAPTER 321– A LITTLE FISH IN A BIG POND

"It's 6:41."

A diminutive voice, off to the left, broke the melancholy.

It was a little old lady, several inches shy of five feet, impeccably dressed in multiple shades of the light blues senior women like to wear, color-coordinated from her scarf to her shoes; the kind of coordination that matters to women her age. She was sitting alone, nursing what looked like a diet cola; sitting at a high-top, her feet dangling in the air, like a little kid at the candy counter.

"I'm sorry, I didn't mean to eavesdrop, but you were talking kinda loud, and I couldn't help it, to hear, I mean. Anyway, it's 6:41....now :42."

"Thanks, no need to apologize; sorry if we were a bit too loud."

C whispered and smiled.

The woman smiled back, the kind of warm smile Cord always got from little old ladies that thought he was somehow sweet, and took a liking to him. It happened all the time, and she was no different.

She took in a breath, ready to chat with her new friends. She wanted to tell them that she used to meet her husband at the clock, too many years ago, and how she loved the ceiling too, and other stories, many more, she thought they would enjoy, but she didn't speak fast enough, and the entourage turned and moved further away. She sighed, widowed once again, to nurse her cola, all alone in a train station, teeming with thousands.

C herded the duo to the top of the marble staircase, gazing down upon the immense *Concourse* three flights below, like a king.

"Okay, here's the plan, you got till 7:40 *[looking at Lilly]*, that's *exactly* fifty-eight minutes, *not fifty-nine*, but fifty-eight. Then we meet at the big clock; got it?"

"What am I gonna do for an *hour*? Why are we splitting up?"

Lilly asked.

"Because Earl and I have something *very* important to do, and I figured you'd want to wander....no? You can stay with us if you're scared?"

"I'm not scared, jerk!"

Oh yes she was, Lilly thought to herself; *she most certainly was scared to death.*

"Why can't I do what you're doing? What trouble are you getting my brother into now?"

"If I recall, last time I left him with *you*, he was attacked by groupies."

"That's right!"

Earl chimed in.

Lilly frowned, seeing she wasn't winning this one. C smiled at her, pushing her gently on the shoulder.

"Go have a little fun, explore, it's New York, you'll eat up an hour in a flash, trust me."

She smirked at him, devilish, and spun on her heels.

"Just remember, *7:40,* and don't be late!"

C scolded, pointing his finger at her.

"Okay, *Daddy.*"

She said it sexy, too sexy, and she saw it got him. And she gleaned, with those two tiny words, that Ay now wanted her to stay. But before C got the words out, she spun and glided princess down the polished marble steps, floating effortlessly onto the grand stage that lay before her, the *Main Concourse*. She had no underwear on, and the breeze flitted up and around her thighs, her open crotch, and it gave her a little jolt. She wondered if people could see that she was pantie-less, and, surprisingly, she didn't care if they could.   In fact, she wanted the whole world to know it, and that she didn't care in the least. That thought made her smile, as she strode confident off the last of the stairs, and entered the throng that milled, to and fro, all around her.

And so it began; the curtains drew, Lillian Liddell stepped through, and New York City got its first taste of a little fish in a big pond.

CHAPTER 322 – THAT LITTLE FISH *OWNED* NEW YORK

She was a little kid swimming doggie-paddle toward the deep end of the pool for the very first time, not holding onto the side, or anyone's arm; no tube, no floaties, all alone, on her own....no help.

She had butterflies....major.

It was from all the taunts Lillian had endured, directly, but mostly indirect, from Carol Crowe. Years of inculcations that she was swimming in a little-shit pond that no one cared about; step outside of Belvidere and you're just another not-so-young face – *no one* will pay attention, no one will give a shit about you. And if Lilly ever dared to come to *her* town, Manhattan, she would be laughed off the street as some airhead, blonde bumpkin. She wouldn't get a second look; she wouldn't even be a small fish in a big pond - she wouldn't be *anything,* she'd be a big, fat nothing.

She would simply be a nobody from nowhere that no one would give a shit about. And there was a name for that, Carol Crowe would say: Lilly Liddell would be *invisible*.

And Lilly would return the venom, and pretend it was simply jealousy. But deep down, she believed Carol; she believed every word of it. That she was an *invisible nothing*.

And now she was in Carol's town, *her* town, and Lilly was scared. She thought this could be all hers when she was dreaming with the top down, driving with the boys through *Times Square,* safely secured in the cocoon of the car. But now, she wasn't nearly so sure.   The doubt ran laps in her head, as she weaved silently through the fabric of bodies, standing tall, shoulders square and walking in a regal, model's gait, trying her best to look composed and sure-of-herself, when she was really neither of those things, on her way to the safety of the *Clock*, like it was home base, or something, like in playing tag....a safe place she could hold onto, breath deep, and regroup.

She needed to get to that *Clock*.

And lost in thought, scared shitless, as she approached the center of the *Main Concourse*, she didn't notice what was happening, the stir, which cut like the wake of a boat behind her.

Everyone around her was doing it.

Busy people, distracted people, hurrying on their way somewhere or another; but regardless, they were all doing it, men and women, young and old; *all* of them.

And most didn't even try to hide it.

They couldn't help but look, couldn't help but notice, the absolute whirlwind as it passed by them. Lillian Liddell was *that* stunning.

Even in New York, even at nearly forty-two years old, walking alone in a simple, white cotton top, short black skirt and red scarf, strolling as if shooting a scene in a movie, Lilly was a show-stopper.

Carol Crowe was successful, confident and beautiful, more so than most, but Carol Crowe *never* got a boat wake like that, and certainly never in her hometown.

And at that moment, although Lillian Liddell was none the wiser, whomever decides such things had already decided.

That little fish *owned* New York.

CHAPTER 323 – THE OLD WOMAN HAD MELTED INTO THE CROWD

Lilly exhaled deep and surveyed the scene, safely anchored to the *Information Desk*, treading water, tethered to a buoy in the middle of the immense marble *Concourse*.

Her gaze drifted to the right, and she saw her brother waving wildly at her. She smiled and waved back.

That's when she first noticed; strangers were looking at her, and more than one.

Oh my God! She quickly looked down at her shoes; could they see through her skirt? That she had no underwear on? Why did she take her damn underwear off! She looked down, patting it, feeling it; it felt fine, no holes, no rips, so see-through fabric. *Oh my God!* It must be something on her face! She frantically wiped around, over and under her nose, her cheeks, her mouth, all over her face. Did she have a loogie in her nose? *Oh my God, how embarrassing!* She fumbled her fingers around, trying to feel anything crusty, anything wet, anything at all, snot or otherwise, that shouldn't be there. *How could this happen today? Here!* Jesus, why the hell didn't Earl tell her?! Is that why he was waving, to say she had snot or something on her face?! All the way from over there?! It must be ***huge!***

Her heart was racing, but she didn't feel anything, not a thing, her face was smooth as silk.

She gingerly looked up and an attractive older woman was standing beside her, squinting, trying to figure out the train times on the informational flier – the *Metro-North Timetables*. She was standing close to Lilly, so close they were almost touching arms. If it had been anyone but a harmless old lady, it would have been too close. She was surprised she hadn't noticed her before, but then again, people were milling all around, in controlled chaos.

"Excuse me."

Lilly said, barely above a whisper, with a look of utter distress and embarrassment.

"Is there something on my face?"

The woman turned to look at Lilly; her eyes were warm, inviting and Lillian could tell, immediately, that she was nice. She didn't know how she knew that, she just knew. Someone was lucky to have her as a mom, or a grandma; she had that look, it had that feel.

The woman's eyes slowly scanned Lillian's face, like she was searching, roaming, drinking her in. She gently placed her hand on Lilly's arm; the woman's fingers were bent with arthritis and trembling a bit, like she was nervous, or just had an old-person's shake - Lilly wasn't sure which. But her hand was warm, very warm, and it felt good, and it made Lilly feel safe, in this big, scary place.

Then, after a bit more ponder, she pronounced a verdict, leaning into Lillian as she whispered.

"I'm afraid something's missing dear."

The old woman said.

"Oh my God, what?"

Lilly gasped.

"A smile."

And the woman cupped Lillian's cheek, and beamed at her, like they were old friends. Lillian let out a sigh of relief, and returned the favor.

"I like your scarf."

The woman whispered, although there really was no reason to whisper.

"Thank you, it was my mother's; we used to fight over who got to wear it - we both loved it....so much."

Lilly wasn't sure why she said that.

"She was *very* beautiful, my mom, the most beautiful woman I had ever seen, and I think it looked better on her, but she always said it looked better on me. I haven't worn it in years, too many years; in fact, today's the first day....I'm so glad I did."

The words just kind of fell, and Lilly felt a little odd, like she was sharing a bit too much information with a stranger, no matter how nice she seemed. The woman didn't reply; she simply kept smiling warm at Lilly, admiring the scarf, and the young girl wrapped inside.

Lilly looked skyward, and got a better glimpse of the unicorn; it was actually kind of cartoonish-looking, with a too-fat neck and a goofy smile. But it made Lilly happy nonetheless. It wouldn't have been goofy-looking if she was eight years old, and it wasn't goofy now either, not to her....no way.

"I've been thinking about that unicorn all my life. I was eight, and my mom told me there was a special unicorn, waiting just for me, hiding up on a ceiling in New York City, peeking out around some clouds. And I believed her. She and I were always gonna come into the City, to come to this *Clock*, meet and say hi to the unicorn together and then take a train to wherever I wanted, a real girl's day. She was my *best* friend, best friend ever. She promised me, some day, and I've been thinking about doing this ever since, since I was eight years old, waiting for that special day. But I never got the chance to do it with her; always wanted to, but something always seemed to come up, and then we ran out of time....we ran out of time a *long* time ago *[Lilly sighed]*. Anyway, this is the first time I've ever been here, first time I've met the unicorn *[Lilly looked skyward and gave a half-wave, with a sad-smile];* I wish my mom could've seen it with me, that would have made it even better....the best. And she was right, he's beautiful."

Lilly looked at the old woman, who had been gazing up at the unicorn with her; their eyes met, and Lillian could see the old woman appeared to be crying, just a little bit, like she was trying to hide it, but simply couldn't. Lilly didn't mean to upset her; she could tell the woman wanted to say something, her lips were trembling, like words wanted to flow, but couldn't. Maybe she wanted to say something to console Lillian, but didn't know exactly what those words should be. Or maybe she wasn't going to say anything at all.

Lilly stopped staring at her; she didn't want her to be uncomfortable. She turned to the west and Earl seemed to be bent over, listening intently to Cord, like whatever he was saying was the most important thing in the world. She smiled at the two of them.

"That's my little brother; he's never been here before either - my first time, his first time. I'm here with him and my boyfriend and...."

That just slipped out.

"I mean C, I mean...."

And as Lilly fumbled with the words, trying to correct herself, she turned back toward the woman with a goofy smile of her own. But the space beside her was empty; Lillian was alone.

The old woman had melted into the crowd.

CHAPTER 324 – DOWNING WHISKY AND DOGGING GIRLS IN *GRAND CENTRAL*

C exhaled deeply, cracked his knuckles – all business.

"Okay, now we're not playing until you repeat the rules Earl. I don't trust you giving out the wrong grades cause you feel bad and all; there's no room for sympathy in this Earl, *none*. It is a brutal business, and this is *serious* stuff, the big leagues! Now I know you memorized 'em, every word, like everything else you do, so spill 'em."

C was staring stern at Earl; this was a serious situation, with serious rules. Earl cleared his throat.

"Okay, Rule No. 1, the most important rule - there are no tens! You can't give a ten, because they don't exist, there aren't any. Nine is as high as it gets; no nine and a halfs either, no fractions allowed. Nine is the highest, and even that doesn't come along very often. I don't want to see any nines right out of the gate."

C smirked and nodded his head in approval. Of course it was a regurgitation of what Cord had just said, verbatim.

Earl continued.

"Five is as low as it goes, no need for any specific number less than that – that's just mean. *Less than* is all you have to say, or a thumbs-down, that covers all the under-fives territory, and there's *lots* of them, trust me."

"Okay, what else?"

C said, administering the oral test. And Earl continued to spit back Cord's words.

"Most girls even worth a look are sixes and sevens, but in this place there will be eights, and even some nines, *maybe* more than a few; that's the fun part. And they only get that if the *whole package* rates; no eights for a pretty smile on a dumpy girl! There's no *but she's probably pretty on the inside*; no room for that kind of sympathy here, no sir!"

"Okay, okay, you got it. Now, last thing; what's the super-most important rule ever, even more important than Rule No. 1."

"We can't tell Lilly!"

"That's right; she'll have our heads if she finds out we're grading girls in *Grand Central* like cattle....this is *our* little secret, okay?"

*[Earl shook his head an emphatic yes, and crossed himself, even though C didn't ask him to....that's how important it was that Lilly **didn't** find out! Oh boy, if she did, they were both in big trouble! Hide-the-forks kind of big trouble! Goners for sure! Earl was so excited, C had told him he played this game all over the world, and would play it someday with Earl when there were some real women to watch, besides the same old-same olds going in and out of Sam's Market or going to church around the Park. This was the big leagues, C said....Earl was in the big leagues!]*

Of course, Lilly knew all about this stupid *game* C played; Ay had told Earl about it a hundred times, usually in front of Lilly, just to get her riled. She thought it was demeaning and childish and told Earl he would be in *big* trouble if he ever played it with C and she found about it; **big trouble** was all she said, it was all Bibby had to say, and Earl's imagination filled in the rest of just what that might mean for him, and there were *no* good endings to that one. The Lilly-risk made playing the game, today, on his birthday, even more fun. He felt like a daredevil.

"What are you smiling at?"

C asked, seeing a devilish grin on Earl's face.

"Let's do it!"

Was all Earl yelped, like a pep talk before the huddle-break.

The two of them settled into a high-top at the balcony bar at *Cipriani Dolci* and ordered two whisky sours, with *Maker's Mark*, well-shaken, on the rocks, no fruit. Earl let C do the ordering; he drank whatever C drank, and usually got drunk on whatever C got drunk on. So today, it was apparently decided they would get drunk on whisky sours.

Earl liked getting drunk with C; he had never been drunk once before Cord came to Belvidere....now he had been drunk lots of times! And getting drunk rating girls like cattle on his birthday – this surely was the best birthday ever! He was licking his lips, spinning his thumbs and scrunching his neck all at the same time; it was *that* kind of exciting....*exciting* overload.

So there they were, the gun about to go off, the horses raring at the gate, two best friends sitting high under the stars of a Mediterranean sky, about to begin the *game*, downing whisky and dogging girls in *Grand Central*.

CHAPTER 325 – A LONG MOAN, DEEP AND DOWN BELOW

Lilly had walked over to the train boards; she was squinting as she read them, concentrating. They were confusing to a novice; she was having a hard time figuring out what they meant and how you actually bought tickets and got to where you wanted to go. She didn't even know where the trains were, where you even got on; she was in one of the most famous train stations in the world, and she hadn't seen a single train yet....not a one.

As best she could tell, there were three lines; the *Hudson Line*, the *Harlem Line* and the *New Haven Line*. She pretended she was with her mom, and tried to figure out what she would have done, which adventure they would have taken, had this all come true....for real.

Okay, first off, she knew she wouldn't do the *Harlem Line;* that just seemed too scary to her, with all the stories she had heard about Harlem as a kid, and as an adult. She didn't even know exactly where Harlem was, compared to where she stood right now, but it didn't matter, coming from Belvidere, it just didn't seem safe – that option was axed with no more rationale than that.

New Haven was in Connecticut, wasn't it? She didn't want to go there. Who wants to go to Connecticut when you're in New York? That was stupid, and boring; Connecticut sucks. Forget Connecticut.

So that left the *Hudson Line;* she assumed that meant it went straight up the Hudson River, someplace north, someplace far. That is where she would have wanted to go with her mom, to the very end of the line, last stop along the tracks, to make the trip as long as she could, to spend as much time as possible with her mom....a two-some. She loved Earl, they both did, more than anything. But Lillian always wanted that long trip alone with her mom, just the two of them, girl-time....alone-time.

She stared up at the board for the Hudson train and looked at what seemed to be the farthest point:

Poughkeepsie

She had heard of that town, but didn't know anything about it: how far it was, how big it was, what it was even there for, what to do when you got there - probably nothing; what could there possibly be to do in a town like that, with a name like that? But who cares? It was probably far, that was the best part, and she liked saying the name; that was good in and of itself.

Poughkeepsie won for no other reason.

She looked at some of the other towns along the way to Poughkeepsie; maybe they could get off and on and off again, do some shopping, some sight-seeing.

She read down the names:

Beacon
Cold Spring
Garrison
Peekskill
Cortlandt
Croton
Ossining
Scarborough

Jesus! She knew none of those towns! Did they even talk about this stuff in geography? Belvidere schools must really suck.

Was Scarborough where the *Scarborough Fair* song came from? She had no idea! She heard of Peekskill, she thought, it sounded kinda familiar, but maybe that was only because it sounded like Poughkeepsie, but maybe not, but why they would have a train stop there she had no idea. She suddenly felt pretty unworldly, and dumb.

Stupid Belvidere, stupid school.

She decided, on her pretend trip with her mom, she would just go to Poughkeepsie....the end of the line. She was sure that was the one she would have picked as a kid, and it was the one she would pick today, if that was in the cards, if this wasn't just a play-pretend game in her head.

Hey wait a minute.

Maybe that *is* what they were doing at 7:40 when they met at the big *Clock*! For a split second, Lillian was thinking the train ride to Poughkeepsie, just a second ago a fantasy, was really gonna happen!

But wait, how would C know that? How would he have known about the train ride with her mom?

But then again, he said coming here was a fluke too! Maybe that was the plan all along, pretend it was a fluke! Maybe her mom told Cord about the whole thing! Holy mackerel, she was going on her train ride! Maybe it was an overnight trip! Earl is always talking about solving mysteries, well, that wasn't so hard, she just solved her own! But wait, she had no clothes! But wait, this is Earl's birthday, not a trip for her, so why would they be going on a girls-day train ride? It made absolutely no sense!

Lilly's head was spinning; she was ecstatic and doubtful and excited and deflated in a span of ten seconds, dreaming of trains and her mom.

Then she heard it; a long moan, deep and down below.

2353

CHAPTER 326 – WONDER IF HE'S ON HIS WAY TO POUGHKEEPSIE

A stomach snarl.

She hadn't eaten but a bite of Manchego and a couple bites of egg salad from the picnic lunch bag in the car; she was too excited, and it finally caught up with her in the *Grand Concourse*. Well, except for the three-quarter bag of *Pizza Supremes* she stole from Earl and scarfed; oh yeah, forgot about those. They must not have done the trick; empty calories.

She smiled; thankful no one heard the hunger rumble, really more of a high-pitched whine. She rubbed her flat belly and spun around, she was now on an treasure hunt, foraging for real food.

"Excuse me, where can I get something to eat?"

A tall fit man in a rush, managed a half-stop, running half-skip, on his way to the trains she still hadn't seen. He pointed east and managed a nice smile at the same time.

"*Central Market*; good stuff."

Was all he said before he was out of sight. He wasn't bad looking, she thought, not bad at all; looks like he works out....nice buns.

Wonder if he's on his way to Poughkeepsie.

CHAPTER 327 – A TRIO OF JUVENILES
HAVING AN ABSOLUTE BALL

Like trick-or-treaters, they seemed to travel in packs. A group of good-looking women followed by droughts of thumbs-down.

But there weren't that many droughts.

A tall, lithe brunette powered by, low-twenties at most, in a short crimson dress; a definite eight. A Mexican waitress lagged a half-step behind, oversized hoop earrings swung as she walked - a solid seven until she smiled, then she notched up to an eight. Earl elbowed C just in time to catch the twenty-something with shoulder-length chocolate hair in black pants before she slipped past them – out of sight, another easy eight. Christ, they were fish in a slipstream, moving too fast!

"Tell 'em to slow down Earl, were missing 'em all!"

C said, exasperated, craning his neck, looking between the rails. Earl shot up and hung over the balcony like a jungle-gym, ready to shout into the crowd to *slow down!* C panicked, and jumped up to pull him back, only to have Earl grin at him, a mischievous little kid.

"Gotcha."

Earl whispered.

In the kerfuffle, they both missed the stately blonde in the muted yellow scarf and pumpkin clutch, with a thin white knit top, tits bouncing in rhythm with each footfall. If she had gotten a grade, it would have been an easy eight, maybe even nine territory.

"Yeah you did, but holy shit Earl, this is *unbelievable*! You never get this many good ones, all coming at ya at once! Christ I'd fuck all of 'em, all of em!"

"Yeah, all of 'em!"

Earl parroted.

"But no nines yet; some close, but still no nines!"

C wagged his finger at Earl, just in case he was thinking of going soft. Earl shook his head no, in earnest agreement.

"But I'd do 'em, Earl; shit I'd do 'em all, riding eights all night long."

"Yeah, I'd do 'em all; riding eights all night long."

Earl repeated, and finished with a *baba ghanoush,* just because he could, and because it was his birthday.

But as he spoke, Earl's eye caught the glint of something moving slow down below, to the right, hugging the ticket counters, out of the main stream. C hadn't seen her; she was an outlier. Earl was excited, like he held a bent rod with a trophy fish on the line, and pointed, well, not really a point, that would have been rude, more of an exaggerated body-nod, at the quarry far below.

C followed the body language and spotted her, swimming slow along the bank of booths.

She was sliding by, a silky-smooth saunter. This one was a bit older, mid to late thirties maybe, but super-thin, in fitted black slacks, pronounced cheekbones, medium bobbed black hair, definite model quality. Her arm was cozily cinched in that of a guy; mother-fucker!

"Holy Christ Earl; you *know* what that is, don't you?"

Earl grinned wide, nodded once, and held up nine fingers in silence. C nodded in appreciation. God, she was a looker. Although Cord hadn't repeated it in his primer, Earl knew the sex-grading; a seven was good for a blowjob at best, an eight meant sex – good enough for sex - and a nine was good enough for sex-plus, the *plus* being whatever else you could think of and get away with....the more depraved, the better.

This one was definitely a *sex-plus*.

And the only suck-ass part was they both saw the guy who *was* getting it, which definitely tarnished the shine. But not much; she was *that* good.

Then from nowhere, came another, and this one was solo. Moving fast, in the middle of the pack, she had an English cap and shoulder-length auburn hair, gray dress slacks and a silk top. She looked up and saw the boys looking at her, and she knew it was her they were spying....girls like that got it all the time. They were busted! But she simply scratched her chin, gave them a little wave and smiled, as she continued on her way.

Another solid nine; the boys were in heaven!

They both fell back in their chairs, started laughing and poking each other, like the two juveniles they were. Time of their lives.

"That was *definitely* sex-plus *plus* my friend, down and dirty dog, just call me *Daddy*."

C said.

"Yeah, dirty dog, just call me *Daddy*."

Mimicked Earl.

As they were savoring the find, acting like horny teenagers, Earl happened to glance to his left. That's when he saw the wicked scowl, and it was *scary*. He immediately clammed up, and started poking C in the chest.

"What?! What are you doing? Don't lose your focus, stay on your game; pay attention down below!"

C said annoyed at the chest-poke; Earl always poked too hard. But Earl kept poking, harder, nodding his head to the left.

And finally C turned, and he saw the diminutive little old lady staring hard at them, the same one from before, who gave them the correct time. And she wasn't wearing a good look, not good at all.

Busted.

"Sorry, that was kinda....sorry."

C said, wondering how much she saw, and heard *[fuck 'em all....do 'em all....sex-plus plus....dirty dog....call me Daddy]*; none of it was good.

"Sorry."

Earl followed suit, sounding more genuine that Cord.

The little old lady didn't let them off the hook that easy. She didn't make a sound, she just stared with flared nostrils and grandma eyes that meant you were in trouble. But after ample punishment had been meted, she let up and gave a half-smile – detention over. Then she demurely held up eight fingers.

C smiled and launched.

"Are you kidding me? I've been playing this game for years; that red-head was a nine, and I don't give 'em away, *trust* me."

"I've been people-watching longer than you've been alive young man, and in this place, that was no nine, trust *me*. She was no more than an eight; you gave her a nine just because she smiled at you; you boys come cheap."

"An eight? Are you crazy! What criteria do you use? Cheap? And you're right, I am absolutely cheap....down and dirty!"

C laughed, self-deprecation.

And with that, the little old lady slid off her high chair and came over to join the boys. Earl saddled a seat for her; she slid between the two of them, Oreo-stuffing, and ordered a whisky sour, *with fruit*, and a Caprese salad - a plate of mozzarella and beefsteak tomatoes, sliced thick, drizzled with extra virgin oil for the table. The game was hard work, and they needed to eat.

Then the three of them proceeded to play and play, non-stop arguments, coaxing, poking, laughing, scolding and cajoling over sevens and eights: short hair, long hair, bobs and ponytails set in a lazy swing, grunge and glasses, librarians and sluts, sophisticated and sexy and mousy and pouty, all shuffling by, across the stage, on their way somewhere else. It was an *olla podrida* of patched jeans and holes in grays, blacks and blue, pumps and boots and flats and jackets and jewels and women in hats, hats of every hue - peach and coral, celadon and all the colors of the sea, skins tanned and porcelain, thin and thinner....a visual overload – thick, sex soup. And that didn't include the avalanche of sixes, fives and *less-thans*....far too many thumbs-down to count. And amongst it all, a handful of New York nines, agreed by all.

They were a trio of juveniles having an absolute ball.

CHAPTER 328 – SHE'D DOWN WHATEVER THAT MAN SERVED UP

A bronze strapping fish, frozen in a tail-flip, hung on the sign above the sleek glass doors. The metal marker announced to all that passed:

Grand Central Market

Lilly coasted confident under the bronze bait, through a door held for her by a svelte handsome young man, dressed to the designer-nines and full of self-import, the kind that rarely holds a door for anyone, but the kind that makes an exception for someone who looks like Lillian. She gave him a small, sweet smile, the kind that says *thanks*, but means *that's all you're gonna get – just a thanks.* He knew the smile, having used it many times himself. He smirked at the rare rebuff, returned a polite grin in regal defeat, and was on his way, and quickly disappeared into the market milieu.

All that information, the silent communication shared between the two, began and ended in a matter of seconds, the time it takes to walk through an opened-door.

A guy like him, Lilly thought, if he somehow stumbled into Belvidere, would be a absolute wildfire, with no equal, absolutely *the* only topic in Town. Woman would faun over him, hoping to catch his eye, on the street, in the market. Stories would soon circle, fester and grow ever-more-fantastic, a *tourbillon*, as sightings occurred and whispers passed: *My God, did you see him - he was all sweaty running by the Courthouse! His chest is shaved clean, his legs too – I saw it, I did! His breath smells like peppermint; I swear, I smelled it, on line, in the Post Office; he breathed at me, on purpose!* And not a single male in Belvidere owned, or could even pronounce, all the designers he was wearing: shoes –

sans socks, cropped, fitted slacks, button-down shirt, light-wool sports coat, pocket square, lapel pin. He would probably get beat up by the local Yahoos just for looking too neat, too perfect....too shaved.

And yet here, in this place, he was merely a minnow. Lilly smiled, but it was only half-about the handsome gentleman-in-passing.

The short walk from the *Main Concourse* to the *Market* had settled the matter; it had become eminently clear to Lillian that she had nothing on her face....it *was* her face, her body, the whole package, that attracted the attention of men and women, young and old, all about her. What had served her so well in Belvidere all her life, those same manipulative tools, seemed to work in this universe as well, and the attention it drew seemed to be on steroids.

And she wasn't even wearing designer; she could only imagine if she did. The smile that creased her face, she couldn't wipe it....it tasted too good. This elixir, it was the best Kool-Aid *ever*.

*I **do** own this City, I really do; read it and weep, bitch!*

She couldn't stop thinking, her mind racing at the possibilities of this big new world. She was a leopard out of its cage, off its leash, strutting and making waves. Oh how she *wished* Carol could see it, so she could wipe her face in it, and laugh. Carol *knew* this would happen if Lilly ever got into the City; she must have known it all along.

I own this place!

She was so caught up in self-revelry, that she glided down the central aisle without a thought as to the delights piled to her left and right.

But the aromas, the visuals, the carpet as it unfolded, finally tugged and made her pause, to pay attention. And before her lay a veritable bounty, the likes she had never seen before.

Sam's, even with the upgrades by Cord, it certainly was not.

Scattered along an endless central aisle were fishmongers, meat-mongers and purveyors of artisan cheese, large wheels of sturdy dairy. Nutty-crunchy women hawked certified organic roots, misted, writhen vegetables Lilly had never seen before, not even in C's upgraded produce at Sam's, plants the likes of which had never grown in Warren County, she knew that for sure. They looked alien, some unpronounceable, and all absolutely wonderful.

Peddlers traded bags of nuts and berries and chocolates and dairy; the din of interaction between scores of vendors and clients filled the air and hung over the space....a canopy of commerce. Lilly, feet planted, figured she could live forever simply on the piles of potato salad and coleslaw, mozzarella and bread – baked in every shape and size - in her sights, as comers and goers darted to and fro about her, carrying their own bags of booty, stuffed to the gills....tonight's dinner.

And as people passed, Lilly realized she didn't understand half the snippets of conversation around her; people were all speaking in foreign tongues. In fact, there was more of other languages than there was of English; some sounded Arabic, some Spanish, maybe French, possibly Russian....she really had no idea, just a guess. She had never experienced *anything* like it in her life.

Lilly continued on, her focus back to food. Everything looked so good, she simply couldn't decide where to stop, what to pick first, so she picked nothing, as her stomach continued to whimper and whine.

And then, up ahead, to the right, Lilly saw him, in profile.

And right at that moment, in less than an instant, she knew she'd down whatever that man served up.

CHAPTER 329 – NICE TO MEET YOU LILLIAN, WITH TWO ELLS

He saw her when she was about fifteen feet away, but was tending to another customer; he never let on.

He was beyond gorgeous; he looked Italian, but was actually Lebanese. But who ever thinks *that guy looks Lebanese?* No one does, especially in *Grand Central*; you think to yourself *that guy looks Italian.*

And this guy looked Italian, *very good* Italian.

He had thick, short-cropped hair – jet black, a bit messy in a perfectly coiffed way. His skin was smooth and evenly tanned, just enough to look healthy....lightly toasted. He was a shade under six-foot, with a gymnast's physique; defined biceps and deltoids, a chiseled chest, not overly big, but sculpted, like an alpha dancer....his washboard stomach hardly hidden behind a super-white fitted, ribbed muscle-tee, untucked in his tailored black dress slacks, summer wool, held up by pencil thin black suspenders, which lay stark against the white of his shirt and the burnish of his skin. He had a too-sexy shadow on his face, the kind women love, just a shade past the smooth from the morning's shave. He wore Clark Kent black-framed glasses, which seemed to be just for show; on anyone else, they would look ridiculous but on him, they were precisely the right gimcrack....tinsel on top....behind which set inviting light blue eyes. He had a beautifully hewn face, with a square chin and a pronounced jawline.

He wore no rings, no jewelry of any kind, and nary a tattoo marred his beautiful, blemish-free skin. And a constant, ever-so-slight smile creased his closed lips. His hands, even his nails, were smooth, clean, but strong, masculine....perfect.

He must be minutes off a magazine shoot, that was the look; not a single item was out of place....even Lilly couldn't help but stare. He was a full step above Button Pierce, and Lillian didn't even know such a step existed, that a man could be this handsome, this perfectly put together.

He was *that* good.

A line of four women, all quite attractive, hugged the front of his kiosk, trying to stay out of the general flow of foot traffic. He peddled a variety of Mediterranean fare: grains, rice, beans and bread in all shapes and sizes, salads and cheeses....a cacophony of flavors, spices and colors: lemon, cardamom, cumin and allspice. And the women couldn't get enough of it, or him. It was clear they were lined up for both, especially the latter.

And he smiled and exchanges pleasantries, asking about the parties they were planning and talking calories and proteins, amino acids and fats....good and bad cholesterol and a string of other healthy topics. It all seemed genuine, or maybe he was just that good. It was clear they were regulars - he called them by name - and knew, for the most part, what they wanted before they spoke – like Frank at Sam's, but without the ugly, and sans rudeness, belly and booze. And they flirted, blushed, giggled and acted like little girls, although they were all in their late thirties, likely forties - fit and pretty - but ten to fifteen years his senior....just like Lillian.

But it was clear that didn't stop any of them from wishing.

Lilly saddled into the back of the line, a bit annoyed she had wait her turn. She lazily glanced over the produce, but the focus was clearly on him; not a stare, more of a sideways slant than anything, a peripheral scout, trying to ascertain how long it would take for him to notice her, to stop in his tracks like the rest of the people that came across her so far, to acknowledge her stunning beauty, like the rest of the City already had, and forget the also-rans in the line in front of her.

And she *waited*.

The line in front moved slow, with each woman purposely drawing out the process; it wasn't a purchase as much as a conversation.   Horny women trying to make small talk with this gorgeous guy, it was *so* obvious, and they were *so* lame; Lillian was embarrassed for the lot of them. And the whole process was getting Lillian ever more annoyed; she was hungry, running out of time before she had to scoot and the young man had yet to recognize her greatness – what is *wrong* with this guy?

He's probably gay; that's gotta be it.

The last obstacle finally shuffled away, and it was then that his eyes first acknowledged hers.   And up close, he was even *more* handsome, not a blemish, nothing out of place. She felt a bit of a butterfly; Lillian had never met someone as good-looking as Button, until now. This guy might even be better looking; Christ, why was she even debating the fact – he *clearly* was. She never thought that would happen....could happen. This man was definitely in a league of his own.

"How can I help you, young lady?"

The words wrapped Lilly in silk, and she was sure they were nothing but sincere. To other customers, it was a shallow salutation, but to her, he meant it, every word, especially the *young* part. Lilly found herself a little tongue-tied; of all people, her! Tongue-tied! Waiting for her turn at bat, she had practiced what she was going to order in her mind, over and over, how she was going to say it, with a few cute witticism thrown in here and there, a bat of the eyelashes, an ever-so-slight parting of the lips, along with a imperceptible tilt of the head....a dance no man could resist.

Instead, Lillian went completely blank.

"Um, um, I've never been here before; what, I don't know....would you suggest?"

*My God; that was **so lame!*** She thought, and immediately felt her face flush.

He smiled at her, knowing she was thrown – he got it all the time. And Lilly knew that pitiful smile; that was *her* smile! She gave that to all the guys who were pretenders, trying to pick her up, and then fumbled in front of her, taken aback by her beauty. *She* threw that pathetic smile around, she didn't get it thrown at *her*! This was quickly becoming a disaster! She wasn't one of the other wannabes in line, she was a Goddess, just ask anybody, and he clearly wasn't getting it!

"You're right, I haven't seen you before; are you looking for a little something to eat? For yourself? By yourself? Or, are you looking for something to share?"

Her mind was racing; forget the witticisms, just say something, *anything,* that isn't stupid.

"Yes."

That was all she got out. Her mouth was suddenly pasty, her pits were wet, and her feet hot and sweaty. He tilted his head, the kind that says: *you really didn't answer the question.*

"Oh, I mean myself, just myself, me....just me."

His smile warmed.

"Fine, I've got just the ticket!"

And just like that, he gently let her off the hook. He spun and rubbed his chin for a moment, looking serious over the bounty before him through his Clark Kents, searching for just the right combination. Then he went to work, quickly putting together a montage of goodies:

a handful of fresh green figs - food of the Gods, imported almonds, in the shell, *dolmades* - stuffed grape leaves, *yemista* and fresh garlic hummus, *falafel*, fresh pita tips and *muffuletta*, hearts of palm, chow-chow, some lupini beans and the most delicate artichoke hearts, mixed with sauteed spinach and extra virgin oil. And lots of feta, crumbly fresh feta.

And then, just about done, he slid around back to the fetch the *piece de resistance,* something extra special, he said, that he kept in the back only for the most discerning customers; he said that with a slight chuckle and a smile, and she smiled in return. He was gone for what seemed like forever, but might have been thirty seconds, maybe less, and rounded the counter and handed her a stapled bag - it was heavy!

"My God, that's gotta be ten pounds of food; I can't eat all that!"

She yelped.

"Yeah, and about ten thousand calories, probably more, so take your time. Unless you want to share it with someone, you know, who really appreciate the bounty."

He said, a not-so-subtle bobber tossed in the water.

Lilly looked for the receipt; it was stapled to the top of the bag. The total was crossed with a pen, replaced by:

N/C

She looked at him odd, and he just smiled.

"The bill's inside, you can pay it later; you look like you're in a rush. I close at ten, and I'm around for awhile after that, you know, just straightening up. I'm in no rush to get out of here, so take your time coming back. Whenever is fine."

Lillian knew there was no bill inside, and she smiled in appreciation. She mouthed *thank-you* to him, and he just nodded.

"I'm Marco, well actually it's Marcus, which is from, derived from I mean, Marek. My real name is Marek, it's from the Romans, you know, the God of War, Mars, but he was more than that, he was also a guardian of agriculture, if you can believe it, it's true, and I'm more that, not the God part, um, or a guardian, but, uh, you know, the agriculture part....I guess. Kinda.

Now Marek felt the fool, rambling on, making a stupid statement, the kind that feels stupid right as you're saying it, but you still keep talking, when you should just shut up.

"Yeah, well, that was kind of, yeah, corny."

He said, blushing a bit. And it was Lillian's turn to let him off the hook with that same pitiful, friendly smile. He acknowledged the touche, and let out a breath of air....a restart. He extended his hand.

"But Marco is easier to remember, most people just call me Marco. It was a pleasure to meet you, and I really hope you like what I packed in the bag."

Lillian extended her hand toward his and simply whispered.

"Nice to meet you, *Marek;* I'm Lillian, but most people just call me Lilly, with two ells."

He shook her hand gently, smiling.

"Nice to meet you *Lillian,* with two ells."

CHAPTER 330 – THE BEST PART SO FAR; THE BEST PART BY FAR

The bag really *was* heavy!

She wanted to dive in, partly because she was starved, but more so to find the special morsel Marco told her he put in *just for the most discerning customers;* she couldn't imagine what could be better than the delights she did see on their way into the satchel.

She whooshed through the glass doors and quickly scuttled off to the right, to peek inside the sack. She slowly slid down the polished limestone wall, the stone cool on her backside, till she stopped a few inches short of the floor. She pulled at the heavy white paper, and the single staple let go. It felt as if she was sticking her hand in the Halloween pillow case, to see what the best-house-on-the-block had snuck in her bag, the one that gave out the best candy – there was always one in every neighborhood – the one that no kid ever skipped. And, of course, that house always had an extra special treat for their favorite trick-or-treater, purposely not letting you see it as they slid it in.

As she gazed into Marek's bag, that was the feel.

On top of all the goodies, neatly folded, lay a piece of crisp white paper, one Marco had never given to any of these customers, *ever*. She read it in silence, as the smile grazed her face:

To the most stunning woman I have <u>ever</u> laid eyes upon
<u>Please</u> do not let this be the last time I ever see you!
I have never done this before; I feel like a little kid
writing a note in class.
Call me, email me, something, anything!
I'm here till 10 pm++; whenever.
I packed enough for two!

She stared at the note, and his business card, stapled to it:

I have never done this before; I feel like a little kid....

She kept re-reading that line.

The most handsome man she had ever met, *ever*, certainly younger than her, probably by more years than she cared to admit, put that note in *her* bag. He was pursuing *her*! Every woman on that line today, and probably every line, every day wanted *him*, and he wanted *her*!

Grand Central was going from unbelievable to something beyond, whatever that word could be. Lilly, still smiling like a little kid, exhaled a confident sigh; she hadn't had many of those in her life, not real ones. And that feeling of superiority rushed back over her, and she savored it.

It was right about then she felt it; it was an almost imperceptible tang, an invisible tug, which signals the presence of someone else, sharing your space. Even though the market doors were in constant motion, people shuffling in and out, it wasn't them; it was something, someone, else.

She rode back up the wall till erect and saw her, on the other side of the hall, about twenty-five feet away, half-hidden behind a lidless garbage can, tucked in a small alcove, not much bigger than her body.

She was stocky and sloppy-looking, with dirty clothes and ruddy cheeks, fair skin and bruised, blotchy, red knees, revealed through large holes in her pants, the result of kneeling on hard surfaces far too long. She clearly lived on the streets; it took less than seconds to gather that. Her eyes were lifeless, staring blankly at the floor. It looked as if she was someone who would be considered slow, or impaired, mentally, in some way; even if she wasn't, that was the look she kept.

She was all alone, and no one paid a bit of attention to her; she was a plant stand, or an extension of the garbage receptacle beside her, she could have been either. She could have died right there, and not a person would have known, or cared.

Beside her was a plastic plate, with remnants of smeared rice and what looked like baked beans, some of the beans spilled onto the floor, other beans, along with the rice, was stuck to the side of the garbage can. She had the same smear on her fingers, and residue caked in the far corners of her mouth.

It took a few moments for Lilly to realize she must have been eating someone's throw-away from the can; she's not sure why she didn't figure that out quicker, but she didn't.

But now she did.

And Lillian Liddell forgot about how beautiful she was, and how much everyone admired her, and how Marek wanted her, and how much Carol would envy her. She just saw a scared, lonely, invisible girl, abandoned, eating out of a garbage can, and how utterly helpless and hopeless she was.

And Lillian realized that young lost girl was *her,* on the inside, just a scratch below the facade, just about all her life, ever since her mom went away. She shook her head sad, seeing herself, shrunk and shoved in an alcove that no one really cared about. Not really.

She picked up her bag of goods and softly walked across the hall, sitting quietly beside the young girl. As Lillian got closer, she saw that her face, hands and fingernails were dirty; the stains were old, permanent, deep in the pores, the wrinkles in her skin, the nails black with street grease and grime. She had acquired the patina of the street; the kind that ages you fast, and ugly.

Lilly opened the bag, and fished out a small plate, fork, spoon and napkin that Marco had folded together. She laid them out, and picked out the first container, which had some pita tips; a second had hummus.

"Here, a friend gave it to me, but I'm not hungry."

The girl looked at Lilly; she didn't smile, or say anything, she just took the two containers and put them on her lap, and carefully, quietly, began to eat.

"You want me to sit with you, for a bit?"

Lilly whispered.

The girl didn't answer, but gave a dazed half-nod, that Lilly almost missed.

So Lilly did.

The girl ate, and Lilly sat quiet beside her, watching people pass, her as invisible as her friend, and she smiled. Lillian reminisced about her mom, and how she hoped her mom would be proud of her. That thought felt good....real good.

And as the medley of thoughts and memories ran round her head, they all seemed to point in the same direction: *this was the best part so far; the best part by far.*

CHAPTER 331 – HANDS ON HER HIPS, SMILING UP FROM BELOW

The trio of juveniles were arguing sevens and eights about a two-some walking along the left-hand side when Earl spotted her; he was first. And he knew right away.

He stood up, silent and put ten fingers high in the air. C spied him, stopped the argue, and pushed him in the thigh.

"What are you doing? *Sit down;* there are **no** tens Earl! **None!**"

Then C turned to see the object Earl had spied, and there, amongst the detritus, Earl was right as rain – this one shone. But C couldn't do it; *no one* is a ten. He held up nine fingers, with the last one bent.

"Nine and a half, and I've *never* given one of those before, ever – halves aren't even allowed. But I'll make an exception in this one case, but that's it, that's as good as it gets Earl."

The woman by now saw the commotion on the balcony and stopped to stare at the trio. She frowned a bit, knowing exactly what was going on.

The old lady, her name was Claire Clifford, but the boys were already calling her Mrs. C, eyed the young lady down below, looked at the two boys and slowly held up her hands; no doubt about it….ten fingers.

C smiled by now, shaking his head slowly, in mock defeat. The young lady had her hands on her hips, smirking, waiting for C to acquiesce.

Cord Brin shook his head one last time and smirked at the beauty below, knowing the other judges were right. He slowly straightened his tenth finger; the first and last perfect score he ever gave.

And Lillian Liddell stood statue, hands on her hips, smiling up from below.

2375

CHAPTER 332 – SHE DIED ALONE, STILL WAITING

The boys gave Mrs. C big hugs and kisses, like leaving an old friend, and promised to stay in touch.

Earl told her that he wasn't afraid of her, not one bit; Mrs. C said she was happy to hear it. He leaned in and whispered *baba ganoush* in her ear, which made her snort a little laugh – half from the word, half from the tickle of his breath. She was *definitely* on his best friend list, and Earl told her so, right then and there. He told her she was right next to Mr. Big B; he never told her that B was a cat – that didn't matter, he still loved Big, and he was way more than a cat anyway, to Earl. Of course, this whole shuffle meant Louie the Lobster dropped another notch, to seventh-best friend, but Earl didn't forget - lobsters don't really mind being seventh-best, they're still happy just being on the list! Plus Louie was on his way to Panama anyway, and what could be better than that?

Earl kept turning around and waving to Mrs. C as he bounded down the stairs toward Lillian. Mrs. C leaned against the rail, kept her hand aloft and stood on her toes, not wanting to lose sight of them one second sooner than she had to.

A perchance meeting that was one of her happiest days in years, new friends, and a new best friend; it made her feel young. She thought of them often, waiting for their call, another trip to *Grand Central* perhaps, and the chance to play more childish games. She even dreamed of Earl once or twice; good dreams, from what she could remember, although she didn't remember much – just him gently holding her hand. Earl was a good hand-holder, and his smile was infectious; she remembered mostly those two things from her dream, mostly, and not much else. But that was enough to make her smile.

But the dreams were as good as it got, because things happen, situations change and best intentions invariably fall by the wayside. In the end, Earl and C never called and never came back to see Mrs. C.

Not once.

Less than a year later, she died alone, still waiting.

CHAPTER 333 – FORGET THE SHINE-BOX SHITHEAD, I'M IN

Lilly looked up and whispered *goodbye....till next time;* nobody heard her but him, but then again, no one was supposed to. She smiled and left the unicorn behind.

The boys hooked her by an arm, one each side, yellow-brick-road-style, and half-skipped down a grand side hall off the *Concourse*, lit by four enormous eggs - gigantic chandeliers set high above the marble floor, a golden allee, lighting the way, the somewhere it led still very much a mystery.

"Shit, we gotta hustle!"

C said aloud, and quickened the pace.

Soon enough they turned a corner and bounded up a small ramp, Near *Track 41*, leading to something called the *Biltmore Room,* or the *Kissing Room,* as it was called years ago, when this area was connected to one of the busy train concourses and bustled with travelers, awash in tearful kisses....for both hellos and goodbyes.

But it wasn't that anymore; someone decades ago decided to reconfigure this area, and this room was sealed off from the train platform - no longer connected to the rails. Now, it was not much more than a pretty blind alley, leading to nowhere. And there were no people here; it was silent and empty when the trio spilled into the space.

A large clock set on the wall, between two oversized bronze torchieres, read 7:44 pm.

C stopped in the quiet, circular enclave, a dead-end really; not so far from the bustle of the *Grand Concourse*, but at the same time, seemingly a world away. It had the feel of a backwater, kind of like

Belvidere, that peculiar, wonderfully weird Belvidere vibe.

The kind that gives goosebumps for no real reason.

Earl and Lillian looked about the room; the space had an air of opulence, or at least did at one time; now, it was half-stripped, and felt faded. There was a newstand kiosk, dark for the day, and a vacant row of shoe-shine stands, seven in series, all quiet. Not a soul but the three occupied this place, and although the newstand and line of shoe-shines were likely open earlier that day, they had a mood, a suggestion of being closed for months....years.

It seemed a lonely, forgotten place. Except for that strangely lit box in the far corner.

It was a stainless steel booth of some sort, tiny – the size of a stubbed shipping container, with a metal ramp, dimly lit in subdued hues of orange and yellow neon. It had that corny, psychedelic look of the future, what the 1970's thought the future would look like, but never did. But somehow it did, *here*, in a shoe-shine dead-end called the *Biltmore Room*.

"We're here; one minute to spare!"

C said, clearly proud of himself.

"*Where?*"

Said Earl.

C pointed silently to the steel, futuristic *Lost-In-Space* shoe-box at the far end of the room.

Just as he did, as if on cue, an end-door opened. Earl was hoping for a spacecraft hatch and maybe an alien or two, that would be pretty cool for a birthday surprise. But, alas, it was just a regular old aluminum door, and a tall thin man, in his twenties, bespectacled and proper, made his way down the ramp, in a regal no-rush, to greet them. He had a set of head-phones draped around his neck.

"7:45? Mr. Brin?"

He said in a pleasant manner; Cord nodded.

"We're recording a birthday….*song?*"

Lillian said in classic drawn-out sarcasm, which C summarily ignored.

"Gee, I hope not, unless C doesn't sing."

Earl added.

"Okay enough already with the singing!"

C said, annoyed at the two of them. He turned to the young man.

"Give us a minute or two, okay? This is a bit of a surprise, so let me explain it a bit, to them.

"Take your time; you're the last one today."

The young man nodded gracefully and retreated to his aluminum and steel cube. The door clicked shut, and once again, it was just the three of them.

"Last *what?* I'm not going in there!"

Lilly said indignant.

"Are we really going in *there*, all three of us, with him *too?*"

Earl asked, the inflection indicating that was *clearly* more than two pounds of bologna shoved in a one pound aluminum sack.

"What is this?"

Lilly asked, this one in a way that expected a real response.

"This, young lady, is *StoryCorps;* remember I told you two about this, from NPR, you know, the radio station I listen to....the stories?"

Both looked at him like he had two heads.

"No, who'd you tell? Because it wasn't *me!*"

Lilly's voice raised an octave, getting instant-angry.

Christ, he did it again. Now C knew he told *someone,* but it didn't matter now: Carol, Margery, Mae; any answer that wasn't Lilly was the *wrong* answer. So he dodged her dart, and pressed on.

"It's a pretty cool concept; it's put on by a non-profit, *StoryCorps,* that's the name, and the concept is stupid-simple. They record stories, short conversations, between family, friends, spouses, siblings, neighbors, whatever. No rules, it just captures a quiddity, the essence, of people's everyday lives. Some stories are funny, some sad, some heartfelt, some all the above, and some just suck. But mostly, they don't suck. They feature one on NPR, that's *National Public Radio*, every week, every Friday morning; they've been doing it for years. They do it at a couple permanent places, like New York and a couple other cities, maybe LA, not sure, and they also have a roving van that drives all over the country, plopping down for a week or so in different bum-fuck towns all over the country. Hundreds of people record every week, thousands and thousands have done it so far, and the *StoryCorps* people pick one to feature on the air at NPR every Friday morning. Kind of cool, but that's not why we are doing it, but kinda cool anyway, don't you think?"

The two of them just stared blank at Cord, like he had grown a second head. So he continued the sell.

"Yeah, that's what I thought at too, at first, kind of stupid; what's the point? The first time I heard about it, thought the idea was a bit queer; who gives a shit about stranger's boring family stories, or neighbors little ditties - stupid people telling stupid stories that nobody cares about. But I listened to the first one, years ago, five to ten years ago maybe, can't remember, and was somehow hooked. Instant. It's not stupid at all; the stories tell you that there are a lot of good people out there, who have had good things happen to them, and really shit things happen to them, some a lot like your own stories – a lot of times they hit home more than you think. And you know what? Most people bounce back. And I'm not a cheerleader for that kind of thing, normally, but it's good, trust me. I rarely miss a week, and if I do, they are on the NPR website to listen to as well. And every one of them, all the thousands they have recorded, are permanently archived in Washington DC, in a museum called the *Folk Art Museum.* I've never been there, that museum, but that's where all the stories are kept, so we'll all be museum pieces, the three of us, *forever;* someone a hundred years from now could download what we talk about today, and figure out what was going on in our weird little world called Belvidere so long ago. We're really recording what it's like to live in this country, on the ground, day-to-day, at this point in time in our history; it's like the oral storytelling the Indians would do, passed from generation to generation, to keep alive the history, their history, and even...."

Lilly had heard enough, and interrupted the dissertation.

"Okay, okay, *Mr. Dictionary,* we get it."

Then she continued.

"But what does this have to do with us? You wanna tell stories to each other? That's what you do *all the time,* and I swear, you make that shit up! That's what we're here for? Really? Are you kidding? I rushed back for bedtime story-time? I left *Marek* behind for this?”

She had to get that in somehow before the night was over. Mission accomplished.

“What's a *Marek*?”

Earl asked.

“Not a what, a who; a drop-dead gorgeous Italian cutie who's *all* into me, that's who.”

Lilly cooed, and smiled like a little girl with a big secret, her eyelashes fluttering at Cord.

“Jesus, whatever; we leave her alone for five minutes and she finds a girlfriend.”

“Yeah, you wish, perv.”

Lilly said, smiling, as she punched him in the arm.

“Come on, it'll be fun; Earl you up for it?

C said.

Earl shook his head an emphatic yes, as if that was ever in doubt when it was something C suggested, especially for his birthday. He was in, with both feet.

The duo looked at Lilly.

Now deep down, Lillian really did think it was pretty cool, or at least, kinda cool, that someone thought of this and was actually doing it, and there was a booth set up in the unicorn building and they were tucked in this weird little room and they were the last ones that day – that alone felt kind of special – she wasn't sure why, but it did. And this was all happening in *her* City to boot, the

City that had quickly adopted her, and her it. But of course, she wasn't going to let C know all that, at least not yet. So she just stared at them, arms folded across her chest in a snit, making them wait.

The door to the booth opened and the young man stuck his head out; now he was a bit annoyed at the delay. C figured his *take your time* was just about up.

"Fine, you stay out here and sit on the shine-box, we'll go in and talk all about *you* to each other. Oh, the stories were gonna tell! There are so many, I simply don't know which to start with; but I know one thing for certain, with *our* Lilly story, we're *definitely* getting on the Friday-radio, for sure! And people can download this stuff, forever! What'ya say Earl?"

And as if on cue, Earl answered rote.

"Welcome to the end of the road, I guess."

"*Neighbors!*"

They both yelled at the same time, high-fiving like teenagers.

"Oh for God's sake, you two really are *so* gay. And *no way* I trust you in there telling perverted lies about me, just to get on the radio. So forget the shine-box shithead, I'm in."

CHAPTER 334 - *SHOVE IT IN!* SHE SAID, AND SO THEY DID

C began.

"Okay, I'll ask Lilly a question first and then...."

"*No way!* No! You're not asking me anything! I'll ask *you* something, though, for sure!"

Lilly jumped in, setting the record, barking at Cord.

"Okay, fine."

C responded, without a hint of push-back. Then he corrected the order.

"Lilly asks me first, then Earl asks Lilly and then I'll ask Earl."

Lilly squinted at Ay; at first blush, that seemed fair, which certainly meant it wasn't, not with C involved – there had to be a trick.

She was still squinting as Earl went through the aluminum threshold, followed, slowly, by Cord; Lilly brought up the rear. The line quickly stalled; it truly was two pounds of bologna. Lilly, ever impatient, barked at the stalled queue in front of her.

"*Shove it in!*"

She said, and so they did.

CHAPTER 335 – ONE KNEW, BUT *BOTH* NEEDED TO KNOW: WHAT'S IN THE BOX?

The young man warily eyed the volume of humanity filling the room, comprised mostly of Earl, and gulped. He politely ran through the interview instructions, a worn drill: relax, please speak *softly* and clearly – no need to shout, please – *no shouting*, don't rush, and most of all, simply enjoy yourself – you are among friends; it isn't a test – there are no right answers. He then sequestered himself as best he could into the corner of the booth, where he fiddled and checked sound levels, audio peaks, control and clarity....radio stuff-and-nonsense. The other three crammed in a space usually reserved for two; with Earl in the mix, it was a sardine-squeeze. As C pulled the door shut, their eardrums muffled in the sound-proof box.

And with that, they simply looked at each other in silence; Earl's eyes were as big as saucers – he clearly wasn't relaxed, panting like an anxious cat on its way to the vet.

"Now remember, ask whatever you want, *nothing* is off the table, and the only rule is, you have to tell the *truth*....deal?"

C said, and the two nodded once in agreement, each with a look one has before turning over a surprise quiz, one you clearly weren't expecting, and weren't prepared for, not one lick.

C then pointed to Lilly; it was as if she was up at the microphone in front of a packed auditorium, in her underwear. She game-show froze. She didn't have enough time to think of a question for C....her mind was racing wild: *no fair, he just sprung this on her, he did it on purpose! I can't think of a single question to ask! I don't even know what to say, or where to start!*

C saw the panic in her face.

"Relax, take a breath; any question will do, no holds barred. You have been waiting for months for just this moment, so here's your chance, nothing is off-limits. And the truth, I promise."

That little pep talk actually made it worse; it was *way* too much pressure. Lillian's mind was going in useless circles; she couldn't focus on a even a single thought! A complete blank.

"You did this on purpose, to fluster me! I, I can't go yet, ask Earl a question! You knew about this whole thing for weeks, months, and I got, like, five seconds! No fair, you go first!"

Lilly was hyperventilating.

"Okay, then I'll ask first. No big deal."

C said calmly, and the young man in the corner smiled, waiting for something, anything, to actually start.

Earl still had that pop-quiz look on his face, mouth agape, his tongue dry and pasty, positively mortified.

"Jesus, relax Earl; it's just like he said, it's not a test, it's supposed to be fun. There's no right answer, just say what you want to say, okay?"

Earl nodded a slow, unconvincing, yes.

"Wait!"

Lilly suddenly screamed.

The young man ripped off his earphones; Lilly's yelp blistered his eardrums, but good.

"Sorry."

She mouthed, shrugging her shoulders like a little kid looking for sympathy. It worked, like it always did; he smiled, rubbed his ears, shook his head a bit and gingerly pulled the muffs back in place.

"I know now; I got a question….two really."

Lilly whispered.

"You just get one, so pick *wisely*."

C gently wagged his finger at her.

She was in a quandary; first no questions, now too many, clogged her brain. Once the pressure to decide had passed, with no limits imposed, the floodgate broke. The first one that came to mind was the black girl, Selena, Selena from Belize. Who was she, *really*? She had to hear that story. And many questions followed. Why did she come to Belvidere? Why'd she leave Belize? Where'd she go in that Volkswagen with the wad of Cord's cash? Has C talked to her since? What does she know about C's past? What name does she even call him; is it Cord, or some other name he made up? Does she know his *real* name....the real story? And that was just the first major question, made up of at least a series of seven sub-questions. And then there was a second major question; where is C *really* from, for real? And where did all that money come from, in the foil packs? And then there was the third major question; wait, she already forgot what the third question even was….*shit!* And then there was the *fourth* major question, and maybe that was the most important one of all; maybe that was the one that finally needed to be asked, and the answer, the truth, revealed.

And before she could think, before she could twirl the myriad options in her head one last time, to decide which question won out, the decision was already made, and the words simply spilled from her lips, as if they had a life of their own.

And so it was, major question number four, the last
question, became the first question, became the *only*
question. Because one knew, but *both* needed to know:

What's in the box?

2389

CHAPTER 336 – AND SO BEGAN A FANTASTICAL TALE

C sighed through a long exhale, looking past his friends.

Given the question could have been *any* question, anything under the sun, and there were many good questions he had failed to answer in the six-odd months he had known Earl and Lillian, he figured it was gonna be a tough one.

But he had hoped it wasn't going to be *this* tough one.

But it was, as he figured it likely would be. And in the end, it was a relief; it really needed to be *this* question....Lilly deserved it, as did Earl. In all the years of playing the game, no one else ever deserved an answer to that question, but *they* did. They surely did. And, frankly, he was tired of keeping the secret to himself.

What C didn't fully figure, at this point in time, sandwiched in the aluminum box at the farthest point in a dead end formerly known as the *Kissing Room* were the rules, the unwritten rules about both the box, and the game. No one outside the game-players knew the rules, and although no one told him, per se, the real contents of the box, and the rules that put those contents into play, were off limits to ones *outside* the know. Cord should have figured as much, he should have known better. But he was careless, and tired, mostly of the game itself. And that, in the end, would be a grave mistake, one of several he would make that night.

It was a slippery slope, and he was soon to find himself knee-deep. But maybe that was *always* the plan, decided long ago, by others; who's to truly know?

But for now, right or wrong, those cautionary thoughts didn't enter his mind. For now, he was focused on Earl and Lillian, and keeping his promise, of the truth, to them both, within the confines of the booth in which they sat.

And his thoughts turned to Carol, the dead one.

Awhile ago, after the hag first appeared, C realized she was a player in the game that he somehow had never met, as strange as that seemed, considering the game had run for years, decades. And that got him to thinking; was Carol just another player in the game that he never met? And why was it that both Carol and the hag first surfaced here, in the strange place called Belvidere? It was here where they were first dealt into the hand, but for what reason, he had no idea. Such decisions were clearly made on a need-to-know basis, at a pay grade much higher than his. He was convinced the hag knew all the rules of the game – she had to. But he also figured Carol probably knew them too. And to that end, she probably knew what was in the box; he wasn't sure what kind of things she could, and couldn't know, but he was pretty sure that was one of them *[Carol's mouth creased sad, as she hung her head]*.

C refocused his gaze on Earl and Lillian, and began to speak.

"I told you both that there is no lying in here, not here, so I won't. And because of that, a backstory must be told, and explained, which will likely make this answer a bit longer, I'm afraid, than you are used to *[C tilted is stare to the guy with the headphones, who gave a small, acknowledging smile]*. But please, to *really* understand the answer to the one question you asked, you need to be sure you don't interrupt me; just let me finish, okay, no matter *what* you hear, or how crazy it sounds....deal?"

Brother and sister jointly nodded, and the young man in the corner shuffled in his seat; it was the end of the day, he was tired, and just wanted to go home. But with *that* preamble teaser, an unexpected scene seemed to be in the offing, the kind that may warrant attention, and he tabled the end-of-day, shut-the-lights-off anticipation that had been dancing in his head for the last hour-plus. For now.

C sighed again, for at that instant, somehow, the issue of full disclosure about things he shouldn't say aloud came to the forefront, in his noggin. It was now a conscious thought. How that suddenly happened, and who pushed that thought to the forefront was unknown; no one stood up, no one took credit. Maybe *It* did it; who knows?

But C was clearly about to crack a faucet, giving information he probably, likely, surely, wasn't supposed to share. What would be the consequences? He didn't know; maybe none, maybe much more than none. But the albatross, worn for years, forever weighing him down, disabling, had suddenly, inexplicably, became unbearable. And the question by Lillian, and the aluminum box *truth-be-told* setting he queued up, provided him the excuse for which he was desperately searching.

So, on he went; there was no turning back.

And so began a fantastical tale.

CHAPTER 337 – THE BOWL WAS FULL OF BLOOD

"You know, Lilly, yesterday, in the woods, after you left, that was pretty sad. For me anyway. And I resigned myself that I would never see you again, for real. I really believed that was the course we were on, the two of us, a dead end. And I accepted it; it was what it was, and what wasn't, or didn't, happen, just didn't….it's my lot. I stopped trying to figure it out, make sense of it, a long time ago *[C sighed through a long exhale].*

God, that was only yesterday, in the woods; it already feels like a hundred years ago. Anyway, sitting on that rock, by myself, after you had run away, I tried to remember all the details of your face, every one: your eyes, nose, cheeks, chin, and I wondered, how long it would last in my memory, *you* would last in my memory, until all those beautiful details, and you, *all* of you, faded away, like they always do.   But I was hoping, maybe you'd be different, because this place, your place, Belvidere, is different, so *very* different from anywhere I have ever been. I was hoping, maybe, I wouldn't forget you, ever. And maybe, you wouldn't forget about me. That was my hope, sitting alone in the woods, on that rock, looking across the river at *Couch Rock [Earl gasped, but didn't say a word].*

I certainly wasn't planning on today. So thank you, for today....for everything today *[Lilly smiled and nodded at C; he smiled back, and it looked a bit sad. Under the table, Earl squeezed Lilly's hand, like he did whenever he was way-happy, and she squeezed back, which she rarely did. It felt like a mom-squeeze, that is what Earl thought when Bibby did it, which sent a little chill up his spine].*

Okay, about the box.

To understand the box, you need to understand Jenny – a woman I don't know, and whom I've never met; a woman who shows up in my life at random; when she visits is not decided by me; I don't even think it's decided by her, but by others. Jenny controls me, in a strange sense, at least her words do, and they have, for as long as I can remember.

This is what Jenny whispers to me:

Some days you awake and immediately begin to worry;
Nothing in particular is wrong;
It's just the sense that forces are aligning quietly;
and there will be trouble.

I read that passage, those words, on a wall in the *Museum of Modern Art*, right here in this City....many, many years ago. It's not exactly right, I mean I didn't remember it and just say it out loud to both of you correctly, the words, they're not exactly what was written on that museum wall so many years ago, but it's close enough....it gets the point.

Anyway, a famous artist named Jenny Holzer, whom I've never met, wrote that, the right version of what I just recited to you both, and they stuck it up on the wall in the museum. I found out later she had, and has, written lots of sayings, snippets just like that, hundreds probably, and I couldn't quote the first word of any other one she ever wrote, and I could care less about any other one she ever wrote, *just this one*. I stumbled upon it wandering around alone; I was at the museum with a married woman I was seeing, but at that moment, when I first saw it, I was alone – she had wandered off somewhere else.

The whole episode felt like it was planned, like I was supposed to stumble upon those words up on the wall in that museum, on that day, all alone. It was like Jenny, or someone else, maybe the puppet, probably the puppet, arranged it just so. Maybe, likely, payback for the fence, getting off that fence. Maybe that chit finally came due.

Anyway, it stuck like gum, to my brain, and for some reason, that I don't understand, that *gum-stick* came with specific rules, *lots of rules*, that I didn't make up, and that don't make a lot of sense and many times, contradict one another. But no matter, they just showed up in my head, the rule book that is, in its entirety, committed to memory, de facto. I don't think she made up the rules either, Jenny, that is; I don't think she really has anything to do with anything; her words were just a serendipitous vehicle. Serendipitous is the wrong word, a nightmare is more like it. Anyway, the game-wheels were set in motion, and haven't stopped since. Frankly, I think it was all the work of the puppet, or the crickets, or the flies, or whomever controls them, in my head. Anyway, somebody, or something, flipped the switch, but it wasn't me. For sure, it wasn't me.

But who *actually* invented the game, and made the rules in the first place, and enforces the rules, doesn't matter, because the rules are the rules, and they *can't* be broken. And *that* is rule number one – the most important rule of all.

Those are simply the rules to the game.

And I have never broken them, the game rules, that is; one of the few absolutes, maybe the only absolute, I can claim. At least until now, maybe. I'm not sure if this, what I'm doing now, is a rule break, but I'm thinking it probably is. But you asked about the box Lilly, and a promise is a promise.

[C sighed long, then continued]

Jenny leaves me alone most of the time; I don't think of her much, if at all, except when I get a sense she's lurking, in my brain, like she comes out from hiding, from behind a tree. That's the feel. And usually when I get that sense, I'm right.

And I got that uneasy sense in the woods, not long after you left yesterday. It was just a brief brush of a feeling, a taste of a sense that she was on her way, but I know that taste well. She's coming, she's definitely coming soon. She's *very* near *[Lilly and Earl scrunched their shoulders a bit, and sat closer together; they got a sense of the puppet story C told them so long ago. But this didn't feel like some fake story time, which made the creep worse]*.

Jenny always visits in the morning, during that twilight when you're not quite asleep, but not awake - there should be a name for that time; if there already is, I don't know it.

When she comes, she simply talks to me, whispers to me actually. She says her ditty, the way I remember it, not the right way, but it isn't really her, it's another voice, in my head, spoken by someone else, some woman that I don't know, even though she has visited me, and spoken to me, for years. She's an enigma. I always thought it should have been the puppet speaking those words – that would make the most sense, but I know what the puppet sounds like, and it isn't that voice, it's a woman. And her voice is different – it's beautiful actually, hauntingly beautiful. It's the kind of voice you pay attention to, one you *have* to listen to – you simply don't have a choice.

And when the voice is done, I know it's time to open the box. That's why I wrote those words on the box in black marker so many years ago, Lilly:

Open When You're Ready

Because those are the rules.

And that beautiful voice, from someone I don't know, living in my head all these years, reciting Jenny's right words, which over the years have morphed into Jenny's wrong words, that's the *Ready*.

I wish it had to do with your mom, Lilly, and the note, her note to you, I really do, then somehow, maybe this would all make sense, why I ended in Belvidere, and met the two of you, which is one of the best things, no, *the* best thing, that has *ever* happened to me. But it doesn't, at least I don't think it does, not sure how it would, or could.

And if your mom knows the answer, if she has more insight than I do, she's not spilling, not to me, anyway. I've never spoken to your mom; wish I could say I have, but I haven't.

So I open the box.

Now Lilly, when I told you about the darts in the box, and throwing the darts, right before I came to Belvidere, I told you, maybe you don't remember, but I told you I get drunk, really ripped, every time after I opened the box, *after a little while anyway.*

And that's all true. Every bit of it.

But I never told you what the *after a little while* really means, or really was; that was an important part that I failed to mention, because *that's the real reason* why I have the box. Getting drunk and throwing the darts only happen after the main part is done, after I fail.

And I fail *every* time; I've failed for years, one hundred percent, perfect attendance….perfect failure.

I always keep the box on an upper shelf, above my head, it has to be high, just another stupid rule. When I take it down, I'm in my underwear, my boxer-briefs, always am. I slice open the tape on the box very carefully, like

I'm opening a special Christmas present. When I was a kid, I opened my Christmas presents by cutting the tape with a super-sharp cutlery knife, a special one with a white plastic handle; I used the same one every year. It was a nothing-special cheap knife, don't even know where my parents ever got it – I just found it in the kitchen utensil drawer one day; it didn't match anything else we had in the drawer, but I remember it was super sharp, sharper than a little cheap knife like it should've ever been. And nobody else ever used the knife, for anything, not eating, nothing; not like they couldn't, anybody could use it, it wasn't *my* knife, but for some reason, no one ever did....no one ever used it that I can remember, but me.

Anyway, at Christmas, I'd use this little white knife to cut the tape on the wrapping paper for each of my presents. It was a precision process; after all the pieces of tape were carefully cut, and the box slid from the paper, I would fold the wrapping paper neatly, so neat it could be reused. My family would always get annoyed with me, since we opened presents one at a time, going around the room, person-to-person, each person opened one present, and everyone watched, then you went on to the next person, and so on. So whenever it came to me, it was this long, drawn-out production, holding up the line, so to speak. And the more they yelled to hurry-up, the slower I went; annoying people was half the fun. Still is *[Lilly and Earl shook their heads a collective yes to that one; C smiled]*.

Anyway, using that same white knife from when I was a kid, I've kept it all these years – you've seen it Earl, in my kitchen drawer *[Earl shook his head yes]* – yeah, that's the one, I open the box just like I opened my Christmas presents, slow, neat....precise. Which makes sense, because, in a strange way, the box is kinda like a special Christmas present to me, from me. And no one gets annoyed at the process, because no one's there, no one's *ever* there, just me, alone. That's the rule.

I slowly peel back the cardboard flaps, like I've never seen what the box holds, and I remove a sealed envelope and a set of clothes, the same set of clothes I wear every time, faded jeans, a light green button-down Oxford, a navy-blue blazer, and my tassel loafers.

And I get dressed, fasten both buttons of the two-button sack jacket, then check my look in the mirror, straighten the collar, pick off any lint.

I carefully, neatly, set the sealed envelope on the table or desk in front of me, whatever table or desk that happens to be, wherever I am, set exactly square and parallel with the edge of the table. Precise.

I pull out the flip cellphone, pop in the battery, power it up and hit *Speed Dial No. 2*; it is the only time I ever call that number, the only time it's appropriate. No one ever answers; they aren't meant to; they know the message, and I tell them exactly where I am, exactly where I'm sitting; that part is critical.

And I end the message the same way, every time:

"So, I guess, once again, it's time. Maybe I'll get lucky. No word in a half-hour, you know what to do; be good my friend."

I flip the phone shut and place it by, and perpendicular to, the envelope on the table. They have to be aligned just right; that's important; to me.

Then I reach back into the box and remove a velvet sleeve, navy, and slip out the contents.

I always forget how utterly beautiful it is. It has intricate carving on the hand grip; it's ivory, and I would *never* think to use such a thing now, but when I got it, years ago, I somehow didn't focus on the ivory part, and how wrong that is, that an elephant or rhino lost its life for such an utterly worthless purpose, and that I should never use such a device for just that reason, but I can't switch it out now....it can't be done. So I deal with it, and in a strange way, if I succeed, maybe the ivory, the elephant, the rhino, gets a bit of revenge. So that part makes it somewhat bearable. It has detailed engraving on the nickel cylinder, the barrel, the frame, painstaking, delicate artwork. It is truly a piece of art; and I always handle it as such, gently, with reverence.

I swing open the cylinder and ensure the single bullet is there; it always is. It waits patiently, and has for years....it has all the time in the world. And it will wait for as long as it takes for our next date. It never tires of trying. I like that part. It never gives up.

I give it a hearty half-spin, which will spin it about two full turns, usually just a bit shy. The same every time.

Seventeen percent

Those are the odds; too much in my favor, frankly, I would change that if I could, but again, I didn't set that rule.

I place the revolver on the table, with the barrel facing away from me; then I neatly close the box flaps, settle in my seat, crack my knuckles one last time, exhale deeply, close my eyes, and get to the best part.

I ponder....a mental walk in the woods, so to speak.

I take a free-form ride in my brain, remembering my life in no particular order, no particular memories, just whatever my brain decides to serve up that day. My own private road-novel, so to speak. And this isn't a worrisome fester, just the opposite; it's a calm, lazy jag through what has mostly been an utter mess of a life, but it is calming, and good, because I mine the scraps, here and there amongst the detritus, that were worth saving. And, inevitably, I remember scenes, snippets from my life, about water, invariably, there's water: oceans, streams, lakes, whatever....water, lots of water. But good water, not bad water....good memories.

And although the trip through the fields is different every time I open the box, the ending is *always* the same, the same vision at the finale – that of a skinny, little, blonde-haired, knobby-kneed girl I knew when I was eleven, whom I met on the school bus, the first day of class. She was the first girl I *ever* loved, the only girl I think that ever truly loved me, who slipped away thirty-odd years ago, before the puppet, the crickets and the flies arrived, crowding my brain. And for that, for losing that beautiful little girl, I was always sad. Somehow, if I had been able to hold onto her, maybe my life would have been different, better....not a mess. Maybe.

Anyway, her name is the last word I ever say, when I put the revolver to my temple; I close my eyes, smile and whisper to her as I pull the trigger, hoping, maybe somehow, she will hear me."

C had been staring blankly at a spot on the wall behind Earl and Lillian as he answered the question. He shook the glaze from his eyes and looked at his friends, who sat quiet, shoulders touching, mouths agape. He looked at the gentleman in the corner, his eyes, too, were extra-wide. Thoughts of going home after a long day were gone. He was thinking of the gun.

They were all thinking of the gun.

Even Carol.

Lillian started to speak, but Cord held up his hand to stop her fast, and she stood down. C chuckled a bit to break the tension and stated to the room.

"I'm rambling, I know; a bit longer response than *StoryCorps* usually gets, or maybe allows. Such a simple question to ask, is not so simple to answer; but I promise, I'm almost done."

He cleared his throat and continued.

"Anyway, I've pulled that trigger countless dozens of times, dozens on top of dozens. What are the odds of still sitting here today, to tell the tale? Not too good, for sure. But I lose, and survive, every time. And then I get drunk and throw darts, and move on.

And the last *move-on*, you two know all about, because the last *move-on* brought us together, in a little Podunk nowheresville called Belvidere. And it's where I've been thrown a wicked curve, called Earl and Lillian, two integers I hadn't seen before, nor planned on. The kind of players that are never part of the game *I* play*[C smiled at them, but they didn't smile back; Carol hung her head, for her kids]*.

So anyway, after you left me yesterday Lilly, given Jenny's subsequent peek-a-boo in the woods, I fully expected to hear her whisper in my ear this morning, and to open the box one more time. But she didn't come; Jenny didn't whisper her fateful words, and that's troubling, because that's what's *supposed* to happen. Instead, I have a nightmare about the hag again, a *real* bad one Lilly - worse than last time, *way worse*....I can almost taste her. She was on the other side of a fuzzy glass wall, translucent, with weird flashing white lights behind it; I can't see her, but I *know* she's right there, inches from my face, waiting at some sort of one-way gate, the way in, with no way out, and she's looking for *me*, to drag through to the other side.

I woke up screaming, chest heaving, hyperventilating; it scared the bejesus out of Chick – she went running out of the bedroom, abandoned me, the little bitch. So for this one, I was on my own *[C chuckled a bit, but no one else was laughing; the four of them stared at Cord, in silence]*.

But for some reason, the hag went away, dissolving behind the opaque wall, and Jenny hid in the weeds, inexplicably, and I drifted to thoughts of Pastina, and my mom.

My mom used to make me Pastina when I was a little kid - five or six years old; it was my favorite. To me, Pastina *was* my mom; thoughts of it meant always led to thoughts of her. I haven't thought of Pastina in years. But here, I've thought about it. And with it, comes my mom. And in this little Town I stumbled upon, she has started visiting me, through wisps of memories, smells and foods, nowhere else but here....Belvidere, New Jersey. And I still don't know why that is; it makes no sense.

And because of the Pastina, and my mom, the darkness of my dreams last night, and the hag, started to fade, just a bit.

So I got up and took a shower, feeling lousy about yesterday - about you Lilly - and it being over, before it really ever started; about the dream, the hag....*everything*. And then, in the shower, I saved a small flying ant from drowning....sure death. It was in the shower, on the wall, and the water nearly got her, but I saved her, put her safely outside the shower, and the little ant, that little save, which I never thought I'd ever tell a soul about, started to draw the curtain a bit further back, to lift the cloud.

And then I remembered about today, about Earl's conte and was amazed that I could have ever even forgotten, even for a second, this very special day. I was so wrapped up in my own sorry state, that I almost forgot. Sorry Earl; there was no excuse for that. But luckily, I didn't. And then I got excited, about seeing my best friend again *[C raised his hand and gently cupped the side of Earl's face]*, and you are, Earl, my best….kindred….best friend.

Okay, back on track.

So I get out of the shower, I'm excited and now feel like I'm running late, you know, so I figure I gotta rush around, but before I can get going, what happens? What always happens? Of course, gotta take a dump *[Lilly stared at C with a 'really – you just said that on record' look]*. Sorry, always happens that way *[C shrugged; Earl did too, just because]*.

So I do, and then, *finally*, I realize why I'm here in Belvidere, why today is today, why it happened, why my mom, her essence, is close, and why everything is going to be okay *[Cord looked at the two of them and smiled, a small uptick – his signature]*.

The bowl was full of blood.

CHAPTER 338 – IN THIS PLACE, IT COULD BE ALL OF THE ABOVE - ONE BITE

It felt like a real cry.

She had felt happy, felt sad, angry, content - all the above, and more, in this place, and they felt real, as real as they ever did before. But she had never cried here, not that she could remember, even though she should have, she should have cried often.

But she didn't.

Crying, for some reason, some unwritten rule, felt off-bounds. Not that there was a rule book to read or a *Welcome* pamphlet to study when you showed up.

There was nothing, except mostly silence....most of the time.

But *time*, in this place, was different. It wasn't even really time, like she remembered. Twenty five years in this place meant nothing; there was no *twenty-five years* in this place.

Here, to her, it always seemed to be *now*, and yet it always seemed to be *then*, and always *next-up*, simultaneous....layered, like a cake you cut through and eat in one single bite. *Then, now* and *next-up,* stacked together, bite after bite. All at the same time, *all* the time. It was the only way she could describe it, to herself, since there was no one else here, in this place, wherever she was, whatever it was called, to describe it to, or talk to, or discuss it with.

It was just her, alone, always, forever.

Except a fleeting manifest, here and there, an interjection into a dream, a whisper in an ear, an attachment to a thought, a fleeting meet on a bench, or in a train station, a small note left in a cemetery, a hand-squeeze in the dark. But those things she didn't really control, they just kinda happened; more so when she wished *hard* for them, but that didn't always work. And sometimes it worked with no wish at all.

The exception, of course, was Earl. Her only real two-way. My God, she missed him.

Talking to Earl was the *highlight* of her life; but of course, it wasn't a real life, it was whatever it was that she was. But regardless of all that, there was no crying, till now.

Like an amputee that feels legs where none exist; a tear tracked a cheek she didn't have; it was a curious feel. And she focused on it, as it ran over her skin to the side of her nose, dead-ending at the top of her lip. She rubbed what should be her lips together to capture it, taste it, absorb it.

And then it was gone.

She wondered what type of tear it was, because she was both happy and sad, angry and relieved; in this place, it could be all of the above - one bite.

CHAPTER 339 – LET'S GO FOR DOOR NO. 3

C took a deep breath, and continued; a bowl of blood needs a bit of explaining.

"All these scars, all over my body, that's another story, many stories, for another time. Well partly, I guess it's time, for some. The skewers, the fence, you know about those. Many of the others are from what you likely expect they're from; endless altercations spanning the globe. Some regrettable, most not; reminders of one mess after another....*one big mess*. But I always walked away - shouldn't have, shouldn't have made it through many of them, but somehow did. It always seems to work that way. The others, they didn't walk away, not-so-much. In fact, in the end, they never did.

Those seem to be the rules.

But that, or those, don't need to be discussed, not now, not today. Probably not ever.

But there are other mementos adorning my body; I call those Door No. 3, so to speak. And they matter to the story today, this story, right now.

So let's go for Door No. 3.

CHAPTER 340 – AND NOW SHE WAS, ALL OVER AGAIN, NOT OF, BUT FOR

"Some of the scars, mostly the round, melon-ball looking ones, and some of the Frankensteins, they're from a different puppet, living and crawling around inside my skin; Door No 3.

I've had a load of nasty malignancies, at least a dozen times, maybe more....lost count, for real. And some of those long jagged scars....remnants of the excisions. The melon balls are the defense, to stave off the Frankensteins. I've had hundreds of them done....*hundreds*. Buckshot spread over my body, blind shots trying to find this particular puppet; find where it will raise its head....next.

Doctors were baffled. Said I should be written up in medical journals, some *Aesculapian* freak. No one has that many melanomas, malignancies and somehow manages to dodge them all, *no one*. They said they seem to come on like no tomorrow, arising on my body from nowhere, grow, start to metastasize, get ugly quick, but then somehow stop and wait, like they're marking time, waylaying till chanced upon and smoked out, excised and discarded, all before they spread to a point where they simply can't be *unspread*.

And so it goes, over and over, a game, waiting for the next *Wack-A-Mole* to pop.

The doctors, a bunch of 'em, have said they never saw anything like it; the cells should have spread like wildfire - they had plenty of time to move out of my skin and mushroom everywhere, attack all my organs, go Stage Four, no cure, and kill me quick, but they never did, like they were stopped by something. But there was no *something* that they knew of to stop it, nothing tangible they ever found, nothing that made any sense, at least that's what they said, what they've told me....over and over.

Anyway, I've been fighting off this particular puppet for years. And why do I fight it? Simple, because the rules say I have to. So one set of rules says to kill myself — put a bullet in my brain; the same rules say save myself, excise the cancer. Completely conflicting, yet the rules nonetheless. But then again, when do the rules we all live by ever truly make sense? They don't.

Rules don't have to make sense to be rules.

You know, stupid as it is, I yell at him sometimes, usually in the shower; funny it's a *him*, not a *her*, it should be a her, the malignancy that festers inside. But for some reason, over the years, it has been a *him*. I call him a pussy, goad him to step up and just be done with it — I don't care, done caring, done fighting. Just get it over with."

And Lilly finally realized that rage in the shower she witnessed so long ago, where she thought C was gay, then she thought he was mad at Carol, or Mae, or her; it was none-of-the-above. She wished it had been. And she remembered being afraid.

And now she was, all over again, not of, but for.

CHAPTER 341 - THE WHITE FLAG, IN THIS CASE, IS RED

"The doctors always told me, after I dodged yet another cancer bullet, that the true Rubicon, the bellwether *no-turning-back,* the point where you crossed over the ability to *unspread* the spread, was simple – blood. Specifically, a special type of bleeding, that was pretty hard to miss. See that, in my case they said, and there's no reason to come back and shoot the shit with them anymore. That was Stage Five they used to joke, because there is no Stage Five, but for me, maybe there was – and that meant you were pretty much fucked. They didn't say it quite like that, a little more refined, dignified wording, but that was the gist, that was what I needed to know.

And sure enough it happened; Stage Five *finally* happened.

The puppet behind Door No. 3 finally delivered a knock-out punch, before I had a chance, got around to, stopping him. I didn't knowingly break the rules, although I threatened, I didn't wait any longer to deal with it than I normally do, which is in-time. But this time was apparently not in-time. Which was, and is, fine by me.

And for some reason, he, or they, whomever *they* are, whomever decides these things, decided to give up the game, at least when it came to me. And for some reason, lost to me, they picked Belvidere as the place to hopscotch the Rubicon.

The fight, as of this morning, is finally decided. Times up; game over.

The puppet finally lost, because the other puppet finally won. And he left his calling card this morning, the one-way ticket that no excise, no Frankenstein can fix, in the bowl.

And because of it, the box is no longer needed.

Raise the flag; but the white flag, in this case, is red."

2411

CHAPTER 342 - YOU DON'T NEED THAT BOX ANYMORE

"Okay, that's it, times up!"

Lilly yelled and she slammed her hand hard on the table. The young man saw it coming and pulled the earphones before she scorched him a second time.

Lillian yanked C by the arm and dragged him up and out of the booth. Earl knew to sit still, so he did, like a good dog. The young man caught Earl's eye and gave him a goofy half-smile, a *some story huh?* kind of look – the kind that thinks the whole thing has got to be some sort of lark, right? This bald guy had to be some kind of actor, bullshit street theater or something, and playing him for the fool; he wasn't falling for that gig. Or maybe this guy really had more than one screw loose. Either way, he wasn't falling for it; boxes and guns and puppets and blood....*come on!* People will say anything to get their story picked to make it on air, and he'll get fired for buying in. Fuck that. But it *was* entertaining, he had to give it that. Although, in the end, he figured this little confessional just might have to get accidentally erased.

Earl just shrugged his shoulders, not sure what else to do. This guy was kind of funny-looking, with those earmuffs, and he wasn't about to talk to him, or anything. He saw the gentleman get up, as if he was going to go out to stretch. He pulled out a crinkled pack of smokes and was going to sneak out and cop a quick drag behind the safety of the booth; no one at this time of night, would catch him smoking indoors, a perk at having the aluminum box in the dead-end *Biltmore Room*. But Earl caught his eye and quickly shook his head a defiant no; it was *dangerous* outside that booth, spelled with a capital *L*. The young man heeded the warning, tucked the pack back in his pocket and quietly sat down.

Smart man.

"Are you fucking kidding me!"

She yelled in his face, up close.

"What?"

Without warning, she slugged him hard in the chest.

"Ow! Fuck!"

"I'll give you *Ow!* Seriously C, seriously?! When were you going to tell me any of that? What kind of fucking story is that?"

"The truth."

He said flat.

"Seriously? You were, are, just going to die on me? On Earl? Seriously?"

She said for a fourth time, shaking her head as her voice trailed off. No more words came.

A single tear emerged and tracked her cheek; he watched it run over her skin to the side of her nose, dead-ending at the top of her lip. She rubbed her lips together to capture it, to taste it, absorb it.

And it was gone.

He pulled her in and hugged her hard, to squeeze the cry out. And it worked, for now.

"I'm calling a *new* doctor tomorrow; doctor's *can* be wrong, they're *always* wrong. And I'm throwing the fucking box away! Rules *can* be broken, I break them all the time, and so will you! End of game, *end of story, and if you even try to stop me....*"

She didn't need to finish the sentence; no ending to that phrase coming from Lillian Liddell was good….a bullet would be better.

She pulled away from him and looked up with eyes that cared.

"You don't need that box anymore."

CHAPTER 343 - I LOVE YOU – DELIVERED EXACTLY THE WAY SHE WANTED IT

"Lilly, I'm sorry about all that, in there; *StoryCorps* is not supposed to be a confessional, at least not like that – Christ! But you asked, and I had to answer, and the answer got kind of convoluted and complicated. But I owed it to you and Earl; it was time to step up....it was just time."

She stepped back into him, eyes puffy and red and sniffed, her nose starting to run.

And she did it.

She kissed him, passionate, long and hard; the kind that says whatever it's supposed to say, with pile-on emphasis.

She pulled away and sniffed her runny nose again....harder. He smiled.

"Wow, that was a sexy end to a kiss; want a tissue?"

She leaned forward and rubbed her runny nose back and forth on his shirt.

"Nope, took care of it."

She smiled and finally did what she needed to do, after six long months of anxiety, selfishness, doubt, mixed messages, missed opportunities and mistakes....plenty of mistakes. Yet it was all healed with three simple words, leaving Lillian's lips:

I love you.

"Yes! Finally! *Let The Wild Rumpus Start!"*

Earl pumped his fist like a Superbowl win and howled as he blew open the spaceship door. He was eavesdropping at peril *[Carol had planted a small suggestion – he would have never dared otherwise]* – at the slightest hint of trouble, he would have gone turtle, clammed right back into his seat. But those words from Lilly signaled a safe zone, temporary perhaps, because these things always have that risk when dealing with his sister, but safe nonetheless....for now.

Safe, and good. Earl was so, so happy.

Lilly and C smiled at their brother and Cord squeezed her ass, then gave it a loving pat....rights of ownership.

She proceeded to slug him in the chest – harder.

"There's your rumpus."

She deadpanned.

That's all it took. Earl dove back in the rabbit-hole, the door slammed shut and C was on his own, swinging in the wind, like usual.

She chuckled, looked into his eyes and tenderly kissed him again, the kind that seals the deal. For added measure, she squeezed *his* butt, which he let slide.

"Don't you have something to say, *in return*?"

She quizzed, throwing the trailer on so he wouldn't get the answer wrong.

He looked at her and sighed, one of happiness, and utter relief.

"Lilly, I've loved you the moment I saw you through the glass door of Sam's, with that stupid apron on, you know that; you've *always* known that."

She smiled; of course she did.

"Say it anyway. I want to hear it, without any wisecracks or anything, just say it, and it better be good."

He kissed her, pulled her back in and gave her a tight, enveloping embrace; the kind her mom used to give her, shared warmth, shared skin, shared everything.

She pulled away, a bit startled.

"That was a mom-hug C. I mean, that was *just* like my mom used to give, really; that was the best hug *ever;* thank you....thank you."

Her voice trailed off.

And then the line came, a line he rarely, if ever, dished, and certainly not this way, without any hint of a wisecrack, delivered the way it was supposed to be, the way it should be....the right way:

I love you.

Delivered exactly the way she wanted it.

CHAPTER 344 – HE SLIPPED BEHIND HER AND SLID BACK INSIDE

"We really need to get back in; our guy wants to go home sometime today."

"Nice try. Let's try this again; who was the married one, in the museum? What happened?"

"Does it really matter? Another one that ended badly, because I'm a dick….next."

"No argument there. Okay, how about Selena, from Belize; what's her story?"

"Again, she's not from Belize; she's from London."

"Okay, whatever. So who was in Belize then, on that little island you wanted to take me to and do God knows what? Never mind, forget that, for now. Okay, what's her story then, this Selena chick from Belize, with the bad hair? *So*?"

"So nothing."

Lilly put her hands on her hips; she could wait all day.

"We had a rough patch in London; she was happy to see me."

"She didn't look happy. And you; happy to see her?"

"Alive? Yes. Please Lilly, too many confessions in one day; my head's starting to hurt. We got plenty of time for this….later."

"You're not getting a pass on this stuff, just so you know."

C sighed and shrugged his shoulders.

"I know, I know."

"What's in the envelope, in the box? What's in it?"

"I thought we were done with questions for now?"

"I didn't say we were done."

C sighed again.

"The call I make, that person takes care of the mess, so to speak. Putting a bullet in your brain can be a bit messy. And if they run late, or someone else stumbles in, on me, that would create some problems, so the envelope is kind of an instructional to that unfortunate soul on who to call. But it shouldn't be necessary, since the speed dial person kinda travels in tandem with me, staying kinda close, but not too. And *never* interfering. The speed dial person has all the other numbers of people to call, and a recipe of what to do next, starting with me.

"Selena!"

Lilly solved a small piece of the puzzle. C sighed a third time, and frowned.

"Not usually; in fact, not ever. But this time, the whole fourth dart thing, it felt different, and Selena and I went through some pretty bad shit together, so I found her and asked her, rather than the person who has taken care of this sort of thing for me for years. I asked, and she, reluctantly, said yes. But she's a one and done. I shouldn't have ever asked her, shouldn't have subjected her to this nonsense, but I did. It was a mistake. It's a long story. Anyway, I couldn't take it back; but I won't do it again."

"What again! There is no *again!* Call her up, tell her to ship out, back to Belize, or London or wherever she came from; services not rendered, services not needed! The box is gone! *Done!*"

"Done."

C parroted, not too convincingly. Abandoning the rules? Ditching the box? Telling this story was one thing, but *that* was something entirely different, a decision not to be taken lightly. There would definitely be consequences, and he couldn't imagine what they would, or could, be, but *not good* was pretty much written all over it. That was a given.

Lillian sensed the dilemma, and stared at him serious.

"C, I know it's not easy, living with demons, trust me on that one, but you gotta give it up. Seriously, me or the box; you can't have both."

He knew the right answer, and how wrong it really was. He grabbed her loosely around the waist.

"I know, it's just….I know."

She looked him square in the eyes.

"Your *lot* in life is *not* to be alone, not anymore. You won't forget my face and I won't forget yours, because *you,* you're not going *anywhere*, without me. I've decided that, so it's settled. Don't give away a keeper C."

She leaned forward and kissed him on the lips and whispered.

"And what *hasn't* happened, still might happen, maybe *much sooner* than you think, and I'm not even drunk."

She kissed him again and smiled wry. He returned the look and whispered.

"Christ, last time we got this close, it was a disaster, need I remind you."

"That was a different life; that Bibby doesn't exist anymore."

"You promise, Bibby?"

"Yeah, that's a promise."

She responded soft. And C continued.

"That, by the way, wasn't very satisfying, not at all. I don't like calling you by that name - Bibby - just wanted to do it and not get stabbed with a fork."

Lilly smiled.

"Agreed, no stabbing, but don't say it again; doesn't sound right coming from you….kinda creepy."

He kissed her on the nose.

"Agreed."

And Lillian threw the next cast into the water.

"You know what? You *were* right about one thing; meeting me was the *best* thing that *ever* happened to you, even better than that little knobby-kneed girl, right?"

Oh boy.

C just smiled goofy, buying time, but didn't shake his head yes. He couldn't; he just wasn't ready to say no to Kristine yet, not aloud, anyway. She was the only thread he had to life before the puppet, the crickets, the flies, the only one-way ticket to a simpler, better time. She had *always* been his only hope....salvation. Kristine was a tough give-up, no matter how much he loved Lillian.

Lillian saw the hesitation, and surprisingly, let Cord off the hook, for now.

"Well what's her name anyway, besides knobby-kneed girl, this eleven-year-old competition?"

"I don't think she's eleven anymore, more like forty-three, if my math's correct."

Lilly slugged C hard in the chest.

"You're doing *math* with her?"

Lilly huffed indignant.

"Whatever, she's probably an old fat cow with wide hips, a paunch and cankles; cankles are the worst."

Lilly added, scrunching her face for emphasis.

"And you're sure she has 'em....cankles?"

C said, sarcastic.

"Most definitely. And a load of kids and a dork husband who wears too-white sneakers all day and drives a gay minivan. No reason to think about her; I wouldn't bother with the math."

C cocked his head. Funny, he never thought of Kristine in that way, even though it was certainly reasonable to do so, reasonable to think of anyone who grows up, to end up, that way: fat, with cankles, a dork husband and a minivan – the whole pathetic package. More do than don't; they walk the streets every day, lots of sub-fives.

Lillian continued.

"Anyway, there's a second girl, against her better judgment, that truly loves you, and this one isn't slipping away....*ever*."

Lilly slipped her arm in his and they made their way back to the booth; that made them both smile – Cord….and Carol.

The door busted open and Earl yelled.

"Come on! Earmuff guy wants to go home and I got a question to ask!"

Cord kissed Lillian on the forehead and, single file, he slipped behind her and slid back inside.

CHAPTER 345 – SHE CLOSED HER EYES, STUCK IT IN, AND KEPT GOING

Earl looked nervous, but determined, more nervous than determined. Carol slowly slid her hand in his and told him it'd be alright. That was all she had to do, all she ever had to do.

Now Earl just sat and smiled, waiting for Lillian to take her seat. This was the *big* one, the biggest one ever, and he kept practicing his line in his head, moving the words around, this one sounded better, no that one....no, the first one.

Cord and Lillian settled in, both smiling and a bit giddy, like high-schoolers on a date. All was right with the world, Lilly thought.

Jokingly, Lilly squeezed C's hand.

"My God, this feels like a test; I got butterflies! Hope I studied the right stuff!"

Nothing but nervous ran through her voice.

"You'll be fine; it's supposed to be fun."

C said warm, squeezing her right hand in support. And he kept it there.

"Are you kidding? I just listened to your's."

She deadpanned.

"Well, it needed to be said, it was, and in the end, *outside* the booth, it was pretty fun."

The young man raised his eyebrows, and C smirked.

"Oh my God! We forgot to talk about the doctor, the blood, the...."

Lilly exclaimed; C put his hand on her shoulder, then back on her hand.

"Don't worry about that, we'll talk about it later. I'm done, test over, your turn….now don't get *nervous*."

She punched him in the arm.

"I am nervous! Cut it out!"

"Don't be nervous Bibby, it's okay."

And the way Earl said it, even, assured, adult, startled her, and she did a double-take. Then recovered.

"See, he can say Bibby and it doesn't sound creepy; it sounds just right."

Lilly giggled, but Earl could see her hand was trembling. She was so scared, so he cradled her left hand; the right was still beneath Cord's.

Earl gently looked at his sister, and said what was ready to be said.

"Lilly, take it out."

"Take *what* out?"

She said, her voice lilting, halting. But she knew *exactly* what he meant. And she started to cry.

"I can't Earl, I can't, I…."

And she lowered her head. The booth was silent. After a bit, without further prompt, Lilly softly spoke, head down, talking to her shoes.

"She used to write notes, little slips of white paper, folded in half, or fours….we both did, to each other, and hid them around the house, like a treasure hunt. Hidden

2425

in a book, under a sofa cushion, in the fridge, under the Kleenex box. Our own little language. When we wanted to just say *Hi,* or *I love you,* or *I'm sorry.*"

Lilly choked up on the *sorry.* The word came out crooked, staccato, in a half-whisper.

"Sometimes, I would just put one word per note, with a number next to each, a puzzle, a riddle to solve; those were some of the best. Some she never found; she'd have to give up and say *uncle;* only when she said *uncle* would I give in and tell her where the missing note, the missing number, was. I was *so* stubborn; she *had* to say *uncle....so stubborn.*

Lilly shook her head, still angry at, and disappointed in, herself after all these years, as the words trailed off to silence.

"You know, she left me a note, Earl, it must have been the night before, 'cause I found it before school, the next day....*that* day. It was in her favorite book, on her favorite page....page 90, I always knew to look there first, it was an easy one. We had a fight over that, over this *[Lilly shook her head and started to say stupid, but she stopped]*....red scarf. I wanted to wear it somewhere and she said no. I don't even remember where, or why it was so important, she rarely said no to anything I asked, especially if *I* thought it was important. Anyway, she did this time, and I got mad; she was probably right, of course, but I still got *so* mad.

So I did what I always did when I got mad at her, to *hurt* her; I gave her the silent treatment....all night. I wouldn't talk to her, stay in the same room, I wouldn't even look at her, to *punish* her....to make *her* apologize to *me,* even though I was in the wrong. That was always the way it went; I could wait for days, it didn't matter; no matter what I did, I'd wear her down and she eventually would apologize to me, and *I* was the jerk who did something wrong in the first place. But it didn't matter, I had way more patience, more staying power, than her, and I could always tell she was crushed when I did that to her - it broke her heart if I was mad at her - she couldn't take it, but I did it anyway, all the time *[Lilly started to cry]*. I just dug in and waited it out. It was my best weapon; it always worked, one hundred percent, never failed. I hurt her every time.

So I found her note in the book that morning, on page 90 – the first place I looked. It said:

I love you always, miss you a lot.
You can wear it whenever you want Sweetie….

Love, Mom
xxxxx oooo

Anyway, I came to the conclusion I was wrong and she was right about this stupid scarf, her favorite, but it didn't matter, she gave in, like always, to make me happy, always to make me happy.

I always wondered why the last *o* was missing, why there were five *x's* and only four *o's;* did it mean something?

I wrote her a note back and put in on the same page in her book:

Hi Mom!
Have a nice day!
♡
Love, Lilly

With a heart over the *i*; I always did that on her notes."

Lilly shook her head.

"I always thought, later: *what a shitty lame response;* I could have done so much better, written such a better note. She deserved a better note.

But it didn't matter, she never found it anyway. I ripped it up and threw it away. She died Earl, thinking I was still mad at her; she died, *we died*....fighting. I'll never forgive myself for that."

Lilly raised to head to look to Earl for help; he smiled, and that was all the help she needed.

"Earl, the note, the envelope, it's the *last* time we're ever gonna talk. It's still 1981 inside that envelope, it's April 7th *forever.* I'm afraid of what it says, or doesn't say; I promised myself I would *never* read it, 'cause then it's *really* over, and mommy's gone, really gone, forever. And I can't handle that. I never got to....I just can't; she's still *alive* in that envelope."

Earl kept smiling. He knew how hard this was for Lilly, and he was so, so proud of her, for talking, for trying. And she was trying hard.

He reached into her purse and pulled out the crisp, white envelope; even though it was a bit brown and scuffed on the edges, it still looked surprisingly new. Cord stared in awe; that was it - Carol, his friend Carol, had touched it, sealed it with her mouth....owned it. Her words to Lilly lay the thickness of paper away, and had, for twenty-five long years.

Earl handed it to Lilly.

She held the envelope firm, as if she was afraid she'd drop it, break it, her hand trembling. The weight of a feather felt like a brick.

Lillian stared at it, really looked at it, curious, as if she was truly seeing it for the first time.

It simply said:

Lillian

Not Lilly.

That was the first hurt, the first clue the insides probably weren't good. Carol never called her *Lillian* in notes; *Lillian* usually meant trouble, a scolding, not a mushy loving note. That word alone, as far as she'd ever gotten, was enough to give her pause for the past two decades plus, and pause right now.

She looked at Earl for help. He kept smiling; it was a good smile….the best he had.

"Go 'head Lilly; it's okay, I promise."

And she knew that wasn't Earl's okay; that was from her mom.

And that was the okay she needed to slowly slide her finger in the far left end, where the glue didn't take, big enough to put the tip of her finger in. Of course she knew this; she had checked that exact spot a hundred times over the years; stuck the very tip of her pinkie in, and then quickly out, a tease to herself, knowing she'd never go further….being sure never to damage a thread of paper, in any way.

Except for today.

This time, she closed her eyes, stuck it in, and kept going.

CHAPTER 346 – SHE GASPED….AND NOTHING MORE

The top was ripped open, slowly, but not neatly, not like C's Christmas presents.

Lilly stared at the open envelope, somewhat detached from what she had just done. She saw the top of a single folded sheet of thick cream stationary inside, her mom's favorite paper. She had held it up to a light a thousand times, to try and read the words, at least see how long it was: lots of words, that would be bad, a scolding; too few words, that would be bad too, dismissive, a scolding. But the light gave nothing away, not a hint revealed….no secrets betrayed.

Till now.

Lilly's hand was shaking as she slowly extracted the paper from the safety of the torn envelope. She closed her eyes, held her breath and flipped open the crease, to reveal the words to the light of day, twenty-five and a half years after her mother's pen last lifted from the paper.

She gasped….and nothing more.

CHAPTER 347 – MOMMY?

The message was short:

I ___________ _ _ _ _ _

—

_ _ _

____

An *I* followed by a disjointed line, drawn haphazard across and down the page in a jagged prescription; an overdose-induced scrawl.

Carol never remembered putting pen to paper, sealing the envelope, writing Lillian's name on the front, or handing that horrible albatross to her daughter. She didn't remember a single moment of the entire act. And Lillian had been tortured for twenty-five years because of it.

Carol never forgave herself for that, for a lot of things, but especially for that.

But she was glad she never finished the note, never started the apology to Lillian and Earl about Button, the one she knew she could never live with - for what she had done with him, for what he had done to her....for what she had, growing, inside her.

Unforgivable, all of it.

And Lillian would never know, nor would Earl....ever. And for that, Carol was grateful.

The booth was silent, as that single, horrible word, and a scratched lifeless line, sunk in. But before Lillian could react, could scream, or cry, or anything, Earl gently cupped her hand and closed his eyes.

And she finally, softly, spoke, barely above a whisper, into her daughter's ear.

Lillian began to cry, her lips trembling, as she slowly whispered a single question, set inside a single word:

"Mommy?"

CHAPTER 348 – EASY! TODAY! BABA GHANOUSH!

They were on foot, C in the lead, hustling up East 43rd, a short block, and hanging a right on Madison. Lilly never paid a shred of attention to the stores they passed: *Coach, Brooks Brothers, Burberry,* nothing but a blur; she was walking on air, her body still numb. The street was throbbing with people, going here and there, to and from, in a hurry; that was the City, that was *always* the City.

Cord had waited till now, but couldn't wait any longer. It had been about fifteen minutes since they left the booth, and Lilly was still aglow, a battery recharge like no other. He swore she wasn't walking, but floating, down the street. Ay whispered to her, but loud enough for Earl to hear.

"So, what did she say?"

"What I needed to hear."

Was all Lillian said, and then she smiled and squeezed C's arm tight, the kind that says don't ask any more questions, life is grand, and I'm happy, happier than I've been in twenty-five years, in forty-one years....*life is worth living.*

"Wow! Did you see earmuff guy go down when mom talked to Lilly? ***Bam!***"

Earl said, for at least the sixth time, slapping his hands together for effect, before prattling on.

"He's lucky he didn't hit his head on the table....that's a very sharp edge! I think those earphones broke his fall. Thank goodness we didn't have to give him mouth-to-mouth, right C? Because that guy woulda been a goner for sure! I'm not kissing any guy, especially with earmuffs! Right C?"

C chuckled.

"Right; goner for sure."

"Those were the best *StoryCorps* stories ever, right C?"

"Yeah, well, *StoryCorps* is not always so….dramatic, that's for sure. If those stories don't make the Friday addition, I can't imagine what will."

"I told him not to, when he woke up. I told him to chuck 'em, please get rid of them."

Lilly confessed.

"Is that what you were jabbing about?"

Cord asked.

"Those are *our* stories, not for everybody else. Plus, he told me he didn't believe them anyway; he thought we were all actors, some hidden camera thing, pulling his leg. So I bought in; told him he figured us out….I fessed up. Anyway, no one would believe those stories, on the radio; they'd think we were a bunch of drugged-out wack-jobs, or something. No thanks. They served their purpose, *for us*. Anyway, too late, done and gone. I watched him destroy them; told him I wasn't leaving till he did, so he did. He just wanted out of there, trust me. He had his fill of us, for sure. Christ."

"Lilly, they're meant to be listened to, that's the point, stories about everyday people."

C said, less than convincing; Lilly just looked at him, head cocked, like he was a nut.

"Well, yeah, okay, they were more than a bit out there, for sure. And they're gone, so water under the bridge; who cares."

"Yeah! Who cares?!"

Earl yelled, hands over his head in victory, for no particular reason.

"Yeah, easy for you to say, you didn't have to take the quiz!"

Lilly snapped.

"That's right, I got out of it! Thank God that guy fainted! Class dismissed!"

"Not so fast Earl."

"**Neighbors!**"

Earl yelled at C's line, plucked from the movie. His hands, once again, over his head, as the trio skipped down the sidewalk, weaving in and out of the crowd.

C smiled; Earl was right, that *was* a line from their favorite movie, but that's not why C said it, so he continued.

"Just 'cause we're not in the booth, doesn't mean you get a pass, birthday or not."

C talked stern.

"What?"

Earl said, suddenly nervous at the game-changer.

"Here's your question, Buddy, no chance to run!"

"Wait! No! Not ready; *no!*"

Earl went to cover his ears and close his eyes, the ultimate question-block. But C threw out the query before Earl could complete the deflection.

"What's the very best day of your life?"

Earl suddenly stopped on the crowded sidewalk, forcing a sea of people to stream left and right, like a wake. He slowly pirate-smiled and whispered the answer to the easiest quiz he ever took, just loud enough so they both could hear.

"Easy! Today! Baba Ghanoush!"

CHAPTER 349 – LEGS CLAMPED HARD; IT WAS THE RIDE OF HER LIFE!

At West 50th they hung a left.

Before them lay the largest church in the world, at least the largest Earl and Lillian had ever laid eyes upon. It was a medieval fortress, with Gothic spires spiking deep into the night sky.

"My God."

Lillian whispered, her eyes trailing the spiny stone skin as it expanded, seemingly forever, down the Avenue. It engulfed the whole City block, half-shrouded behind a line of large trees, dwarfed by the edifice.

"*St. Patrick*s, pretty famous."

C said.

"*St. Patricks*?! That's the same church as in Belvidere!"

Earl yelped.

"Not quite the same; I think this one's *just* a bit bigger. Here, let's duck in for a quick peak, no charge to look; those pesky Catholics are pretty generous that way."

C took Lillian by the arm, and with Earl in tow, they half-skipped the granite steps to the side entrance off 50th, passing through thick, massive wooden doors.

Just inside the portal it felt dim, opaque, even though it wasn't particularly so. An amalgam of smells greeted them: timeworn oiled wood, the cold dampness of shadowed stone and the sooty wax of burning candles, all mixed with the snuff of parchment and worn leather from hundreds of hymnal tomes, scattered amongst the endless pews populating the nave. The space was simply cavernous – the arched, ribbed marble columns and ceiling felt as if they'd been swallowed whole into the belly of the beast - the sinewy insides of a ribcage of rock, half a football field tall, and one-plus long.   It seemed impossible to Earl that a church could be so big; probably *everybody* in Belvidere could fit inside, plus the whole herd of cows at Marty's farm, the chickens too! Who would build such a thing, for the whole town, and the cows and chickens? Earl wasn't sure why he thought that, he just did. He looked to his left and saw a pipe organ on the far wall; it looked to be floating in the air, way above his head. It seemed the size of their old house on Fourth Street, bigger even. There must have been hundreds of people walking about, and although some knelt in pews, bent in prayer, most others milled and gawked about the perimeter; the utter size of the space simply engulfed them, and made their presence seem insignificant....small. Lillian and Earl were afraid to even speak; they craned their necks up and down, left and right, trying to take in the architectural overdose: acres of stained glass – in deep shades of blue; blood-reds everywhere – from garnet-velvet roping to crimson Persian carpets to rows of flickering vermilion glass – votive fleeting flames devoted to unspoken hopes and unanswered prayers; reliquaries full of aged paintings – replete with golden halos; saintly sculptures carved in marble filling every darkened alcove: Anthony and Andrew, Elizabeth and Rose, Joseph, Bridget and Bernard....Saints galore. It was garniture atop spangle, heaped upon embellishment....everything outdoing everything around it. And it was all sprinkled in gold, aureate highlights pole to pole: chandeliers, candle pikes, brackets, baldachins and more, which seemed to mass and coalesce at the enormous High Altar, the gilding flickered in pious amber light.

It was utter excess, somehow dignified by the divine, shared by the hushed humanity which quietly shuffled through the space....an endless, faceless wave.

The throng, in toto, guided by some unseen hand, following some unwritten rule, circumvented the altar in a counterclockwise rotation. The three of them were swept along, captured by the tide, slowly drifting with the flow. Earl had wanted to light a candle, there were a whole pack of pretty gold votive set beside a carving of the *Holy Family*. He had done that once in St. Patrick's in Belvidere and made a wish; he figured a wish was probably called a prayer in such a situation, and lit a candle - Marty had lent him the quarter. But he didn't have a quarter here, and he was sure *these* candles weren't quarter-candles anyway; this place was way too fancy for just a quarter. He couldn't even imagine what a prayer would cost in this place. Anyway, he was afraid to ask C, because he was afraid to even speak.

So the candle and the quarter and the prayer, came and went, along with the *Holy Family*.

Eventually the crowd steered them out the front doors, depositing them onto the steps along 5th Avenue, across from an enormous, forty-five foot bronze statue of *Atlas*, holding the heavens aloft.

Only then did Lillian speak, and she whispered two words, shaking her head in disbelief.

"*The money.*"

And that's all she said about the Catholic experience.

The trio made their way down the steps and hooked a left, taking C's lead. They skipped across the Avenue, defying the blinking red hand.

"What's next?"

Earl asked, safely on the far curb.

"Yeah, tough to top the last one; not the Church, although that was pretty amazing, but I meant before that….pretty tough to top *that*."

Lillian said, and finished her sentence with a long kiss, planted on C's neck.

"I could get used to *that*, real easy."

C said.

So Lillian planted another kiss on him, even longer, just as they found themselves at the mouth of a long, lovely corridor; sloped and stepped stones made up an expansive walkway between two large edifices, crafted from the same rock, with a raised planting bed running ribbon down the center, filled with a medley of greenery and October flowers in bloom.

"The Promenade."

Was all C said.

"Where's it go?"

Earl asked, excited.

"Let's find out."

C answered through a sly smile.

And the three of them made their way down the gallery, arms hooked, on their way to Oz, moving closer to what, Earl and Lillian simply didn't know. At this point, everything was still, very much, a surprise.

The Promenade deposited them at a knee wall, which looked down upon the most famous rectangle of white in the world, beyond which was set a large gold sculpture of a recumbent young man, leaping alongside a large ring, holding something, which wasn't exactly clear, in his hand.

Earl stared at the spectacle below in awe.

"Holy mackerel; *skating*!"

Was all Earl could muster. But that was enough to make C smile. The very best day ever kept getting better.

"Is this really the....."

Lilly started to say; her mom had skated here once, just once, in borrowed skates, as a kid. She remembered the story, told many times over.

"Yep, ice skating in Rockefeller Center; can't get much more New York than that."

"What's *that*?"

Earl said, pointing at the golden giant.

"*Prometheus;* he was a Titan, in Greek mythology. He stole fire from the Gods and gave it to man, and was punished because of it, tortured forever for it, by Zeus, King of the Gods. Zeus chained him to a rock, where an eagle came and ate Prometheus' liver – ate it while he was alive – eaten alive. Then the liver would grow back and was eaten again by the eagle, every day. Prometheus was tortured by being eaten alive, daily, *forever*....and that's a pretty long time. Prometheus supposedly created man from clay. But it was worth it, to him, because Prometheus was a champion of humanity, or an idiot, one or the other, or both."

C said, sarcastic.

"Is he real? And why is he here, guarding the ice?"

Earl asked.

"Looks real to me. And good question; why's he here - who knows?"

C said, shrugging his shoulders.

It was only October 7th, but the rink was already teeming with skaters.

"My God, it's only October; it's not even cold out! When do they open this?"

Lilly asked.

"This weekend actually; it's the first weekend of the season. Just dumb luck, for us, but since it was open, thought you'd like to see it."

C said, shrugging his shoulders a second time.

And they did.

The trio made their way around the rink to the *Rock Center Cafe*, a small bistro ice-side, with a floor to ceiling room-length wall of glass overlooking the rink....eye level.

Skaters, young and old, circled beyond the glass in an endless, counterclockwise procession, some fast and talented, most slow and cautious. Three lithe men gliding effortless across the ice stood out amongst the crowd; a small group of young girls held hands as they laughed and screamed - a swirling, spinning, turning patchwork of colorful garb. The lot of them would release their loose-knit fishnet of hands as they overtook slower skaters, and struggled to reconnect, only to break grips again at the next obstacle....an endless, blissful cycle. Rump-drops rained regular, followed by adult laughs and children wails. A few tip-toed on their skates, grasping the perimeter rail in a death-grip; one old man, a permanent scowl etching his face, skated round, round and round....an automaton, grumbling at anyone close enough to grumble at. Enormous white and blue snowflakes, five feet wide, produced by some hidden projector, danced on the side of the skyscrapers nearest the ice....forever flying and falling around the skaters in an endless loop of film.

It was beautiful, comical and mesmerizing; New York, wrapped in a schnitzel.

Menus came and a montage of food was ordered; Lilly was famished, since she gave her Marek-booty away. She smiled to herself; that she even met Marco already seemed like a distant memory. She had already forgotten him, and his was not a face to forget, till her stomach whined for food. Woman would kill to be with Marco, and he was already less than an afterthought; such was this wonderfully wacky day.

She wouldn't trade it for the world.

Across the table was spread a melange of dishes: mushroom soup, set beside mushroom risotto, marinated olives and garlic-infused broccoli rabe. Kir Royales graced the table, along with a tall, dark blue bottle of *Saratoga* sparkling water; Lilly simply loved the bottle, and ordered it for no other reason. She never drank a sip.

A warm smile graced Lillian's face and she stared upwards, at nothing in particular, oblivious to the throng circling on skates just feet beyond the glass.

"What?"

C said.

"*What?* Are you kidding me?"

Lilly responded, incredulous.

"Do you think it'll happen again, like it does for Earl?"

C whispered.

She grabbed Cord's arm and shimmied close to his face.

"I don't care, it doesn't matter. I talked to my mom, C; it was *her*! For real C, for real; it wasn't wishful thinking, it wasn't my imagination....it was **real**. Once is enough, another is good, more would be even better, but it's all just icing from here on in. Once is more than enough for me. It's what I needed....I'm content."

She leaned across the table and kissed C.

"Hey, where's Earl?"

The big man's absence was delayed-notice to Lillian; he had been gone for the last ten minutes, at least. C smiled wry and pointed through the thick glass.

"The man who's afraid to talk to anybody just found a new girlfriend and convinced the ice-skating rink police to let him on the ice in his street shoes, go figure; *baba ganoush* must really, truly work, especially when you're the size of your brother."

Earlier, as the bounty arrived at the table, and Lillian was searching for the bathroom, Earl had noticed a little girl, no more than six, in an all-pink jumpsuit, with little silver stars sewn all around. It was hard to miss her, since she was holding onto the rail just the other side of the glass, directly in front of the table, less than five feet away, wildly waving at Earl....*right at him*! At first he was scared and pretended not to see her, but she was a bit hard to ignore; she was persistent, relentless....a little Lilly.

By the second loop around she was smiling and waving so vigorously, Earl was afraid her arm would fall off.

By the third loop, Earl was in love.

And his immense size didn't scare her in the least; every time she finished her pass by the window in front of Earl's chair, she pulled fiercely on her mom's arm, to quick-skate the other three sides of the rink, a little girl pushing people out of the way, so she could, once again, stand in front of Earl, smile and wave.

She had never seen someone so big. It was very first crush; she was in love with a giant.

Her mother was oblivious, gabbing incessantly on a cellphone, paying no attention to the affair at hand, holding her daughter's hand like holding a leash, and skating entirely too slow, for three-quarters of each loop, for little Patricia's liking.

On that third loop, Earl was smiling and waving as frantically at Patricia as she was at him.

By the fifth loop, her mother had stopped by the rail at the opposite end of the rink, a world away, and began unlacing her skates, never missing a word on the cell, pinched in the crook of her neck. Patricia was in an absolute panic, shrieking and pulling on her mother's leg, kicking at her skate, trying to stop the unlacing. The mother never once glanced at her daughter; tuning out the wails and paying no mind to the kicking, tugging, jerking and yanking. She stuck and wiggled her fingers beneath the bootstraps to loosen their grip on her feet. This bit of New York fun was clearly over.

Until that is, a large tree trunk appeared beside her, casting a long, dark shadow across her face.

The mother looked up, and up, and almost fell backwards on her rump. Earl stared down at her; it took all his courage to do so, but he did, repeating *baba ganoush* to himself, in his head. It made him feel safe.

Patricia instinctively latched onto Earl's calf, the size of the woman's waist, and simply refused to let go.

Earl, trembling, nervous, and speaking barely above a whisper, explained his *relationship* with her daughter, his honorable intentions, and pointed to Lillian and Cord as witness, as if the two smiling Snapperheads in the *Rock Cafe* meant anything.

But apparently they did, as did Earl, because the mother granted him not two, but three go-rounds in the rink, paying for the skates Earl did not don, Patricia riding high on the giant's shoulders, a world above the ice, eye to eye with Prometheus….a true queen.

"I don't have a daddy."

She said. They were the first words she ever spoke to Earl. She didn't say it happy, or sad, it was rather matter-of-fact, more to simply get it out of the way. Which Patricia thought was an important thing to do.

"Me neither."

Earl's first words to her.

"Maybe you can be my daddy! Or my boyfriend!"

With that, she smiled sly and put her tiny hand over his eyes, so he couldn't see. He grabbed her legs tight, then pretended he was stumbling and going to fall.

But she wasn't scared a lick. Patricia laughed and shrieked, her legs clamped hard; it was the ride of her life!

CHAPTER 350 – KISSING HIM REPEATEDLY ON THE TIP OF HIS HEAD

They were nearing the end of the third lap and Earl was taking the *babiest* of baby steps, *barely* inching forward. It was still too fast.

"Slower!"

Patricia yelled frantic, wanting the last lap to *never* end, as her mother held her hands on her hips, sans phone; she was ready to leave two laps ago.

"You know, it's my birthday today."

Earl whispered.

"Mine too! Mine too!"

Patricia shrieked, but it wasn't really; it wasn't for....she didn't know how long. But it didn't matter, it felt like a birthday, to her.

"Really?"

Earl said.

She put her head down and shook it a sad no.

"Well it doesn't matter, your birthday is coming up; it's *always* coming up, right?"

She raised her head, smiled and shook a hopeful yes.

"Well, here's a present for you."

And in his pocket, Earl pulled out the best present ever, a beautiful, huge gray and white herring gull feather, the biggest, most beautiful feather Patricia had ever laid eyes upon.

"Now let me tell you."

Earl continued, entrancing his new little friend.

"This feather is *magical,* and brings the best luck *ever!* My best friend in the whole wide world, my brother, see him in the window over there?"

Earl pointed at C and Lilly; but they weren't looking.

"He's got no hair, like you!"

"That's right, the short one with no hair; he's pretty short, trust me on that, but that's okay, 'cause he's a *kindred spirit*; do you know what that means?"

Patricia shook *yes* at first, then shook her head the truth - *no*.

"Well, me neither, at least I didn't, at first. But it's good stuff, *the best ever!* My mom says so, and if she says so, then it is, and *that's that*!"

Patricia agreed with a vigorous shake of the head; she was sold.

"Anyway, my brother, his name's Cord, but I call him C; C gave it to me, as a gift, and he says that this feather will bring me good luck, the best luck ever....and it did! Lots of it! All day today! And the luck just keeps coming, better and better! And I just got the feather today, for my birthday! From C! Like saving *Louie the Lobster,* and he's going to Panama and I'm meeting him there soon, swinging in a hammock with C, and because C and Lilly, that's my sister, right over there, the *real* pretty one - she's so pretty isn't she? Anyway Lilly and C, they love each other, they even said so today, and that's the best ever too! And Lilly talked to my mom, for the first time in a *long* time, and they're both real happy again, and nothing is better than that! And I got to come to New York and solve a real mystery and I saw real dinosaurs and it's my birthday and I learned all about *baba ganoush* and a bunch of other bestest stuff I can't even remember....but you know what the **best of the best of the best** of all of it is?"

Patricia just stared at Earl, bewildered; she never heard someone talk so fast!

"Well I'll tell ya; I got to meet **you**! And go ice-skating, with shoes on! Three times around!"

Patricia shrieked in excitement; she loved Earl....she loved him *so* much.

Then Earl whispered to her, like it was a super-secret.

"So you see, this is the *best* day ever for me, ever, *ever, ever*; I couldn't squeeze any more good luck out of this feather even if I wanted to, and I don't....any more best luck and I wouldn't even know what to do with it! Besides, I want to save the rest and give it to you, so you can get a brand new dad and we can be friends forever and ever! And you know what?"

Patricia shook her head no; she couldn't possibly think what.

"I'm gonna come skate with you next year, on my birthday, and every birthday after that, just you and me, forever! The feather seals it....deal?"

Patricia reached down her hand and it was engulfed in Earl's mitt; a shake and sealed-deal if there ever was one. He carefully took the feather and gently ran it down her cheek, barely touching her skin; it was the best feeling ever, one she never forgot.

"I love you Earl."

"I love you too P."

No one had ever called her that before, and she never let anyone ever call her that again, no one but Earl.
Ever.

Earl shuffled the last quarter lap in silence, a satisfied smile tracing his face. Patricia clutched the feather like her life depended on it, smiling and kissing him repeatedly on the tip of his head.

CHAPTER 351 – IT DOESN'T WORK THAT WAY....DREAMS NEVER DO

The three little girls shrieked, arms locked, stumble-skating round the rink. Patricia looked at her watch; it was just about time to go.

"Come on girls, three more laps....that's it."

"Oooooh!"

Came the collective whine, as if on cue. But it wasn't unexpected; it was always a three-lap warning, not two, not four....always three. That was Aunt Patricia's rule. It just was, and the girls never knew why, nor would their aunt ever tell.

Patricia didn't skate anymore; she hadn't for years. She simply stood by the rail and watched the grandchildren circle the familiar ice. Exhausted, cheeks cherry red, they bustled up next to her.

"Can Diane *please* see it....*please???*"

One of the little girls pleaded like little girls do, as if their life depended on it.

Patricia huffed; it was another ritual. Her granddaughter's needed to see it each year; a skating date at Rockefeller Center wasn't complete without it....and to show it to whatever new friend tagged along.

Patricia clicked open her pocketbook and carefully removed the object of desire.

"Can we have it?"

"No."

Patricia said, dismissive.

"Can we touch it?"

"No, you can look at it, and that's it; it has special, *magical* powers, way too powerful for silly little girls like you."

"Wow!"

All three little munchkins breathed together, which made Patricia crack a small smile, just a small one, one nobody would notice but her.

The three little girls stared in wonder at her hands, holding the delicate gray and white feather, from a herring gull. It was a bit worse for wear, but not too bad, considering it had traveled with Patricia, to and from this place, for the past seventy-three years.

It came out but once a year, on October 7th, Earl's birthday, and only at the rink where *P* first rode high on his massive shoulders, and fell in love.

It was a skating date she never missed.

Patricia ran the feather lightly across her cheek, just like Earl did to her that very first time, and quickly sequestered it back to the safety of her purse. At times she wasn't sure if Earl was even real, if it *really* happened....if it all wasn't just a little-girl's dream.

But there was always the feather; the feather made it real.

And Earl was right, as right as rain; it *was* magical. And for the seven decades since, it brought *P* the best luck ever. She had a full, fantastic life, dreams fulfilled many times over; she was without want, without regret.

Well, except for one, one *big* one.

Not that she hadn't seen him, she did, once a year as promised, usually on October 7th, as planned, but not always. Sometimes it was a day or two early, but never late.

Earl was *never* late.

And with each visit, they skated, and held hands tight, and went for walks up and down the *Promenade* and giggled like little kids. But the best was riding high on his shoulders, and the only thing better than that was simply holding hands. *That* was the best.

And Earl and *P* always held hands.

At least until she opened her eyes; she hated opening her eyes on those mornings. She would quickly close them again, trying to recapture the last scene, to get back to where she just was – a restart.

But it doesn't work that way....dreams never do.

CHAPTER 352 – SERVE UP WHAT'S NEXT....*BITCH!*

Two double-espressos sat empty on the table; a tawny, coffee film lined the tiny white porcelain cups. The bill was paid and sat on the table, waiting to be retrieved.

The two of them watched Earl through the glass, parting with his new-found friend, giving her a hug, and then another, and then just one more. Lilly smiled at the spectacle and spoke fondly to C, as she stared at her brother through the tall bank of glass.

"Little girls always seem to like Earl, I don't know why; they should be afraid of him, he's so big, like a giant. But they're not....they never are."

C smirked, surveying the same scene.

"That's because little girls like little boys, and Earl's a *very big* little boy, the best *little boy* ever. Big girls like Earl too, the innocence of little boys that he never lost, that he'll never lose."

Lillian turned to C and squeezed his hand.

"I love my brother."

"I know you do; I do too."

C said, and squeezed her hand a bit.

"I know I need Earl, but Earl has always needed me, we needed each other, and he always needed me more than I needed him, at least that's what I always thought, always wanted to believe. It was my crutch - what got me out of bed and through the day, every long day, since my mom went away. And now I know he doesn't, he doesn't need me *more;* I'm not sure he even needs me at all, and that makes me scared and sad. And the fact that it's *her*, Carol, makes it even worse. But I have to get my arms around that somehow, someday. I just don't think I'm ready yet, maybe I never will be, but *ready* is coming whether I want it to or not, isn't it?"

C smiled subdued and shook his head, a single nod, that said *yes*, that *someday* had indeed arrived.

And then C said something without thinking, it just came out, on its own. He's not sure why, it just did.

"You know, change happens, whether you want it to, or you're ready for it, or not; it really doesn't give a shit. But it's not all bad, it really isn't. You know, that wacky little Town of yours has changed me, for sure….a dead-end on its way to nowhere. But there's something about it that's just different, but in a good way. You know, I find myself more and more with wet eyes, kind of a happy cry, a pre-cry really, over the simplest little things: stories of goodness, stories of family, stories of friendship; stupid little ditties about you and Earl and Sam and Buck, Marty and Ji-Sue, and all the rest of the characters I've run across - stories I wouldn't have bothered to notice in the past. Strange - does that happen when you get old? Have I crossed the old-man threshold, or have I simply grown a conscience, or a soul, whatever that means?"

"Maybe you've just grown up."

Lillian said, giving him her own hand-squeeze. Cord looked at her, cocked his head and gave a tiny uptick smile.

"Maybe….maybe. It feels good just the same. If *that's* change, I'll take it."

Cord and Lillian stood to go, just when Earl came prancing back in.

"See you found a girlfriend, a little short."

C snarked.

"We said the same thing about you!"

Earl blurted; Lilly laughed and high-fived her brother, jumping a bit to reach his hand.

"And she said you have no hair!"

Earl threw in, for good measure.

"Yeah, yeah; you don't have any yourself pal."

C said, not amused. Then Earl went on one of his famous benders, sucking in a big gulp of air.

"Her name is Patricia, not Pat, not Patty, not *anything* but Patricia, but I call her *P* and she said nobody can call her that but me! She likes that! But her mom didn't, so I just kinda stared at her, all serious and stuff, and whispered *baba ghanoush,* and she laughed, kinda nervous-like, and then everything was okay! Baba ghanoush is the absolute best! It solves everything [*C just smiled*]! And *P* can be *pretty* bossy you know, but I don't care one lick, because I'm used to it, because I have a sister who's kinda bossy, so I know how to handle *bossy [Lillian looked at her brother cocked, in mock anger],* just saying, and I love *P,* and she's not *too* bossy, just a little bossy, because she didn't want the skating to end, but neither did I, so I guess that might make me a little bossy too. But I'm not sure about that."

Then Earl took in another big breath and looked at C and Lillian, who were smiling at him. It was then he noticed them holding hands.

"Hey! You two are holding hands! *Boyfriend-girlfriend; girlfriend-boyfriend!*"

Earl taunted while smiling, like a kid on the playground. But despite the tease, C and Lilly didn't let go. Then the smile drained from Earl's face, and he got a bit serious, since he had something *very* important to confess.

"Hey C, I kinda did something that you might get mad about, and I don't want you to be mad at me, especially not on my birthday."

Earl put his head down, expecting a scold.

"I saw it; it's okay Earl – no worries. I gave it to *you* buddy; it's yours to do with as you wish. That's what gifts are; there are no take-backs."

"Yeah, but I had so much luck with it today, and I figured I was all lucked-out, for me, except bad luck, and we don't want any of that! So I figured *P* could use it; she doesn't have a dad, me neither, so I just figured a magic feather…."

Lillian tugged on Earl's shirt and he bent down; she kissed him on the cheek and whispered in his ear.

"Really? You think so?"

Earl beamed. Lillian smiled and shook a single *yes*, and that was the end of the gull feather talk. C never did find out that little secret.

"Holy shit! It's 10:45! We gotta get going! Stuff to do!"

C yelled.

"Stuff to do?! Are you kidding? I'm going to bed! I'm tired, and this has been a really long, really great day, the best ever, for both Earl *and* me. Thanks C, really; but more?"

C kissed her on the head.

"Earl's gets just one 40th birthday, young lady – one and done! And he's got seventy-five minutes left; the day is not nearly over! He can sleep all day tomorrow, right Earl?"

"Right!"

Earl would have said *right* to anything C said, and Lilly knew it.

So she laid out her next line, the money line, as if an actor on a stage, as both Earl and C lay in wait.

"Okay, okay, serve up what's next....*bitch!*"

CHAPTER 353 – ONE OF THE BEST, FOR LIFE, FOREVER: *AMERICAN PIE*

The Mustang was a rocket headed west; topping out at one-hundred-ten miles per hour along empty stretches of pavement on its one-way to Exit 12 - Hope and the *Land of Make Believe*.

C kept the radio to a whisper; the cabin rumbled low, a metronome of pavement and rubber running under the car. Earl was on the kip in the back seat; Lillian was asleep shotgun, her limp hand slipped neat inside C's.

In the quiet of the cab, C gazed over at her. Eyes shut and lips curved in the subtlest of smiles, she had the look of a little kid coming home from the best field trip ever; peaceful, content, sleeping in her white cotton short-sleeve top and short black skirt. She had kicked off her flats; her thin bare feet with aubergine-painted toes stretched and disappeared into the darkness under the dash. She had flashed her digits earlier in the trip and bragged to him about the fancy French name of her expensive polish, *way better* than any polish Carol would ever have – *aubergine;* the word rolled off her tongue like silk, until C smirked and told her it was eggplant – the word meant *eggplant* - she had eggplant feet. She was furious at the insult, but more so, secretly, at being eggplant-ignorant. And with that, she refused to share her toes with him the rest of the day, until now.

He smiled at the honor.

Cord's eyes drifted up and down the length of her body; she looked as beautiful as the first day he laid eyes on her through the glass at Sam's.

Even more.

He rubbed her palm gently with his thumb as he stared out the windshield at the narrow path the headlight's cut in the ink; her hand was soft and warm in his – the best hand-hold he ever remembered.

Her being up front, beside him, asleep, made him smile, a small uptick; what a ride it had been - April to October.

What a wild ride.

I'll Stand By You

seeped softly from the radio, a second play today, and he thought about how songs like that light the radio, sometimes, just at the right time, and *this* was the right time. Because it was how C felt about the both of them, and how he felt that way about no one else *ever* before.

He would stand by both of them, through thick and thin, without question. He smiled at the memory of talking to Sam that first time at *Nonpareil*, at *The Palace,* and he shook his head a silent yes to himself in the car; yes, he most certainly would step into the path of a bus, for either one of them. Without question.

And that was a great thing.

The song quietly ended and

My Girl

followed. Another song, tailor-made for him, for her, for this day. He just shook his head....serendipity. And then wondered how many other people, driving across the country, or lying in bed, or sitting on a porch were also listening to that song, right now, thinking the same exact thing....a song playing just for them, and no one else.

But it didn't matter, because right here, right now, that song *did* belong to C and Lilly, and no one else.

Baba O'Riley

That song always reminded C of squatting heavy weights when he was younger, twenty-something, it had that association from a first-play in a forgotten gym long ago. And that memory morphed into C and Earl, squatting that first day at Margery's gym; he still couldn't believe what he witnessed, what Earl did in that one half-assed workout. He shook his head in disbelief and turned to see the big man snoring in the back of the Mustang. Never squatted before, ever, and after one workout, *after* kick-boxing with Lilly, taming eight-hundred-thirty pounds like it was a warm-up. Earl was the world record holder in the squat, in a world that had no idea who he was, what he had done, what he was capable of, or that he even existed.

Amazing.

Earl let out a sleep-snort and half-turned on the back seat. World record holder, snoring oblivious in the back seat; C shook his head and smiled at the thought.

The expansion joints clicked, the traffic was light and C's mind continued to wander alone.

If I Can't Have You

From *Saturday Night Fever*. That was strange; it was the second time he had heard that one today - the first was on the way to Sandy Hook, or New York....the details of the long day's events started to blur. He enjoyed listening to it alone; the kind of song a guy can enjoy alone in the car, but would never admit to amongst his friends. A group of guys in the car? That song gets turned off with a dismissive laugh as quick as you can reach the dial. For sure.

He was fast approaching Exit 12; he spied the slight brown sign beside the Exit:

Land of Make Believe

for the 1950's kiddie amusement park, just outside Hope. C smirked when he saw it, because that sign, to him, was no amusement park marker - it represented everything that was *Belvidere*, lock and stock.

The Mustang hugged the exit ramp curb at sixty miles per hour and came to a hurried stop at the base. C took a left onto Route 521, heading south. He was still a few miles north of Carol's Halloween tree, but closing fast.

China Girl

C thought of Ji-Sue; he snorted a laugh, thinking about how he wanted to tag that one at one time....a lifetime ago, it seemed. *Well, if the opportunity presented itself, he still might nail it;* he thought to himself, but it was an inside joke. He smiled, knowing he would do no such thing, and knowing in any other place, at any other time in his life, he would *absolutely* do such a thing, repeatedly, if possible. The more depraved, the better.

He looked down at his hand, which was still resting on Lilly's.

That was no joke.

He just passed through the blinking red light in *downtown* Hope, which consisted of exactly one block of vintage limestone and wood-frame buildings. He found himself just passing Carol's big sycamore, flipping the radio mindlessly, looking for something good.

And he found it, for him, one of the best, for life, forever:

2463

American Pie

CHAPTER 354 – DISAPPEARING INTO THE DARKNESS OF THE REAR VIEW

American Pie.

That song, from the very first note, in the time an instant takes, opened the door; wherever he was, in she walked, smiling and knobby-kneed, right into his brain. Right into his heart.

That song *was* Kristine, always was, always would be. Funny it came on now, as he was holding Lillian's hand. It made him feel a bit strange, as if he was cheating, on her. He never felt that way before, with any of the women he had been with over the years. And there had been many....*too* many.

What would he do in that situation, if the two ever came face-to-face? Kristine was *always* his fail-safe, where he invariably turned for refuge, to feel better, feel normal, feel right. But that was before there was such a thing as a Lillian Liddell in his life.

And now?

Kristine, Lillian? Lillian, Kristine?

He shook his head; he simply didn't have an answer to that one. That hand was still in play, as the majestic sycamore faded, disappearing into the darkness of the rear-view.

CHAPTER 355 - THE PARTY BEGUN, WAS ABOUT TO BEGIN

The Mustang stealthily slid into the only open space in the parking lot, the premium stall, set beside the right-side front door, reserved, tonight, for the most extra-special VIPs.

C left out a sigh of relief, and smirked. The dashboard clock just flipped to 11:58 pm; two minutes to spare, as he turned the key left, and the calescent engine went to sleep.

He could hear, through the wall before him, the percussion of a gathering well under way, with booze flowing freely, voices and laughter rising and falling in allegro.

And he realized, the party begun, was about to begin.

CHAPTER 356 – A CODFISH MUFFIN SANDWICH

"Hey, wake up!"

C rumbled in the dark of the car.

Lilly half-cracked her eyes, groggy, trying to gauge the destination.

"....the *Log Cabin*?"

Earl was trying to wake up fast, herky-jerking his head to shake away the sleep. He was ready for Round Two, or whatever round they were now on; no way he wanted this day to ever end.

"Hey, that's Marty's truck; cool, he's here! I can't wait to tell him all about today!

Earl rubbed his hands together, excited-fast.

"Hey, wait a minute, that's Woodies van, and Moe's Cadillac; what the? They never come to the *Cabin*."

Lilly said, still half-groggy.

Brother and sister bum-stumbled from the Mustang, punch-drunk from the exhaustion of the day. Neither noticed the big white sign with the bright red lettering that Cord tried to stand in front of, the one that said:

PRIVATE PARTY - YEAH FOR YOU EARL!
HAPPY BIRTHDAY!!

The trio passed through the door, into the bar and saw every high-top and bar stool occupied by people they knew, most already half-tanked, some beyond. It was midnight, but this party had ramped hours ago.

Lillian and Earl were spotted walking in behind C, glasses raised in unison and a ripple quickly spread through the bar, which seconds later erupted in a singular, sonorous roar:

HAPPY BIRTHDAY EARL!!!

Lilly startle-jumped and Earl fell back into the wall; they were both awake *now*.

Only then did they realize they didn't know *some* of the people in Earl's favorite pizza dive, they knew *everyone*. Every single one. And the mob surrounded them like rock stars….true-to-life groupies.

"Hey, nice to finally show up; my dad's usually in bed three hours ago."

Woody said, sticking a freshly cut *DeMuth* in C's mouth.

"But he's okay with it, anything for Earl. And of course, he's up to his eyes in too-young tits and ass; what's not to love? Right pop *[Moe slipped a small smile]*? And everyone thinks he's a harmless old man, so he gets away with it all, rubbing and groping all the jail bait....lucky bastard!"

Woody cracked, as he slapped Cord on the back and Moe smiled wide - a kid in a candy store, stealing at will.

C looked over and saw Buck and Linda together at a high-top on the far end of the bar. They both raised their beer mugs – a salute to the trio. Linda's skirt was faux-alligator, skin tight and a bit too short, just the way it should be, C thought, as he grinned. If that was him sitting next to her, that alligator would be off in no time; Buck, the lucky fuck.

A bear hug half-wrapped Earl from behind.

"Happy birthday buddy! You're an old fart now!"

Marty yelled as he shook Earl left-to-right; Marty's dad, shy and ever the gentleman, gave Earl a so-slight farmer's smile, along with a hearty shake, his hands rough-hewn and strong from years in the fields. A real Jersey farmer. Ji-Sue jumped up on her toes and kissed Earl on the cheek, giggling the whole time, at what, no one quite knew.

Shit, she was looking mighty sweet too, C thought. Jesus, he was *surrounded* by pussy, all belonging to someone else.

C scoped the room; a lot of the folks he simply didn't know....people in and out of Earl's life that Ay had never met. But one and all, they embraced the big man; the affection was contagious. And surprisingly, Earl wasn't running for the back door, in terror; little did C know that Earl kept repeating it to himself, over and over:

Baba Ganoush

and it worked like a charm.

There must have been over a hundred people jammed into the bar area, wall-to-wall, yet surprisingly no one, not a single one, had spilled into the adjacent dining room. Tables were set herky-jerk around the perimeter, but the center was left open, for dancing yet to come. And at the far end, tucked catty-corner to the fireplace, which was lit and roaring despite the mild outside, was an old jukebox. And the music box didn't look like some cheap knockoff, but the real deal, circa-1950's, and neon bright. The *Cabin* didn't normally have a jukebox on hand. This one was brought in special....just for Earl.

2468

"Sambo!"

Earl yelled, seeing Sam bellied up to the bar, beside Uncle Frank, who was already skunked, eyes three-quarters closed and his face puffed and distorted from the booze. Frank was holding a cheap bottle of beer in a way that looked ready to slip through his too-loose grip. He was the only person who seemed annoyed at the whole affair, wishing to be drinking alone, at home on the couch, with his hand slipped in his unbuttoned pants, cupping his balls....standard fare.

Sam smiled as he rose slow from his bar stool, nursing his bad knees, and hugged Earl, kissing him hard on both cheeks, like good Italians do, even though neither one was.

Cord eyed around some more, scanning the room, and spied Sue, the codfish from Sam's; he remembered meeting her that first day in Town....God, that was a lifetime ago. Standing by the bar, she was poured into a mid-riff shirt, showing lots of porcelain skin, and a skin-tight leopard-mini; Jesus, she didn't look half-bad, for a cod. Her ass seemed smaller, and her belly, even though it protruded a bit over the top of her skirt, was, in a strange way, sexy. Her twin sister was with her, and she looked even better, in a matching cat-skin mini, with less of a belly, and a better ass; to this day, he never knew her name.   The twin twosome was somehow transformed, and didn't look bad at all, and he wasn't even tanked. A couple of drinks and he could see himself gyrating with a white-man overbite in the middle of a twin two-fer mixed with some....*Christ*, who would *ever* take the time to spread and stroke either of those codfish, he thought with contempt that first day at Sam's, and here, a mere six months later, the answer was crystal clear - *he* would, right here, right now! How fucking sad was that.

Jesus, come to think of it, everyone around him was looking good and probably getting laid, except him. He needed to fuck Lilly, but good, the last taste he had was Margery, and that was *months* ago.

His thoughts returned to the cod; he stared glassy at Sue and her sister bar-side, as his dick awoke in his pants. His mind was riding a one track rail – a codfish muffin sandwich.

CHAPTER 357 – DROPPED HER HAND TO GIVE THE SACK A SQUEEZE

Thoughts of fucking led naturally to thoughts of Mae, whom he hadn't thought about otherwise. Yet despite the scoping, he hadn't seen her, or Margery, for that matter. But the place was packed like sardines, so they could be hidden in the jam, somewhere. He was sure they would have come; hopefully, they hadn't already come and gone. God he missed them both, especially from the waist-down. He shook his head and returned to the party.

In all his yammering, Earl hadn't looked once into the dining room.

"Hey Earl, look at that, an old jukebox; is that always here?"

C asked, innocent.

"A jukebox? No, there's no jukebox at the...."

Earl said, then stopped; his eyes grew wide as he turned and saw the colored lights casting a mesmerizing neon glow around the empty dining room, competing with the flicker of the fire. The box was beautiful. C patted Earl high on the back.

"Why don't you go take a look buddy."

Was all he said, and Earl crossed the dance floor, a beeline to the bait. Months of planning, months; hopefully, she got it right. And of course she did, every last one....*exactly* right. And as Cord made his way over to the player, it was clear this jukebox was no replica - it was the real deal, with *real* records....the works. He should have expected as much; Carol never cut corners, never.

Earl spied the play list and noticed the first song, labeled No. 1:

Video Killed The Radio Star

"Hey C, cool, looks what's on…."

And then Earl's eyes went wide as he saw the next song, and the next, and next….a steady line, the best of the very best; the songs he had listened to a thousand times over, the songs Cord and he had been talking about, arguing about, laughing about, all spring, all summer long, they were all, magically, in this mysterious jukebox.

Earl scanned the songs, and relived the memories.

Will The Wolf Survive

That was C's earworm that very first April day; Cord didn't know the words, but Earl did, every one, and Earl knew Ay liked the barefoot girl, so he did too.

Fat Bottom Girls

From their first run around the Park, *the* race, C winning the bet and passing out, and becoming friends with Carol; that was the *best ever*, still was. He loved this song, at least now he did, and he loved Carol….he always had, from the first moment he met her.

Tubthumping

The boat ramp with C and Lilly, and throwing C in the water! And C throwing Lilly in after, and Loki, poor Loki; he hoped Loki was okay, and wished he could pet him and kiss him and hug him, right now, and maybe give him some chicken, or a pizza, or a hamburger, or something. He bet he would sure love a hamburger; maybe that would make him happy.

Thunder Island

Lilly laughing at C for liking that song, but it wasn't really so bad, and Earl liked it anyway, because C liked it; that was a good enough reason for Earl. And maybe someday he and Carol could lie on the beach at night in the cool sand, and then maybe they could....oh boy, don't want to think about *that* right now.

Sunset Grill

The song C said he heard when he first walked into Belvidere; C said it always reminded him of the levee rim road that he was gonna show Earl some day, riding the motorcycle and beating the dust on the levee. And his mother telling Earl that he was gonna beat the dust on the rim road, no matter what C said, and his mom was right, 'cause she was *always* right about stuff like that, so C was for-sure gonna be buying him the next two Ken and Sandy books, the ones about the clues of the mysterious marked claw and the coiled cobra....oh boy, he couldn't wait!

No Rain

The chubby little girl, with glasses, in a bumblebee outfit; she's dancing and happy, but then everybody makes fun or her, or ignores her, and she's sad, until she wanders into a field full of other people wearing bumblebee suits too, and she runs to them, accepted as she is, dancing and happy. And that always made Earl extra happy, because he wanted the little bumblebee girl to be happy, and he always liked bumblebees anyway, especially when he got to pet them with his mom, and *especially*, especially when he got to pet them with Carol; she was a very good bumblebee petter.

Africa

Oh Yeah

Baker Street

And the list went on and on, Earl's mouth agape reading every song he and C ever spoke about for all the time the two had been friends....all mysteriously captured in this wonderful neon music box.

"C, this is the best jukebox *ever*! They have all the best songs ever, all our favorites! How cool is that? How can that even happen in real life?"

Lilly had silently saddled alongside C, and whispered.

"Was this? This was the boat ramp that day, wasn't it?"

C shook his head and smiled soft through a whisper back at her.

"And a lot of other times, *a lot,* trust me; what a fucking project....all a big ruse. He never caught on, still hasn't, obviously. That's what I love about your brother; that, and a million other things."

Lillian smiled, watching her brother gaze at the jukebox like a little kid, reading all the songs.

"You were planning *this* day, even way back then? Really?"

C shook his head a proud yes.

"....you're a *good* brother."

She breathed warm into C's ear and kissed him gently on the neck.

It was the first time she ever said those words, and they felt good....they felt right.

"Uh oh, does that mean I can't have sex with my *sister*?"

C asked, in mock horror.

"Come on, this *is* Belvidere."

Lilly smirked.

"Of course, all's good then, *sis*?"

"All's good."

Lilly moaned softly into his ear, as she dropped her hand to give the sack a squeeze.

Earl's eyes glazed; there wasn't a song missing, not a one....except *one*.

A big one, the *most important* one of all. Earl yelled across the room.

"Hey C; this jukebox really isn't perfect. It almost is, but *almost* isn't, you know....perfect. Just saying."

"Yeah? What's wrong?"

C asked coy.

"It's missing...."

Cord didn't let him finish the sentence; the hook was set, he just needed to reel him in.

"Earl...."

C simply said, interrupting him.

"....hit *E 40*."

Earl looked to see what *E-40* was, but there was no *E-40* listed. As hard as he looked, it simply wasn't there. There was an *E-39*: *Bad Reputation*, and there was an *E-41: If It Makes You Happy*, but, somehow, the jukebox people skipped *E-40*!

"Sorry C, but they skipped it, major mistake at the factory – heads are gonna roll! There isn't an *E-40;* it's defective!"

C grinned.

"Trust me on this one buddy, there most certainly *is* an *E-40*. Just punch it in and let's see what the magic box serves up."

"Okay, but I'm telling ya, it's defective; it's not gonna work."

Earl was shaking his head, knowing he was right about these defective things. Lilly looked at C and smiled; she knew what the song was, of course she did. But C knew for sure that Lilly had no idea what E-40 *really* was, not by a long-shot.

That would soon change.

Earl's big pointer carefully, gingerly, depressed the three buttons: *E 4 0;* a quiet, mechanical click, click, click followed in the bowels of the box. Earl's tongue was sticking out in anticipation of just what might happen; it was yet another mystery to be solved – all in one day!

A twenty-five-year old vintage vinyl *45* flipped and effortlessly fell onto the turntable, Carol ensured it was an immaculate, original issue – nothing else would have done – and the fateful music was soon to emerge.

Earl grabbed the front of the jukebox hard and tight, like hanging onto an amusement ride about to begin, and yelled, like new-found religion.

"They didn't forget it! It's there! Joan Jett was really in there C, she was just hiding; she's so sneaky! You were right C, it's absolutely perfect!"

Lilly smiled and hugged Ay.

"You really *are* *t*he best."

C looked at her with a half-smile, and held up a hand, five fingers spread.

"Just remember you said that, in about five seconds."

As the first words left the box:

I saw him standing there by the record machine....
2478

Earl spun to look at Cord and Lillian, arms raised in a touchdown, just as the *Cabin* kitchen door, off to the left, swung open, and Joan Jett, decked head-to-toe in skin-tight original *'80's* red leather, seductively bit her lip and slowly pulled off her left glove, leaning against the wall, by the door.

"What the?"

Lilly said, instinctively clenching her fists.

C quickly grabbed her by the arm.

"Stand down sis, he's been waiting forty long years....for *this*."

CHAPTER 359 – SHE HAD HER RIVAL TO THANK

"But, but…."

Lilly sputtered.

"But what?"

C whispered.

"But this was *our* best day ever! And now she's gotta…."

C spun Lilly and whispered, nose-to-nose.

"Lilly, you left Town, you saw the ocean, saw the City - Grand Central! You *talked* to your mom for Christ sake! Are you kidding? You've been waiting twenty-five years, the last *twenty-five years* has revolved around just that, wanting to talk to her, just one more time, for real….and it happened! It somehow really happened! And it was *good*. *This* was *your* best day, *our* best day, *ever*, it still is, and probably always will be; nothing is ever gonna change that."

C gently cupped Lilly's face in his hands, as he continued.

"But it's still Earl's birthday, and as much as he loves you, and me….he loves Joan Jett, especially *that* Joan Jett, always has, always will. *His* best day ever, keeps getting better and better; let him enjoy it sweetie, your brother deserves it, he deserves *all* of it, including her, and then some more on top."

She shook her head and smiled a silent yes, then the both of them turned toward the jukebox, as the crowd, like the sea, poured in around them.

Clearly everyone had been waiting for this main act curtain-rise for hours, the lot of them getting more hammered by the minute. So it was no surprise that the place erupted when Earl's song started and the *Lady-In-Red* emerged from the *Cabin* kitchen. The whole throng was singing, screaming and swaying along with Joan, with all the juice of a rock concert. The crescendo staggered Earl off-balance, backing into the jukebox. If he could have crawled into the walls, he would have. Lilly covered her ears and screamed at the top of her lungs.

"Jesus!"

But no one heard her, not even C, who was inches away. It was that loud, and getting louder as Joan slinked her way toward her man, through a tunnel of flesh carved from the throng.

Lillian glared at the spectacle, at Carol stealing the center of attention – the spotlight belonged to her rival – Carol *owned* it. She cast an evil eye at C, who was smiling broad and singing along at the top of his lungs; in this chaotic atmosphere, thankfully, no one could hear how horribly he sang.

Lilly went to elbow him hard in the ribs, to throttle his enthusiasm, but sensing the assault, C looked down on her; his smile and small hand squeeze disarmed her. He kept singing badly, as he grinned in her direction.

And Lillian stopped, no follow-through, no annoyed look, no retaliation. She just exhaled loudly, closed her eyes and placed her head gently on his shoulder. But her right hand, hidden by her side, was still clenched tight, an angry Carol-fist. She couldn't let go, despite all that C said, despite the fact that he was right. It wasn't that easy, it just wasn't; fourteen years was a long time to be forever-mad.

Across the room, Joan was in her glory.

2480

She happened to snatch a glance of Lilly and her angry fist, which only made her heap it on.

Actually, Carol Crowe felt a bit bad; clearly this gig was a surprise to Lillian. She was sure C would have gotten weak knees and spilled about Joan, the jukebox, the works, at some point during the day – but he apparently didn't, which made the surprise that much worse for her nemesis.

But *just a bit* bad was all she felt.

Lilly got to spend the whole day with Earl – which ruined Carol's day. The New York trip was always meant to have *her* come along with Cord and Earl, just the three of them, all laughing and wearing the cheap black sunglasses that Carol bought, saving lobsters, exploring the City, *her* City, doing *StoryCorps*....the works. But C told her, on the remote chance that Lillian wanted to tag, and it would be Earl's sole call on that front, that Carol would be a no-go, a casualty. That was the deal, no negotiation, no drama, or he was out, and Carol accepted it - she accepted the risk.

But the risk was calculated, as Carol calculated all risk. C had told her the likelihood of Lilly wanting to actually come on their little conte was zero to none - Lillian was still mad at him, like usual, and in forty-one years, she had never left Town....not really. Not twice, not once....never. So Carol banked on those lottery-long odds all week, came to believe in them, and in the end, was reduced to a casualty.

Instead of a glorious day with Earl, she got to watch from Sam's front window as the Mustang crawled slowly out of Town, blaring *Tobacco Road*, with Lillian wearing **her** cheap black sunglasses! Christ, that alone made her want to scream! Carol got the privilege of sitting home all day, alone with the cats, an alternating current between fuming and sulking, wondering what kind of day the three of them had, what kind of day she missed. And as she walked toward the jukebox, she hoped for Earl's sake, even though she wasn't there to share it, that he had a banner day. And as for his sister, well she hoped that Lillian didn't have a complete suck-ass day, just a big healthy dose of a partial suck-ass one.

She would give her that.

Little did Carol know, she had unwittingly served up the very best day of Lillian's life, bar none; and little did Lillian know, as her mom smiled, that she had her rival to thank.

CHAPTER 360 - HE DID AS HE WAS TOLD....AND BEGAN TO DANCE

It felt like glue on his butt, stuck fast to the slope of the jukebox glass. His heart was racing rabbit, a thousand eyes on him, including hers. The sweat beaded his brow as a sexy red cat slinked its way across the dance floor, coming right for him.

He closed his eyes; when he was a kid, that usually worked....close your eyes and you magically disappear.

He cracked his right eye: **DIDN'T WORK!**

Carol was less than ten feet away, smiling like a snapper-head, closing fast. He was just about to faint, as the room pulsed with an *olla podrida* of music, clapping and static-charged sex, when he somehow, above the din, inexplicably heard that safe voice, the one that had protected him, saved him, loved him, his entire life.

And the message from his sister was simple:

"Earl....dance."

Earl cracked his eyes and saw Lillian smiling at him, shaking her head yes, far behind Joan, at the far end of a tunnel of swaying, pulsing flesh that lay before him. And Earl smiled back, a little-boy's smile. He always loved when Lillian told him to dance.

So he did as he was told....and began to dance.

CHAPTER 361 – LET THE MOVES BEGIN

Earl was a fantastic dancer, because Lillian was a fantastic dancer, because their mom was too.

Mother taught daughter taught brother.

Lillian never did know how her mom learned to dance so well; Uncle Frank certainly couldn't – just her. She learned it somewhere, maybe from her dad, but Sam couldn't dance either, so maybe it was some other dad.

It was one of those questions, one of those many discussions, they never got around to, but it was no big deal, they had a lifetime to talk about it. Till they didn't.

So they never did.

The three of them spent their lives dancing, but only alone, at home, with each other. Lillian wasn't sure why that was a rule, but it was. No one, except Frank, Button – once or twice, by mistake, and maybe Sam, even knew how good they were. It wasn't a secret, but it somehow remained one.

And even when Carol died, the dancing didn't end. It was a rare holdover from that time; one of the few things their mother enjoyed that Lillian would allow to continue in their home. Why Lillian chose that from all the rest of their mom-rituals was a mystery; Earl certainly never asked – it wasn't worth Lillian's wrath, and he was just happy to dance. And he knew their mom would watch them, join them, even when she didn't tell him, he knew she was there, could feel her, right alongside, which made dancing with Lillian that much more special, because the three of them did it together, like they always had, with Lillian none the wiser.

And although in recent years, especially this last year, they didn't dance nearly as much as they once did, Lillian would still, without warning, pull Earl off the couch. And it was Lillian's call - always was - Earl never initiated; it wasn't allowed, just Lilly. And there was no saying no, not that Earl ever would....dancing to him was candy. And it usually put Lillian in a good mood, she would laugh and smile and spin with her brother, and for a short time, anyway, she seemed to have not a care in the world.

And that was nothing but a good thing for both to them....a bonus.

Jazz, classical, ballroom, tango, salsa, disco, dirty, you name it....Lillian and Earl could do it, and likely better than anyone in the room, if they had ever decided to leave their four walls.

And now Earl had; boy, he *certainly* had.

Carol was a pretty good dancer; she had natural moves and certainly looked the part, especially to people who didn't dance, or dance well. She had obviously never seen Earl dance, and quickly found herself deep in the big leagues.

Like he was plugged in an outlet, Earl closed his eyes, most of the way, and went on automatic. He and Lillian, much to her chagrin, had danced to Joan Jett, this song in particular, more times than Lilly could count....hundreds, easily. Suffice to say, it was Earl's favorite, and, to the note, he had the moves down.

So let the moves begin.

Now it was Carol's turn to be surprised, as was the crush behind her.

Earl's was go-go locomotion; endless rolls, shifts, stirs and splits....confident, liquid moves mesmerized the crowd and a hush quickly blanketed the room, with all eyes on the big man, slowly rotating, eyes partially closed and all smile, pumping to the beat from the magic box.

It took all Carol had to simply keep up, to go along for the ride....and what a ride it was. She only matched him in her smile – on that front, they were equals.

Cord stood, mouth agape.

"Holy shit! How did he pull *that* out of his ass? Where the hell did that come from?"

Lilly looked at C and shook her head, arms folded across her chest, smiling self-content at her prize. A teacher watching her pupil perform, flawlessly.

"Where do you think? Me."

"Jesus, is there anything that boy can't do?"

"Live without me."

It slipped out quick, without Lilly even thinking, and she wanted an immediate retract. But none was available. So she shrugged at the room, and continued.

"I figured I'd have to accept it, *her*, someday; it's clear she isn't going away. Anyway, I get it C, *someday* is here. But you know what, I think *someday* is today, tonight, right here, right now, him and her, on the dance floor, dancing to the same song Earl and I have danced to a thousand times. And you know what C? I'm scared, and I'm already lonely, I already miss him. He's the best brother in the whole world; my mom always knew that; I'm not sure if she knew I always agreed, but I always did."

Lilly teared up, and dropped her head. C put his finger gently under her chin, raised her face to his and kissed her lightly on the forehead, smiled and held her face with warm hands.

"I'm proud of you Lillian Liddell, I really am, and so is your mom, and she doesn't have to talk to either one of us for me to know that. Long time coming."

"Yeah, well, I'm kinda tired of this fight; it has been lot of years and the wind is out of the sails, so to speak."

C scratched his cheek, a mix of surprise, and doubt.

"Don't worry, I gotta new fight on my hands. What's her name, by the way? I noticed you *never* gave that up, just changed the subject, like usual. So spill."

And surprisingly, he did.

"Kristine; her name's Kristine, with a K."

Lilly looked at him cocked.

"Kristine, with a K, that's kinda gay. Does this gay girl have a last name?"

"I don't remember."

C said a bit too quick, and Lilly smiled wry.

"Yeah right, whatever."

"Well, doesn't matter what it is, I don't like the sound of it, don't like the sound of it at all *[Lilly shook her head as she spoke]*. Not nearly as nice-sounding as Lillian Liddell; see how that rolls off the tongue....poetry. *Kristine Whatever*....yuck; sounds short and chunky to me."

"Chunky? That doesn't even make any sense; how is short and chunky supposed to sound?"

C said, sarcastic.

"Like *Kristine Whatever*."

Lilly said, dead-pan, and then chuckled, impressed with her own little joke.

"And what did this girl call you when you were eleven, or whatever? Cord? Or Cordelia? Cordelia Brin."

C just stared at her. Lilly continued.

"No wait, let me guess *[Lilly paused, sarcastic, finger on her chin]* Cord Brin is actually a made-up name, made up *many* years after *Kristine Whatever* with a K left the scene, one of many made-up names along the way, I'm sure. Were you making them up at eleven? Or did you have a real name back then? What would your little knobby-kneed girlfriend call you back then? When she whispered sweet nothings in your ear, huh? I'm guessing....*Maxwell*? *Mad Max* for short. Close?"

Both of them, engaged in conversation, had missed most of the dirtiest dirty dancing between Earl and Carol, which was a very good thing, for Earl.

Lillian stared at Cord, hands on her hips.

"I'm waiting; I just got a second wind, so I've got all night....*Max*."

She stared hard, her hips wanted to sway to the music, but she held them rigid, in protest.

"My name can be whatever you want it to be."

Weak attempt, and C knew it.

"Not good enough Cordelia. You know, *brother*, I'm thinking *this little* sister is starting to get a bit shy below the waistline, and tonight, that would be such a shame, for you that is."

"Ah, the old reliable, the go-to tool in Lilly's little toolbox; are you *always* going to use *that* against me?"

C shook his head and huffed.

"Will it always work?"

She answered in a self-assured snark. C smiled; they both knew the answer to that one.

Cord exhaled a slow sigh, leaned over, formed a whisper, and a big sweet nothing slipped in her ear.

CHAPTER 363 – THE SONG SERVED UP, AND THE SHOWDOWN BEGAN

It was no small deal.

It was the first time in decades that he had willingly given it up, that he had trickled the truth, to anyone. No one had heard that word, just Lillian.

And she knew it was real.

"Really?"

She said in a little laugh, a mix of surprise and glee, knowing she had a treasured tidbit, for sure. He frowned and nodded, once.

"Is it with a G, or a K?"

She let slip a little laugh, more of a snort, which made her laugh some more.

"It really isn't that funny."

"Yes it is."

She snickered.

"Well, I haven't answered to that in quite some time….long time."

"Good thing for you! Musta gotten beat up on the playground with a name like that! So that's where all the scars are from? It's all coming together now."

"Enough already, *Bibby.*"

"Hey, that was because Earl couldn't say my name right, a little different than being named that, *on purpose*! By your parents! Good God! Or was it the nuns?"

"Well, the word was that my parents didn't pick a name for close to three weeks after I was born. They, the family, just passed me around and called me *the baby,* kind of like *the cat.*"

"They took three weeks and the best they could come up with was *that?!* They should have stuck with *the baby,* or better yet, *the cat.*"

"Okay, okay, fun's over."

"Are you kidding? The fun's just beginning! I'm calling you that from now on!"

"No you're not."

Cord said, short. Lilly pondered a moment.

"You know, you're right, I'm not. For once we agree. You're a lot of things, but you are definitely *not* that name. Plus, I couldn't keep a straight face, or be seen in the same room. And there's no good way to nickname that one, for sure; my advice, keep it under your hat."

"Thanks for the input."

C said, sarcastic.

Two minutes and fifty-seven seconds, give or take; that was the limit for Song No. 40 on the jukebox, Joan's toll of time, and it was getting close to the end.

But the last part, the final forty-nine seconds to be exact, was Earl's favorite, the over-and-again final stanza, when the jam of bar patrons in the video sing, pulse and fist-thrust, as Joan walks atop the bar, playing guitar, skinned in red:

I love rock and roll,
So put another dime in the jukebox baby;

I love rock and roll,
So come and take your time and dance with me.

Five repeats of the same four lines.

And with the start of the first stanza, Linda jumped in spontaneous and joined Carol and Earl, singing, smiling-wide and fist-pumping to the thumping beat.

And with each of the succeeding stanza, the female coterie grew, surrounding Earl like groupies. The cod-twins were next, dancing, kissing each other on the lips, twirling tongues, and rubbing bodies pornographic – Moe was about to pass out; followed, emerging from a crack in the crowd, by Margery. C couldn't take his eyes off her; porcelain-white, lithe, tight and....

A quick sock to the gut ended the thought.

"Hey, one and *so-done*! They'll be no more *squatting* with that one....***ever***!"

Lilly yelled in Cord's face. C still smiled; that would always be the best squat workout he ever had. He deftly stepped back a pace, outside of Lilly's swing range, in case another roundhouse was coming in response to the sly smile.

The final stanza began, and out of thin air, Mae enter the ring, dancing beside her daughter, smiling and swaying to the beat of the guitar. It was the first time Cord had seen her since the dinner date at Margery's, and the news of her and *Toolbox Joe*. It seemed a lifetime ago. He wondered if the little, wrinkly munchkin was in tow tonight. He spied Mae up and down; *she looked a little thicker through the middle*, he thought.

Guess he was still in range; a second sock brought him back.

"Hey, and way too many with grandma; equally done! And by the way, having sex with old wrinkly people with no teeth? *Yuck!*"

As the song wound down its final seconds the room whipped into a frenzy, girls bumping and grinding each other, hands overhead, clapping, laughing and enjoying the birthday boys show.

Earl was simply amazing, a dancing wunderkind.

"Time to have a little fun; can't let that dirty display go unanswered. And it **better** be on there, C, that's all I'm saying; it ***better*** be on there!"

Lilly punched Cord chest-hard for a third time; she was getting good at that.

"Fuck! Stop the God-damn punching! And I thought you were done with all that, with her. You know, tired of the fight? Wind out of the sails? Remember saying that, about five minutes ago?"

C said, exasperated, rubbing the skin-sting in his chest.

"It might be done, but it's not *done-done.* Close, but you know, but the whole *getting in the last-word thing*, it's a bitch."

And before Ay could snatch her, Lillian gave a quick shoulder-slip and darted across the room, saddling-up to the music box, her butt swaying to the music and her finger impatiently scrolling the songs, in a frantic search.

Found it! She whispered to herself, a great grin creasing her face, just as Joan went quiet, and the record clicked to reset.

Lillian bellowed to the room at the top of her lungs, a primordial, guttural cry, loud and clear, so there would be no mistake in the jungle.

"Clear the fucking floor!"

To this crowd, Lillian Liddell didn't need to ask twice; all dutifully did, including Earl.

All except one.

"You too."

She waved dismissive at Carol, who stood her ground, trying to look all Joan-tough in her red skin-tights.

Cord skipped over quick and hooked Carol's arm. She could see Earl getting a bit frantic, and for that reason, and that reason only, Carol reluctantly ceded the floor, escorted by Ay.

Arm horizontal, rigid, she pointed hard at her brother, jabbing her right middle finger at him; it was clear this was not up for discussion.

"Earl, let's show 'em how it's done."

And with three quick clicks, the song served up, and the showdown began.

www.ingramcontent.com/pod-product-compliance
Lightning Source LLC
Chambersburg PA
CBHW060616310726
48982CB00003B/578